BRIDES OF CHRISTMAS

A Collection Of Holiday Mail Order Bride Romances

CHARITY PHILLIPS
FAITH-ANN SMITH

Copyright ©2015-2019
by Charity Phillips and Faith-Ann Smith
www.hopemeadowpublishing.com

All rights reserved. Printed in the United States of America. No part of this book may be used or reproduced in any manner whatsoever without written permission except in the case of brief quotations embodied in critical articles or reviews.

This book is a work of fiction. Names, characters, businesses, organizations, places, events and incidents either are the product of the author's imagination or are used fictitiously. Any resemblance to actual persons, living or dead, events, or locales is entirely coincidental.

CONTENTS

Beatrice's Christmas Blessing	1
Millie's Christmas Surprise	77
Amelia's Blessed Christmas	169
A Christmas Mail Order Bride For Samson	259

BEATRICE'S CHRISTMAS BLESSING

BEATRICE'S CHRISTMAS BLESSING

ALBANY, NEW YORK - 1880

Beatrice Miller's world comes crashing down when her husband dies suddenly from a terrible accident. Her life has shifted without notice, and she must deal with not only grief, but the worry of being a burden on her late husband's already poverty-stricken family.

But her late husband has left her with a small bundled surprise; one she fears she may not be capable of taking care of herself. Her child is due around Christmastime, and instead of bringing only joy, he brings worry and heartache.

In a desperate attempt to find stability for herself and her child, Beatrice answers an ad from a rancher seeking of a marriage of convenience. Certain she could never love again, she makes the long trip to Wyoming and is shocked when she begins to feel an immediate connection.

But it isn't with the rancher whom she is to marry; it is with his ranch hand who is nothing but kind to her and has the warmest smile she's ever seen.

Is it possible that a Christmas miracle will arrive not only in the form of a bundle of joy, but in a second love?

CHAPTER 1

Beatrice Miller would be hard pressed to ever forget that unhappy day. She was mending at home, her employment as a seamstress over since marrying her husband Thomas, when the young officer stopped at their door. It was Susan, the oldest of Thomas's sisters, that had answered the door and it was a good thing that she called to Beatrice before the man had a chance to tell her what had happened. Beatrice would never have forgiven herself or that officer if he'd told Susan, only seventeen, that her beloved brother had died.

"Mrs. Miller?" inquired the officer when Beatrice had put her things aside and gone to the door.

"Yes? May I ask why you've come knocking here, scaring my poor sister witless?" Beatrice asked, nudging Susan playfully. The other girl scowled, but there was no bite in it.

But the levity Beatrice worked to instill vanished as the man removed his black hat and held it in front of him, playing nervously with the brim. There was no doubt that he truly was the bearer of bad news. His eyes darted to Susan, then back to Beatrice. Clearing his throat, he asked, "May we have a word in private, Mrs. Miller?"

Beatrice didn't even glance at Susan. The tone and the expression of the officer was certainly enough to convince her that whatever he might say, it wouldn't be a happy thing. "Susan, dear, go and start supper, will you?"

Susan, though normally well-behaved, pouted slightly at being sent away; she could guess they wanted to speak on all manners of important things without her. "But it's early, still—"

Beatrice waved her off. "Hush and do as you're told!"

Susan huffed a little, but turned on her heel and marched off through the small home towards the kitchen. Pulling herself up to her full height, Beatrice inhaled deeply to calm herself, then asked, "What troubles you, officer?"

He winced, unhappy all around. "Ma'am, I hate being the messenger of this news, and I wish it were otherwise, but I'm afraid I must be the one to tell you."

Cold had settled across Beatrice's shoulders and was steadily slipping down her body, trailing over her spine and along her arms, saturating everything. "Please, don't drag it on further. Just tell me."

With a world-weary sigh, he shook his head. "'Tis your husband, ma'am. I'm afraid he's dead."

The officer continued, explaining it was a traffic accident that caused his demise; that the horse stampeded poor Thomas and that the carriage driver felt terribly sorry. He said that it wasn't anyone's fault; that it was awful, but there wasn't any helping it.

But those words slid in one ear and out the other. Beatrice was lost to grief that she thought she might never know; a grief so powerful that it numbed her body and mind, a means of protecting her from its full intensity, lest it devour her whole. Vaguely, Beatrice heard the man apologize and mention a few things about the body before he left. She must have closed the door, though she hardly remembered, and she must have gone to Susan, though she scantly recalled that, either.

It was her obligation to tell her sisters-in-law, Susan and Lydia, and together they cried until Mrs. Martha Miller—Beatrice's mother-in-law—returned home to share in the unhappy news. By the time Mr. Joseph Miller arrived, the entire house was in mourning.

Unhappiness swallowed the Miller residence, and while it was heartfelt, brought on by the loss of one of their beloved, it was in part practical, as well. Thomas had brought money to the family. He was by no means wealthy, being only twenty-three and a half years of age himself, and he left nothing to his poor widow, Beatrice. But that money had greatly helped the Miller family, who had only Mr. Miller working full time at the rails and Mrs. Miller working part time in the kitchen of one of their wealthier neighbors.

Now, these two incomes would simply not be enough for the family.

They sat at the dinner table only two weeks after Thomas's passing. The table was quiet, often as it was these days. Beatrice sat beside Susan who sat across from Lydia. Next to Lydia was Mrs. Miller. At the head of the table was Mr. Miller, and across from him was only an empty place setting. Thomas's seat would not be occupied again.

The meal was lean—a hunk of bread and a meager portion of fowl apiece—just enough to keep everyone from going to bed hungry.

"I've spoken with Mrs. Carrington," commented Mrs. Miller. "She said she could add in dinner, as well." Mrs. Miller had been inquiring about additional hours since Thomas's death.

Mr. Miller frowned. He had a weary face and cracked lips; time did not favor him well. "That'll have you home late, Mattie."

Letting out a sigh, the older woman nodded. "There's just no getting around it, Joseph. We need the income."

"I could search for a job!" cried Lydia, only fifteen and determined to be the eldest already. "My needlework is quite good and—"

"Hush with your nonsense," chastised Susan. "You're not worth much at needlepoint. I bet no one would even hire you as a nanny."

"Mother! Susan's being awful again!"

The two sisters bickered, and it was actually Beatrice

who calmed them. "That's enough out of both of you. Mother and Father haven't worked this hard just to come home to the likes of feral children. Behave." When the two girls quieted, Beatrice fixed her eyes upon her father-in-law's. "Besides, I think it's best if *I* return to work."

For a long moment, the table was quiet. Mr. Miller didn't disapprove of women working; they were too poor for that. He didn't want his daughters to toil unduly, however. But Beatrice wasn't a blood relative, and she had worked before. After contemplating the notion, he nodded. "Alright, then. With any luck, it'll be enough."

CHAPTER 2

Still wearing her black mourning dress, its petticoats beneath weighing her down and adding volume to her wide skirt, Beatrice left early the following morning. She instructed Susan to mind Lydia until their mother returned that afternoon; Mrs. Miller was scheduled to work from breakfast through lunch.

Beatrice had been a very good seamstress, expertly manning the sewing machines with the ease of a true professional. Of course, there were many other ladies with equal skill, but Beatrice had hoped that her old boss might need her services once again.

Mr. Wilson was a portly man in his fifties who had gotten into business with his father. He had a building downtown in the business district that was little more than brick siding and a large open room with a dozen or so sewing machines set up on tables. Beatrice had worked for him for nearly three years before meeting Thomas.

The thought of her husband—her *late* husband—made her heart clutch in grief. Two weeks was no amount of time to move on; she couldn't imagine that a *thousand* weeks would be enough.

I must, she thought with as much courage as she could. *For the sake of my family.*

The Millers had welcomed her into their home upon marrying their only son, and despite his death, there was absolutely no question that she should stay. The least she could do was pull her own weight.

Pushing forward, she opened the door to the warehouse and headed inside. Mr. Wilson's room was on the fourth floor. Beatrice climbed the first three flights heavily, but had to stop on the landing just below the fourth. She found herself winded and almost dizzy.

Could my bodice be too tight?

This dress had been purchased upon the death of her father only a couple of years earlier and she wondered if perhaps she had outgrown it. *But all my dresses are this size!*

Deciding it was only her grief—and her lack of sleep as a result—that had her winded after only three flights of stairs, she allowed herself a moment of rest, then proceeded to climb the last flight to the fourth floor. There, she knocked on the door where the office of seamstresses was located. Normally, one might first inquire downstairs and then find the office of the employer, but Beatrice remembered how often he spent his time in the office with the girls. She also worried that she might be refused if she stated her business in the lobby; these could be hard times for everyone, after all.

Beatrice knocked again, worried that the faint sounds of the sewing machines running on the other end were drowning her out. She might have tried merely entering to get herself noticed, but she knew from experience that the door was often locked. After another moment of waiting, Beatrice lifted her hand to knock again only to have the door open abruptly.

"What is it, woman?" demanded a short, portly man with a well-maintained mustache and a pocket watch gripped in his hand. He checked it twice before Beatrice even had a chance to answer. "Well? Out with it! I'm very busy."

Recovering, Beatrice smiled and offered a very small curtsey to be polite. "Beg your pardon, sir. I was inquiring after Mr. Wilson?"

The little man checked his watch again, rolled his eyes, and let out a loud sigh. "I haven't the time to answer your questions." He tried to close the door on her quite rudely, but she managed to wedge herself between it and the jam. He had neither the malice nor the strength to catch her in the frame. Sighing again, he muttered, "Persistent little thing... Fine. What is it you need?"

Beatrice tried again, speaking quickly. "Mr. Wilson. I

worked for him once before and was hoping he might have another available job for me."

The man snorted. "Mr. Wilson sold the business a year ago. It's mine and I assure you I don't have a need for a pestering woman like you. Good day."

Beatrice's shoulders slumped, but she nodded and backed away from the door. She'd imposed on the man's time long enough, and clearly, he wasn't going to budge. When she was fully in the hall again, he slammed the door in her face.

Dejected, she made the long trek home—still unemployed.

CHAPTER 3

THE NEXT MORNING, BEATRICE awoke to find that her stomach was twisting uncomfortably. It was only the nearness of the washbasin that kept her from emptying the contents of her stomach there instead of the floor. She couldn't fathom what sort of illness this was, but her stomach felt touchy for the rest of the day and she couldn't eat much at all, though she managed to force down a little bread at dinner.

The following day, Beatrice found herself in the same position. In fact, over the course of the next week, Beatrice woke up with terrible nausea. Her appetite had improved, but only slightly. At the beginning of the following week, when it was once more the same morning routine, Beatrice dropped heavily into the couch. There she stayed for at least twenty minutes before young Lydia joined her. Being only fifteen, the girl had little control of her tongue, and at times, would say the wrong thing. It wasn't out of meanness, but out of a lack of understanding. So when she dropped down onto the couch beside Beatrice, she turned to her and smiled slyly. "Sick again, sister?"

Beatrice only nodded. She was feeling worn out. She knew by the afternoon, things would be fine, but afternoon seemed a long way off.

"Could you possibly be...with child?"

As soon as the words left the poor girl's lips, the air in the room seemed to be removed. Beatrice found it difficult to breathe; her eyes widened, and suddenly, the world seemed to be too much for her to bear.

Pregnant? Oh, Lord, not pregnant!

It was not that Beatrice didn't want a child. Ever since she was very young, she had felt that her true calling was that of a mother. It showed further when she joined the Millers, helping to tend to Lydia and Susan. Occasionally, she even helped the neighbors with their young child, who would be turning six years of age this Christmas.

Christmas.

Beatrice found her thoughts tumbling over one another rapidly in an effort to make sense of everything in her life right now. Her husband had died only three weeks ago.

If I am pregnant...I will be due in December.

It was only April and nine months might give a child a

late December birth. Not that Beatrice could embrace the concept that she might, indeed, be pregnant. Not now. Not when life had just taken something so wonderful from her, leaving her to fend without him. And the family! Oh, the poor Millers! They would feel obligated to help with the child, but they could barely feed their own. It seemed terribly unfair to Beatrice that they should have to bear the burden of supporting both her and a child on top of what they had lost.

No, I can't be pregnant!

"Oh, Beatrice!" cried Lydia, her delicate hand covering her mouth. "I'm so sorry! I shouldn't have said that; 'twas wicked of me. To speak of my poor brother—" Her voice broke off with a squeak and a sob. Tears brimmed in her large eyes and she failed to blink them away as they trailed down her flushed cheeks. "I'm so very sorry. Please, forgive me, sister."

Beatrice was wracked by her own inner turmoil over the prospect of truly being pregnant, but she tried to focus on young Lydia instead. Forcing a smile, she patted the other girl's hand. "It's alright, Lydia. You meant no harm."

When the girl had calmed the onslaught of sudden tears, she nodded. She was pitiful as she offered a watery smile in return. "Of course you are not pregnant, but perhaps it would not be so terrible if you were? It would be a piece of Thomas returned to us."

Beatrice agreed, but she fretted, still. She had but a week to know for sure.

A week came swiftly, but her monthly visitor did not. Beatrice comforted herself that there was time still; late did not mean absent. Several more days passed, but still, she did not show any signs. By the end of another week—a week past her cycle—she knew the truth.

She was pregnant.

CHAPTER 4

AT THE REQUEST OF MRS. MILLER, WHO HAD MANAGED TO garner a few more hours from her employer, Beatrice and Lydia were out in the market to pick up a few things for dinner that night. They had only a few coins in their purse, but it would be enough for a sparse dinner for the lot of them.

These things greatly troubled Beatrice, as did her own condition. She was sick in the morning, almost always, and ate just a small portion at dinner. She tired easily and her clothing was often constricting now.

Her thoughts were plagued with worries of money and an upcoming child with no father. The intelligent thing to do might be to find another suitable father for the child, but her heart was still so full of grief that she could barely even think it, lest she cry for whom she had lost.

Still, she knew she must do something. Even if she were to find a job, however, she knew that it would be a waste of everyone's time. She would only be able to work for nine months, and she didn't even know how much of that would be good work. A seamstress was afforded the luxury of sitting down at least, but already she was growing weary. How would she feel around the time of her child's expected birth?

Sighing, Beatrice shook her head.

"What are you sighing about?" inquired Lydia who was easily distracted by a woman selling flowers. "Oh! I would love these so!" But she didn't even ask Beatrice if she might be able to buy some. She knew the answer as well as any of them: their money was for food, not flowers.

"Nothing," Beatrice said in answer to the first question. "I'm only a bit tired."

Lydia spared her a glance; her eyes dropped to her belly. "Oh." Her cheeks flushed and her eyes grew glassy. The Millers knew of Beatrice's condition, thanks to Lydia who had been watching almost as closely as Beatrice for some confirmation. The news was a mixture of happiness and sadness for everyone, so they spoke little of it.

Spotting a small boy up ahead, Beatrice had a moment where she imagined he might be hers. He was selling papers, smiling and apple-cheeked; Beatrice was quick to buy one.

"For Father," she explained when Lydia's eyebrows rose in question.

It was one of the few luxuries they might still indulge in,

for Mr. Miller felt it was of the upmost importance to be aware of the goings-on of the world. Lydia did not need to know that Beatrice also found herself thinking fondly of the little boy who might look like her own.

As soon as the money had exchanged hands and the young boy had scampered off, Lydia gave a squeal of delight. Beatrice looked just in time to see the Lydia rushing forward, embracing another girl that Beatrice recognized as Miss Mary Scott. She was out with her mother that afternoon, and as the two young girls went to look at the flowers from earlier, gossiping as girls do, Beatrice was left with Mrs. Scott.

"Good day, Mrs. Scott."

The woman smiled warmly. "Mrs. Miller! How are you, dear? Things must be so hard after everything that has happened."

Beatrice felt the familiar tug on her heart, but she forced herself to be brave. "Yes, it is, but we are strong. Please, cheer me with happy news of your family."

The woman eagerly did so, diving right in to explain that one of her distant relatives had boldly moved out West only three weeks ago.

"Out West?" Beatrice asked in surprise.

Mrs. Scott nodded quickly, happy to share in this bit of gossip. "It's quite scandalous, really." She leaned forward and dropped her voice to a stage whisper. "She found a husband —in the paper!"

Beatrice smiled and shook her head. "Oh, Mrs. Scott,

that's hardly scandalous! Women do so all the time. It's quite acceptable in this day and age."

As soon as the words left her mouth, she glanced down at her own paper. It *was* acceptable, she reasoned. Westward expansion was encouraged by the government, offering acres of wild land in exchange for cultivating and living upon it. As a result, many strapping young men were heading off into the wild West in search of land upon which to build their own fortunes. And it was hardly reasonable for young women to make such a trek with these men, with no stable place to call home. Thus, it became necessary to encourage women to head West to join them in marriage.

Perhaps women like me?

Beatrice realized that Mrs. Scott had continued to talk about her sister's husband's cousin while she contemplated the wisdom of using the paper in her own hand.

"...and after only three letters!" exclaimed Mrs. Scott. "That's hardly an appropriate amount of time for a young lady to get to know anyone at all! Courting should take years, if you ask me." She lifted her chin in emphasis.

"But is she well taken care of?" asked Beatrice. She was just about to ask about the other woman's happiness, but that was irrelevant to Beatrice's situation. She was not looking for a new husband to love; no one could ever take the place of her beloved Thomas. Instead, she wished only to know if it were a viable option.

Mrs. Scott first seemed startled by the question, then honestly considered it. "Well, I suppose so. From the letters we've received in return, the girl's quite happy. Her husband is fairly dutiful, despite his crass way of courting her."

Thankfully, before the women could continue their conversation further, Lydia and Miss Mary returned. "Mary, dear, we must be going." The Scotts bid the Millers good day and went about their business.

Lydia and Beatrice went on to do the same, but for the rest of the evening, Beatrice thought of the paper and the ad that had taken one woman out West.

CHAPTER 5

THAT EVENING, BEATRICE AND SUSAN PREPARED THE meal. Mrs. Miller didn't arrive until late in the evening, thanks to her additional hours, and it didn't seem right to anyone that she should have to cook after toiling away in a kitchen all day. When dinner was served, the family ate in relative silence. Each had their own thoughts to occupy their minds; Beatrice's thoughts centered on the paper. Mr. Miller read it every night after dinner as ripples of nervousness washed through Beatrice. She wanted to look through it in search of the ads—matrimonials, they were called. But she didn't want the others to know of her aim just yet. She worried they might strongly oppose and insist she stay with them. It just wasn't economically feasible. And if she were truly honest with herself, there was a part of her that needed to go; to get away from this house and this family with all of its reminders of her dearest Thomas.

The end to dinner could not come soon enough. When it did, the girls sat on the floor, working on their needlepoint. Mrs. Miller sat on the sofa, focused on her knitting while Beatrice dutifully held the yarn straight as she worked. Her eyes were trained on Mr. Miller, however, as he sat near the fire in his old rocking chair. He leisurely read through the paper, taking ages before he was through. When he finished, Beatrice was horrified to see him begin to crumple it into a ball.

"No!" she all but shouted.

All eyes turned to her, shocked by her outburst.

Calming her racing heart, she put down the yarn carefully. Lydia quickly put her own needlework aside to take it up as Beatrice rose. She walked toward Mr. Miller, smiling faintly.

"I apologize," she said sincerely, smoothing out her skirt. "I only meant that I wanted to search the ads. For a job," she added quickly.

Still a little bewildered, he handed her the half-crumpled bit of paper. "Of course."

She thanked him, then retreated to the kitchen where there was both a chair and a candle—and, most importantly, her solitude. Lighting the candle, she licked her lips nervously and began to search.

Beatrice was initially hopeful, but as she perused the ads, she felt that hope dwindle. There were many; more than she expected, and most seemed very earnest. Only a handful seemed scandalous to her. However, even the legitimate ones had her spirits waning. They all seemed to want something she could not provide.

A loving wife.

Beatrice was many things. Dutiful. Honest. Loyal. Respectable. But she had loved only one man in that way, and now that God had taken him from her, she did not think it would be right to search for that same love again in another man. Thus, she did not feel she could possibly respond to an ad posted by some poor, lonely soul. No; she needed a man who wanted a wife to take care of his home, not his heart.

Almost giving up, Beatrice promised herself that she would look at only one more. If she found nothing, she would give up her foolish quest; then, she would actually look at the ads in the hopes of finding a job.

As it turned out, that final ad would change the course of her future.

MATRIMONIAL—Rancher seeks hard-working woman in search of comfortable and stable living arrangements. Must be of a marriageable age not to exceed thirty years with a respectable reputation. Will provide travel expenses. Should be family oriented with the intention of ultimately providing an heir to the ranch.

His name was listed as a Mr. Frank Foster from Wyoming. Beatrice considered the ad. The rest asked for dutiful young wives in search of a loving husband, but this ad seemed concerned only with stability, security, and the practical things that come with marriage.

A marriage of convenience—just what Beatrice had been searching for.

Finding her fountain pen and ink well, she fetched a sheet of parchment, and by the fading light of the candle, she wrote him a response. It was short and to the point, explaining her situation.

Dear Mr. Foster,

My name is Mrs. Beatrice Miller and I am a widow at only twenty-two years of age. My husband passed only recently and I seek stability for myself, as well as a means of easing the burden on my late husband's family. I do not fear work, but I worry my condition will hinder my ability to contribute for too long of a time.

I am only a month pregnant. My child is due to have a Christmastime birth, and my hope is only that he will be born to a stable, warm home.

I cannot offer love, but I am well equipped to clean, cook, and mend. Other chores I would learn easily.

If my situation sounds amenable to you, please respond promptly.

Best,

Mrs. Beatrice Miller

Beatrice signed her name quickly and set the letter aside to let it dry. This also allowed her a few more minutes to truly think of what she was doing. Was she ready to become a wife again? And if she was, could she stand to live as a wife to a man where there could be no love?

Sighing, she began to remove the pins from her hair in preparation for sleep, allowing her long, brown locks to fall about her shoulders and down her back. The rest of her family had already gone to bed; she was the only one still awake at this late hour. Slowly, she braided the soft strands until they fell together over one shoulder. She checked the drying ink to be sure it had finished, then folded it up carefully. Stuffing it into an envelope, she copied the address from the paper and sealed it. Tomorrow, she would mail it.

CHAPTER 6

Within only another two weeks, Beatrice received a quick reply from Mr. Foster.

Mrs. Miller,

My sympathies for your situation. I accept your proposal. Send word of your planned departure, and I will pay for transport.

Mr. Foster

The reply was without inflection or any sort of warmth, but that was what Beatrice was in search of. She wanted only the bare bones of a relationship that would provide each party with what it was they needed. That same day, Beatrice responded again, giving him less than a month before her projected departure. Even sooner than his last reply, she received the letter containing her ticket.

At this point, she had already told the Millers of her

plans. They disagreed at varying stages of vehemence, but each one in turn eventually came around. It was actually Mr. Miller that ended up being the most opposed, and it was he who accepted to her way of thinking last.

"You won't reconsider?" asked Mr. Miller, his mustache bristling.

Beatrice smiled warmly at him. They were at the train station now; it was a bit late for reconsidering in her mind. "I've made up my mind. It's for the best. I'll send word as soon as I can."

He puffed out a breath, then let it go in a whoosh. He still wasn't thrilled with the thought of her leaving. "I wish you'd let someone accompany you, at the very least."

In all honesty, Beatrice agreed whole heartedly with this sentiment. She felt exposed and insecure traveling alone, but she felt confident that the train and those who worked on it would provide her a modicum of safety. She would not be scared off so easily, she promised herself. To her father-in-law, she stuck simply to practicality. "Father, you know that's simply not an option. You cannot leave work; the girls are too young to travel with me and then return on their own. And it would be just as preposterous for Mother to chaperone me, only to return with no chaperone of her own."

He frowned, but nodded. "Of course, you're right. It just doesn't put me any more at ease."

They embraced then before the whistle blew. She had

bid her farewells to the rest of the family already, and the girls had been in tears. Finally, she got on the train and settled in for the long ride that would take her west to Wyoming and her future husband.

CHAPTER 7

Wendover, Wyoming – June, 1880

THE TRAIN ARRIVED MID-AFTERNOON. IT HAD BEEN A long journey, the constant motion of the train cars making the nausea Beatrice was already experiencing all the worse. She was grateful when they finally stopped and hurried off to see this new world she was meandering into.

It was June and summer was in full bloom. The area was mountainous, although the particular town she had stopped in was flat and plain-like. Grass could be seen in the distance, trees were scattered about, and a river that the train had miraculously traversed lined the far edge of her vision. It was quite a beautiful place; she approved of it immediately.

It was hotter than she had expected, however, and it seemed as though she was instantly sweating beneath her dress. Frowning, she brought out a small hand fan and did her best to keep the heat at bay. She hoped she would have a moment to freshen up before engaging too thoroughly with Mr. Foster; she wanted to make a good impression upon him.

And now that the thought had occurred to her, where *was* Mr. Foster? She had received only two letters from him, neither of them including a description of himself—nor had hers, admittedly—and he hadn't described much beyond the dates of her arrival. All she knew was that she would be met at the station.

But by whom?

She left the platform, but curbed her desire to wander. She wanted to look around, but didn't want to chance missing her would-be husband. That would be the worst scenario her mind could come up with.

Her large, brown eyes began to scan the area in search of a man that might be her Mr. Foster. It was difficult, as she was essentially pairing him with writing. Quickly, she gave up; this wasn't working. Letting her shoulders slouch slightly, she sat with her meager belongings and breathed slowly to keep down her growing sense of unease.

Where is he? she wondered, feeling more and more concerned.

Just as she stood, prepared to find *someone* that might direct her to the Foster Ranch, she saw a young man waving a wide brimmed hat. She almost let her eyes drag past him, except that she noticed, even from this short distance, that he was smiling. Beaming. Such a warm smile...

She'd stopped to stare at him long enough that he actually started towards her. A blush rose to her cheeks and she looked away. *How embarrassing,* she thought. This was hardly how she wanted to begin her life here, catching the eye of some strange man—

Or is this Mr. Foster?

A strange hope blossomed in her chest as she glanced over at him again, and in only moments, she reached him. He was younger than she expected with sun-streaked brown hair that was pushed back away from his handsome face. His smile was broad and there were small lines around it already, as though he smiled often. His eyes were a dark, sparkling brown and they seemed to see her as though she was the *only* thing to see.

"Mrs. Miller?" he asked and her heart thumped against her chest.

"Mr. Foster?"

His smile wavered a little as it turned apologetic. "Sorry, ma'am. Mr. Foster couldn't make it here today himself, so he sent me on ahead to meet you. I'm Lewis Conlin, the ranch hand for Mr. Foster. I apologize for the mix up."

That sudden spark died quickly in Beatrice's chest. Her smile wasn't unkind, but it was practiced and it didn't quite reach her eyes. "Oh, that's quite alright," she assured him, though she couldn't deny the disappointment.

He dug into his pants pockets until he withdrew a folded piece of parchment. "Mr. Foster told me to give this to you, so that you know I am who I say I am."

She accepted the letter, and after she unfolded it, she quickly read it and confirmed all that Mr. Conlin had just told her. With a sigh, she folded it up again. "Thank you, Mr. Conlin. Is the ranch far?"

He stared at her for a long moment, almost too long, then seemed to catch himself. He smiled sheepishly then shook his head. "No, ma'am. Not too far. I'll get your things."

Mr. Conlin quickly loaded up her things, then hurried to offer his hand to help her into the wagon. She hesitated for a moment, but then accepted his offer of assistance. His hands were calloused, rough, but gentle as he eased her up. When she had settled in her seat, he hurried over and sat beside her, taking up the reins. Getting the horses started, the plodded ahead at a slow pace. After a few moments of silence, Mr. Conlin began to chat.

"I've worked for Mr. Foster for nearly five years now. He's a hard man, but fair," he explained. "Helped out me and my family quite a bit."

Beatrice's heart reacted strangely to that statement, but she ignored it as best she could. "Oh, are you married, Mr. Conlin?"

He laughed. It was a good sound; warm and sweet. "No,

ma'am. 'Fraid you misunderstood me. Probably my fault anyhow. My family is only my mother and my sister. Haven't gotten around to starting one of my own as of yet."

"Oh. I see."

A spot of silence spread between the two, but it wasn't uncomfortable. Instead, it was filled with the warm afternoon air, the soft clopping of horse hooves, and the sounds of nature just past the road. It was tranquil in a way that the city wasn't, and Beatrice was taking to it immediately.

"I've never been to New York," commented Mr. Conlin, as though reading her mind. "Is it much different?"

Beatrice nodded. "Yes, very. The city is large with towering buildings and—" She stopped abruptly, blushing. "But I'm sure it's like any city. Didn't you come from a city before here?"

He shrugged his broad shoulders. "Oh, sure. I came from Pennsylvania, originally. It was more city-like than this, but it was still just a little speck in the grand scheme of things. I think of it like a bucket in the ocean and this little place out west here is just a drop instead, if you catch my drift."

Beatrice smiled; she liked that analogy. "Yes, I think I do."

"You got family back home, ma'am? Could I call you Beatrice, or is that not right? I have to apologize again; I've got terrible manners."

Beatrice offered him a laugh. Although she didn't think it was quite proper to be called by her first name by a man that was not family nor husband, she admitted that she enjoyed the way he said her name. And she appreciated his asking her. "No, it's alright. I... I think it might be best if you called me Mrs. Miller, though—at least in the presence of Mr. Foster."

His eyebrows rose a little in response to that and Beatrice blushed. She didn't even know why she added on that last bit; she hadn't intended to. There was just something about him that was welcoming and familiar.

After a moment, that warm smile of his returned and she felt the tension ease. "Very well. Then since it's only us, I'll just say it would be nice if you might call me Lewis, Beatrice."

Her flush deepened and they did not converse for the remainder of the trip, but Beatrice felt comfortable—and welcomed.

CHAPTER 8

Foster Ranch, Wyoming – June, 1880

THE TRIP WASN'T TOO LONG, BUT THEY ARRIVED LATE IN the afternoon. Thankfully, the sun was going down later in the evening still, so there was plenty of daylight to see by.

Mr. Conlin—Lewis, were it not for the presence of a man standing on the porch of the main house—offered his hand to help Beatrice descend from the wagon. She accepted once again, the feel of his weathered hands warm and comforting, despite only sharing a short carriage ride together.

"I'll get your things, Bea—Mrs. Miller." Mr. Conlin's

cheeks grew rosy and he ducked away from her quickly. He'd nearly slipped, but caught himself just in time.

That was when she really thought it might have been truly foolish of her to allow him to use her first name—even in private. But she wouldn't focus on that right now.

The man on the porch was older than Mr. Conlin. He looked to be in his thirties, his beard sprinkled with the lightest dusting of graying hair already, wrinkles lining his eyes and his mouth. He stood with his arms folded across his broad chest, scrutinizing her.

This time there was no question; this was Mr. Foster, her future husband.

Something dropped within her, a settling feature of disappointment. She tried to shove it aside, knowing that she would have to embrace this life and this man in some fashion if she were to hope to settle here. Moving forward, she reached him in just a few steps. "Mr. Foster, I presume?"

He nodded. "That's right. And you'd be Mrs. Miller."

Beatrice mimicked his earlier nod. "Yes, sir."

His eyes made a quick pass over her, but she didn't even feel offended or much of any strong emotion at all. The gaze was almost clinical; uninterested. "Trust your health is good?"

"Yes, thank you."

"Good. And your condition?"

Beatrice hesitated, glancing back at Mr. Conlin. She didn't know if he was aware of her pregnancy or if Mr.

Foster was of a mind to explain it to him. Until she knew what his feelings were on the subject, she decided to keep any specifics vague.

"Yes, fine. The train provided no complications."

He nodded again. "Alright. The night's yours to settle in. Tomorrow you'll start the chores; Lewis'll help you. Tonight, supper will be provided, but as of tomorrow, the meals will be your responsibility."

Without another word or a moment for Beatrice to even answer him, he turned away and walked inside the large home. She stared at him, a little surprised, and more than a little dejected.

Don't be so upset, she scolded herself. *This is what you were looking for all along.*

That steadied her a little, though despite what she'd been intending all the way back in Albany, she couldn't shake the settling disappointment.

"Don't worry, Beatrice," Lewis said quietly as he came to stand beside her, gathering her belongings in his arms. "I'll show you around. You've got a cottage all to yourself until... well, until the wedding."

Without any other words exchanged, Lewis led her around to the back where a little one room cottage rested. It wasn't much, but it provided enough room for her, along with a roof over her head and a bed. What more had she expected?

Lewis left her for the night, then explained he wouldn't

be staying for dinner, but that he would see her in the morning. She felt a touch of loneliness at his departure, but told herself that would pass quickly once she adjusted to this new home.

CHAPTER 9

THE NEXT MORNING CAME TOO EARLY FOR BEATRICE. It wasn't that she had never had early mornings before—in fact, when she worked as a seamstress, they were often required to start work very early—but even that didn't compare to the wake-up call sounded by the rooster, crowing to the barely rising sun. It roused her from her sleep, though she remained between sleep and wakefulness until she splashed water upon her face. Between the earliness of the day and the nausea that always came with her mornings now, Beatrice found herself struggling.

Though she did not feel well, she began to dress. She was still wearing black, though it was no longer necessary given her situation, but it was difficult to let go of Thomas—even now. As she began to slip on her underthings, then her dress, and finally her pinafore, she noted the tightness of it all. Her belly was still small, the baby having grown only for a couple of months now, but every little shift in her body seemed to be more noticeable these days.

Her hands flattened across her stomach, and carefully, she caressed it. "A Christmas baby," she murmured in a sweet voice. "Perhaps it is a sign. A gift given in return for what I have lost."

She thought of the two Christmases she spent with Thomas and the Millers. The coldness outside coupled with the heat of the hearth; the fresh scents of cut mistletoe and pine; cooked goose and fresh bread; spiced cider and apples baking. And the decorating... The Millers were not by any means a wealthy family, but they had enough to partake a little in the festiveness of the season. Beatrice would string popcorn and Lydia would giggle as she hung mistletoe. Susan loved to tie bows on the branches of the small tree they managed to place in the small living room.

And Thomas... Oh, how he loved to sing carols and lullabies and anything that sounded sweet.

Just thinking of those times had Beatrice on the verge of tears. She inhaled deeply, doing her best to keep the tears from falling. Forcing the images away, she reminded herself that it was still June and there would be no Thomas—or any Miller at all—with her this Christmas.

It is time to move on. For the baby, she told herself silently.

Winding her hair upon the top of her head, she left the

small cottage in search of the larger house. She wasn't entirely sure of all of which her duties entailed, but she knew that meals were her responsibility. And after dinner last night, she at least knew where the kitchen was.

Upon entering the house, she was immediately greeted by the scent of the meal cooking in the kitchen. She followed her nose more than her memory of the night before and was surprised to find that Lewis was almost finished cooking breakfast.

Immediately, she was plagued by guilt. "Lewis! I didn't mean for you to compensate for my tardiness."

He glanced over his shoulder; his smile was warm and inviting, drawing her closer, even before she realized she was moving at all.

"Don't worry about it, Beatrice." He motioned her over. "I figured I would show you what's expected first anyway, so I planned on it."

Smiling, she nodded. "Thank you. But you should have woken me."

Grinning sheepishly, he looked back to the eggs he was frying. "I thought maybe you needed the sleep. Mornings can be early here."

That, Beatrice wholeheartedly agreed with.

They fell into easy conversation focused on the neutral territory of exactly what was expected of her: the meals, obviously, but also feeding the chickens and the pigs, mending holes in garments, keeping the house, and milking the cows. Lewis told her that there would be more, but that Mr. Foster wanted to make sure she could keep up before piling on the work. He reiterated his belief that Mr. Foster was rough, but fair in the end.

"What are your duties?" Beatrice asked.

Lewis laughed heartily. "Oh, a bit of everything, really. Right now, it's mostly taking care of the cattle and mending the fences. I check the grazing sites, too, to make sure there aren't any predators."

Her eyes widened slightly. "Predators?"

He grinned. "Don't you worry. I keep 'em in check. Mostly it's only wolves and coyotes, though there has been a bandit or two in these parts."

"Bandits!" She gasped and covered her mouth.

He nodded, and this time his grin was gone. "That's right... which is why I don't want you wandering off by yourself. Always make sure that either me or Mr. Foster is there with you, just in case something happens."

Beatrice was quite startled by the idea of bandits, her heart hammering in her chest. Lewis must have noticed her unease and felt regret over it, because he placed a gentle hand on hers. "Now, don't you worry. I'll make sure that no bandits bother you."

His words brought comfort, as did his warm hand, but they also brought a flutter of nervousness. What if Mr. Foster were to walk in right then? Her eyes dropped to where his hand covered hers. Realizing what he was doing, he jerked his hand back quickly and immediately began to apologize.

"I'm so sorry, Beatrice. That was very improper of me," he said, shaking his head.

Beatrice opened her mouth to tell him it was alright, that she hadn't minded his gesture of comfort, but before she got the chance to, Mr. Foster entered the room. The two young people jumped further apart, even though they hadn't been doing anything wrong.

Mr. Foster eyed the exchange quietly and Beatrice felt her face burn with shame. Here was the rancher who had paid her fare to come and be his wife, yet she found herself being drawn closer and closer to his employee. *How terrible of me!* she scolded herself. It didn't matter that the touches were innocent or well-intentioned; she was being cavalier without giving a care or thought to anyone but herself. And what did all of this say about her love for Thomas? Was she so easily drawn away by calloused hands and a warm smile?

Surely not! She was a devoted wife and would be again. This... this *connection* to the ranch hand was nothing more than her latching on to the first thing that brought her security in an otherwise new place.

She insisted upon it, even when her heart sent her signals to suggest otherwise. Those, she chose to ignore.

On the verge of apologizing—she wasn't sure to which party at the moment—Beatrice turned her gaze to Mr. Foster. She found that he had already looked away and was sitting at the table. "Good," he said, much to her surprise. "Glad to see you're already learning your routine. I like routine and I expect you to be proficient at your duties very quickly. If you have any issues, I expect Mr. Conlin here will help in that regard."

Beatrice couldn't bear to bring herself to look over at the handsome young ranch hand, so she kept her eyes down as she grabbed the food and began to set it on the table. Together, they all sat down for breakfast, and Mr. Foster surprised her with a prayer of thanks to God before feasting upon his meal. Beatrice appreciated that more than anything.

When the meal was over, Mr. Foster left, and the only reason that Mr. Conlin didn't go with him was because he insisted on Mr. Conlin showing Beatrice her duties. To his character, Mr. Conlin didn't seem to have any protests to this. He showed her where the feed was kept. He taught her how to milk the cows, and while she felt that it was actually much harder than it looked, she was certain she could master it easily. Mr. Conlin showed her the cattle and the horses, letting her skim her hand over their silky coats and through their manes.

Quickly, it was lunch time, and Mr. Conlin went over what Mr. Foster usually expected for his meals. Mr. Conlin also explained that while he often joined him for lunch—for the sake of convenience—he was there for breakfast only some of the time, and that he almost never stayed for dinner. That time was reserved to be spent with his own family, he confided in her.

All through the day, Beatrice found him charming. He was sweet in all the ways Mr. Foster wasn't, and attentive in ways that soothed her. With only one day, Mr. Conlin made her feel as though this place could eventually feel like home.

CHAPTER 10

By the start of July, the weather had become much warmer. Beatrice had gone to town twice with Mr. Conlin to pick up material for new dresses; none were fitting her, and they were all much too heavy for summer anyway. She wasn't very large yet, but the evidence of her child was quickly becoming much more noticeable. She'd managed to make a dress that was a bit loose on her in an effort to make it adjustable around her slowly swelling belly. The pinafore she wore over the dress helped to cinch it down for the time being and kept it from getting too dirty.

As the weeks passed, Beatrice found herself sure of just two things. First, that Mr. Foster was indeed a gruff, uncouth man, and while she believed him to be a fair and just man, she knew with certainty that she could never love him. She reminded herself every day that this was acceptable to her. She hadn't ventured out to the West in search of love, but for a marriage of convenience that might ease her broken heart and provide for her growing baby. Yet even so, she could not doubt that inside, her heart wondered if any of it were true. Could she really live forever in a loveless marriage?

But for all her doubts, it was her second certainty that seemed to steady her: she greatly enjoyed spending time with Mr. Conlin. She found him to be a sweet, kind young man. He was constantly helping her with her chores, ensuring her comfort and asking if she needed anything. He was incredibly attentive, despite his own chores and responsibilities, of which there were many.

Was it wrong to feel so...*grateful* for his presence?

Of course not! She reassured herself with force one afternoon as she tended to the horses. She found that she enjoyed grooming them immensely, and they seemed to prefer her feminine touch. Finishing up with the horses, a majestic flaxen chestnut stallion and a beautiful buckskin mare, Beatrice bid them both good day, returning to the house to begin the inside chores. Lunch was already taken care of, thankfully, so she only needed to worry about the evening meal, which wasn't for hours.

Pausing on the porch, she peered through the windows for any evidence of Mr. Foster, and when she saw none, a decision was made. Her feet begin to carry her swiftly off the porch and out into the fields beyond the house. The

Foster Ranch was quite large, but Beatrice had some idea of where she might go—and who she might find there.

Long strides took her quickly towards the fence where she thought Mr. Conlin might be mending it, however, as she grew closer, the windmill that loomed in the sky appeared on her right side. It was quite tall, with four legs and crossing braces that made it look like a mismatched ladder. She might have continued on past it if she hadn't noticed that several tools lay at the base of the windmill. Frowning, she approached them for closer inspection. Once there, she heard a sound from above her.

"Beatrice!"

Startled, she looked up only to see that Mr. Conlin was atop the windmill!

"Lewis!" she cried. "Get down immediately! That is dangerous!"

She didn't care that she sounded like a nagging mother; she was genuinely concerned for his safety. He actually laughed at her, the wind carrying the sound and tossing it about until it finally reached her ears. She found the sound to be warming—even if she was angry with him for being so very high up.

She didn't have to tell him twice. He quickly began to descend, and in moments, he was on the ground again. Dusting himself off, he removed the thick work gloves he wore to protect his already worn hands. "Beatrice, I—"

Stomping right up to him, she wagged her finger in his

direction. "Lewis Conlin, what on Earth were doing up there? You could have fallen!"

Although he looked moderately chastised, he was still grinning; something that probably had not helped his cause. But before she had cause to grow angrier with him, he held up his hands, palms flat, to show that he was apologetic, at least. "Don't worry so much, Beatrice. I've done this a thousand times. I know what I'm doing."

Beatrice's flushed face suggested that she didn't care how confident he was. Frustrated, she turned around abruptly, her skirts tangling around her feet, and began to march decidedly away from him.

"Beatrice! Where are you going?" When she neither stopped nor answered him, he began to jog after her. "Wait!"

His long strides caught up with her easily and he reached for her arm. Tugging her around to face him, he said, "Wait, please, I'm sorry."

She shook off his arm, and for a second, looked as though she might have scolded him for his inappropriate behavior. But then her features softened. Her eyes glistened. His eyes widened; he was surprised that she felt so strongly about this that she might cry. And she *did* feel like crying. He had legitimately scared her, though that certainly wasn't the only cause.

Letting his hand drop, Lewis removed his wide hat and held it in front of him, fiddling with the brim. "Please, don't be upset with me. I really am sorry. I didn't mean to scare you, but I wouldn't have done something I didn't feel confident about. And, well, that's part of my job."

Taking a deep breath, she nodded her head. Discreetly, she wiped at her eyes and did her best to compose herself. She suddenly felt weary as a result of that brief flash of intense emotion, but she did her best to compose herself. "Of course. I ought to apologize, too. I shouldn't have... This is your job, and naturally, you would be skilled at it. I am just..." She waved her hands about as though she was searching for words in the air. She knew what she wanted to say, but wasn't quite sure about how to say it. Although she had begun to show, her condition had not been openly discussed except for briefly in passing between herself and Mr. Foster. These talks consisted mainly of what might be needed around the house to accommodate the birth. Otherwise, there was little talk at all.

Lewis studied her quietly for a moment, then asked gently, "Is it the baby?"

She glanced up at him from beneath her lashes. It should come as no surprise that he would know of her pregnancy. She was beginning to show, but certainly, he would know it was not Mr. Foster's, as they had not yet married. After a moment, she nodded. "Yes. I find I am more easily upset these days. The baby is beginning to intensify my feelings already, and he is still so young."

Lewis smiled warmly at her. The warmth of his smile seemed to flood her heart, her cheeks blushing furiously; such was always the case whenever she was around him. She couldn't say exactly what it was about him that warmed her grief-stricken heart, or perhaps it was merely that she wasn't yet ready to admit to herself what it was. Thomas had been so important to her. Grief lingered in her heart, but when Lewis around, he helped ease the pain.

"When is the baby due," he inquired politely, "if it's alright for me to ask?"

She smiled at him and nodded. "Of course it is. My condition is hardly a secret." Her pregnancy was something that Mr. Foster didn't seem interested in discussing much; Lewis was the first to really ask her about it. She turned and began to walk slowly, not with any particular place in mind. "I expect the baby to come along near Christmastime." She smiled softly, her hands absently caressing her just-swollen belly. "I have always loved the season, though I don't know how I'll react to it out here. Is it even the same?"

Lewis easily fell into step beside her and shook his head a little. "In some ways. We get the snow, but it's dryer here. The cold seems to bite more—but we'll keep the hearth warm for you this winter, Beatrice." He smiled genuinely, his eyes sparkling. "A Christmas birth," he commented. "A true gift."

Beatrice allowed herself to study Lewis' face. She noticed his faint laugh lines and the weathered skin that came from many days spent outside, working in the sun, the cold, and the heat. His hair was brown, but kissed by the sun, and would often flop into his eyes as though he was in need of a trim. She thought of offering to cut it for him, but wasn't sure if that was appropriate.

"I think you are the first to consider this child as a gift," she murmured softly and it was the truth. Although the Millers hadn't considered the baby to be a problem or anything of the like, they certainly hadn't thought of it as a blessing. They were poor and had only just lost their son. Although this baby was a continuation of him, it was also another burden to be shared on people who hardly had the means to fend for themselves. And Mr. Foster could not care less about the baby. He meant it no harm, of course, and would likely treat her child with the same civil affection that would be considered dutiful. But he would never love it. To him, having a child around was merely a part of having a wife. Maybe it would even be an excuse to not have a child of his own.

But Lewis...

"What else could a baby be but a gift?" he asked her rhetorically. "It is a miraculous thing for a woman to become a mother, isn't it? Why shouldn't a baby then, under any circumstance, be considered a blessing?"

Beatrice's heart swelled at the sentiment behind his words. She had grieved herself when she'd learned of her pregnancy. It had terrified her, the thought of being alone to care for a child who would grow up fatherless. Not through any fault of its own or hers, but through accident. But as Lewis spoke, she felt a tight knot ease inside of her—the one that had been made up of worry and all of the awful emotions that come with the unknown.

"Thank you," she said to him finally, her words genuine. "I had forgotten that this baby could be anything other than a burden."

Lewis's smile softened, sympathetic. "It must be difficult. The father... he's gone?" By the tentativeness of his tone, Beatrice could tell that he was uncertain whether or not he should be asking. And it gave her confidence that he meant no harm and would think no less of her, regardless of her answer.

Beatrice nodded. Though there was a lump of sadness in her throat, she managed to speak past it. "Yes. My husband, Thomas... he died just this past April. It was a terrible accident." Her hand clutched at her breast, willing her heart to stop its aching. "He was very dear to me."

After a moment, Lewis asked, "Is that why you came here?"

"Yes. I... I feared I might never be able to love again." She didn't tell him that she might have been wrong, or that her decision might have been made too rashly. Instead, she only added, "I answered Mr. Foster's ad knowing that neither of us would provide anything more than stability for the other. That was my intention."

Lewis fell quiet. They walked slowly, picking their way through the fields. Perhaps it was wasting time that was not really theirs, but neither could bring themselves to return to the chores still needed to be finished just yet. Instead, they desired to linger in each other's company, happy for these few brief stolen minutes together.

"And now that you're here?" Lewis asked after a while. They were nearing the main house, and as a result, they slowed, neither quite ready to part ways. "Do you still agree with your decision?"

"Yes," Beatrice added immediately, until she noticed how Lewis's expression fell. Quickly, she added, "Yes, I agree with the decision to come *here*. I find that I very much like it here."

The corners of his lips curled into a smile that was slow to come, but warm when it did. "I didn't think you'd come to like Mr. Foster all that much, if you don't mind me saying." His voice was moderately teasing, perhaps guessing to her intentions—more so than she had.

Her cheeks flushed, but she lifted her chin. She glanced over at him out of the corner of her eye to see that he was staring at her. When their eyes met, both looked away quickly. "I... like him just fine. He is a decent man, although I am certain there will be no love between us." As the words tumbled from her lips, she realized how they sounded and quickly added, "Which is precisely what I had anticipated. I do not regret our lack of closeness."

"Of course, that was the plan." They fell into companionable silence once again. They had almost reached the house when Lewis finally spoke again. "Christmas will be cold. Perhaps I'll ask my sister to knit an afghan for you—and the baby. She's very good."

"Oh, no! I couldn't possibly—"

"I insist. You'll need the warmth."

She smiled softly at him. "That is very kind."

"I would do it myself if I were any good at it," he answered a little sheepishly. After another moment, he cleared his throat and said, "I enjoy Christmas very much, but it has lost some of its joy since my father's passing."

Thinking on it for only half a moment, Beatrice boldly told him, "Perhaps you might stay for dinner that evening, then. It will be very lonely for only myself and Mr. Foster. Company would be lovely."

He looked over to her, seeming genuinely surprised, but happy for the invitation. He was about to accept it, it seemed, but in the next moment, his smile dropped and his shoulders sagged. "I am happy to have received the invitation, Beatrice, but I couldn't do that. My sister and mother would be alone for the night and I—"

Before he could go any further, Beatrice placed a gentle hand on his arm, thoughtlessly so, and said, "Nonsense. The invitation is to all of your family. As I said, Mr. Foster and myself could surely use the company. The winter is only cold when one spends it alone."

The eagerness returned to his eyes and he said, "Then I would happily accept your invitation."

"Good. I would have it no other way."

Neither seemed to think twice about Beatrice having invited him without so much as discussing it with Mr. Foster.

CHAPTER 11

Months passed. Beatrice grew accustomed to the early mornings, even as the days became shorter and she found herself up hours before dawn. At the same time, she grew rounder and the weather grew colder. Her time with Mr. Foster was civil, if not wholly warm, and her friendliness with Lewis grew. It never reached beyond friendship, but as Beatrice's heart grew full of thoughts of him and his warm smile, the tiniest part of herself admitted that she wished it might.

It was a foolish wish, but not because of her late husband. He was gone, and while it had not yet been a full year since his passing, she acknowledged that she would mend. The grief that lingered in her breast would not turn her to stone and as her belly grew, and she began to embrace the gift she had been given. A baby. A physical, living memory of the man she had first given her heart to. The birth might be bittersweet, she admitted, but it would hold all of the pleasantness that comes from a memory to be cherished.

No, it was not poor Thomas' memory that made her desire for closeness to Lewis seem foolish. Instead, it was Mr. Foster.

There was no love that would ever grow between them. She accepted that and did not wish to change it. On his part, he felt the same. He wanted only a wife. But Beatrice had entered into a deal with the man and it seemed dishonest of her to now wish for something more.

And despite the sweet affections Lewis seemed to share with her, there was no guarantee that they were any different from affections he might offer to someone else. He was a kind, decent man, and she believed he shared that kindness easily with everyone. Perhaps it was all for the best that the lingering desires in her heart remained there alone.

As the weather grew cold, Beatrice wore more and more layers. They helped to keep her warm, though her hands were often chilled. Lewis's sister—whom Beatrice learned was named Daniella—had knitted the afghan as Lewis had promised. It sat at the foot of her bed, and at night, she curled up with it and it indeed kept her warm. By December, she was using it every night.

On the morning of the first of December, there was snow on the ground. It was more than the few sprinklings that had arrived throughout November; this was calf-deep, and with it came a beautiful silence that was sweet and soothing, if chilly.

Beatrice took time to bundle up, taking extra care around her swollen belly. She was excited for December, not only because her baby was kicking often now, but because it had always been her favorite month. The snow, the scents of baking and of the wood burning stove; they filled the short days and long nights with a kind of magic that could only be found then. December was a special time to her, and she held it close to her heart.

Leaving her cottage for the main house while the sky was still dark, she trekked through the deep snow. It was a little inconvenient and was about the only reason she looked forward to marrying. She would be able to stay in the main house and not have to leave the warmth of the house to make breakfast, but unfortunately, it wasn't quite enough to make her truly look forward to the marriage.

Letting out a sigh that came in a breath she could see before her face, Beatrice moved as quickly as she could through the snow. When she made it to the main house, she kicked the snow off her boots and stepped inside. The house was a bit chilly, but it was beginning to warm which meant that the stove was already lit. Uncovering her hair to keep it from getting damp, she headed to the kitchen. She wasn't surprised to find that Lewis was already there.

Although Beatrice had grown accustomed to making the meals and tending to her other chores, Lewis still insisted on helping her when he could—with breakfast especially, it seemed, though she could hardly fathom why.

"Good morning," he greeted her cheerfully. As usual, his eyes dropped to her belly briefly before raising to her face once more. "How is the baby this morning?"

This, too, had become the norm. While Mr. Foster still referred to her baby as her "condition," Lewis had started to ask how she was feeling and how the baby was daily. It was nice to speak of her child, to treat him or her like a positive thing coming into the world.

"Very active," Beatrice admitted, as she took up her spot beside him. Lewis insisted on doing most of the cooking these days, and she was hardly in much condition to argue. Though she still did chores and cooked meals, there was no denying that the labor was beginning to wear on her. Now that she was very pregnant, it was difficult to get around and she became winded easily. "The baby has been kicking me all morning."

Lewis laughed softly. "He or she's gonna be a morning person. Consider yourself lucky."

She waved him off, spraying small speckles of flour on him. "Oh, wonderful. A little morning person. But what about *my* wishes? I wouldn't mind a little more peace in the mornings, myself."

Grinning, Lewis dusted off a spot of flour. "Maybe you'll become a morning person, too."

"Doubtful," she told him, though in all fairness she *did* enjoy her mornings. That was hardly because of the early hour, however; it had more to do with the pleasant way she began each day, having light conversation with Lewis over making breakfast.

"Have you thought of a name?"

She paused with uncertainty. She *had* thought of a name, as a matter of fact. She'd decided upon it almost immediately and hadn't reconsidered since. "I have," she said finally, cautious.

"And?" he prompted.

"Thomas."

Silence descended upon the kitchen. Lewis, of course, knew who her late husband was. They had spoken of him on several occasions, and in each of them, he'd been quite sympathetic. But now she worried that perhaps her answer might ruin his mood. It wasn't healthy to bring up the dead so often, even when they were your beloved—or maybe especially because of just that.

"Obviously, that is assuming it is a boy," she continued when Lewis did not immediately answer. "But if it is a girl, I thought perhaps Mary. It seems appropriate for Christmas, doesn't it?"

Beatrice worried momentarily that he still wouldn't answer, but then he looked over at her and smiled gently. "It's lovely. And... Thomas is a good name, too. A boy would be so lucky to honor his father that way."

Her shoulders eased, the tension slipping away, and she smiled gently at him. "Thank you."

They talked easily for the rest of the morning until Mr.

Foster came in. They all sat together to eat and Beatrice did her best to not sneak secret glances at Lewis, and he tried to do the same.

Later in the day, Beatrice determined that she needed to begin decorating the house. It was finally December, and she wanted the festiveness of the season to last all month long. She spent time making cider, baking apples, and kneading dough for fresh dinner rolls.

Lewis would come in from time to time bearing small gifts. He'd bring in evergreen clippings for her to make wreaths with; she also tied them together with small red bows to make a festive garland for the mantle. He also managed to gather a small bunch of mistletoe for her, and with his help, she hung it above the doorway.

By the end of the first day, she felt satisfied in a way that she hadn't in a long time. The traditions of Christmas warmed her heart, allowing her to forget about her swollen feet and aching back for a while. They brought her joy, and had her looking forward to Christmastime more and more each day.

Each of Beatrice's December days passed much the same. She would spend her mornings with Lewis, who brought her tree clippings, pine cones, and fabrics from town to be made into lovely ribbons. Her afternoons would be a mixture of decorating, baking, and chores, followed by the evening meal and some quiet time with Mr. Foster, who spent it mostly reading softly by candlelight. They got along well enough, but there was no chemistry between them whatsoever. She wished him no ill will, but she admitted that his presence often made her feel lonelier.

One night, only a few days into December, Beatrice found herself working on her needlework as Mr. Foster read by the fire. It was perhaps the scent of the pine cones burning as they helped the fire along that made her think of Christmas, and she found herself musing on the Christmas dinner that was to come—and that Lewis and his family would be there.

She had not yet discussed her invitation with Mr. Foster, however. Realizing her mistake, she set her needlework aside and worried her hands together. Turning to him, she resolved to inform him of the invitation, but the words had a hard time coming out. He looked up, sensing someone watching him, to find her mouth opening and closing with uncertainty.

He lifted an eyebrow in question. "Well? What is it, woman?"

Swallowing heavily, she straightened up and found her courage. "I wished to mention that Christmas will be here very soon."

He grunted. He didn't dislike Christmas, but he was not a man of much holiday cheer, either. "I'm aware. Hard to forget about it with all these decorations." He waved towards the mantle and the mistletoe above the door.

About to return to his book, Beatrice quickly continued. "I was intending to have a dinner."

He grunted again, but said nothing in response.

"And it is so much better to have company at such dinners, isn't it?"

At this he glanced up again, eyebrows raised curiously. "Is that so?"

She nodded. "Oh, yes. It's a tradition, isn't it?" Before he could agree or disagree, she hurried on. "Which is why I took the liberty of inviting Mr. Conlin and his family for you."

For a second, his jaw worked and his eyes narrowed. He looked angry at this new bit of information and she worried he might tell her to inform Lewis that there would be no Christmas dinner *here* for the Conlins, but then he blew out a long breath that disturbed his mustache. She thought he said several things under his breath, but she caught none of them. Then, with a sigh, he nodded his head. "Yes, of course. Good, good." He went back to his reading and didn't speak to her again until she bid him goodnight before returning to her small cottage.

She felt immensely relieved that he'd agreed to her proposal, and she felt foolish for having waited so long before telling him. But the Conlins were coming for Christmas dinner, and there was little she was more excited for—other than the baby itself, of course.

CHAPTER 12

CHRISTMAS EVE ARRIVED ONLY A FEW SHORT WEEKS later. Snow lingered on the ground, though the skies were clear and blue. Everything was thankfully still, as the wind often made the cold much more brutal. Beatrice was especially thankful because the Conlins would be arriving that day, late in the afternoon, by wagon and she was sure it would be the same one Lewis had picked her up in. It was uncovered and would freeze the lot of them to their very bones. This was the reason behind Beatrice's insistence that the whole family would stay through the night and could leave as they pleased the following morning. She would have it no other way. It was also a comfort to herself that she would have roommates for the night, as the Conlin women would sleep in her cottage.

That day, there were no chores. For once, it was just

about spending time with each other. Sure, there was cooking to do, but Beatrice enjoyed that most days—and today, especially. Mr. Foster made sure that the fire was stoked and made his rounds to check on the animals. Beatrice encouraged him to try decorating, perhaps finishing the string of popcorn she'd been working on, but he just wasn't all that interested. Beatrice had learned by now that he was a hardworking man, but otherwise enjoyed the peace and quiet of being left alone.

Beatrice didn't let his aloofness bother her; not today. She was too busy baking gingerbread and apple pie. There was pheasant, buttered potatoes, fresh dinner rolls, and a variety of other sides that would be sure to fill everyone's hunger tonight. The scents coming from the kitchen combined with those of the pine logs burning in the fire, the roasting nuts crackling within, and more fresh clippings Lewis had brought her only just yesterday.

Her baby was lightly kicking today, and as she was reminded of Thomas with each tiny kick, she felt that similar bittersweet sorrow that always came along with thoughts of him. She wished he was here to sing his carols, but she did her best not to let those thoughts be of sadness only. Instead, she reminded herself that she had a gift this Christmas; a gift from him.

By late afternoon, the Conlins had arrived. "Mr. Foster, Mrs. Miller—" it had been so long since Lewis had addressed her as such that Beatrice started at the formality of it, "—it is my pleasure to introduce you to my sister, Daniella, and my mother, Donna."

The older of the women—lovely, if a little weary—had long brown hair twisted into a neat bun atop her head and stepped forward. "Thank you so much for the invitation, Mr. Foster. You've been nothing but generous to my boy."

Mr. Foster cleared his throat and actually looked a bit flustered by her words. "Of course. He's a decent lad."

Daniella, however, darted right around Mr. Foster and headed straight for Beatrice. "Oh, Beatrice! You're just as lovely as my brother says!" Both Beatrice and Lewis flushed at the comment, but no one else seemed to take any heed of it. Daniella wrapped her arms around her in a warm embrace.

"Daniella!" scolded her mother, but the younger woman paid no mind.

"I am so happy to finally meet you! My brother is so fond of you."

At this, Mr. Foster shifted his gaze to Lewis, whose cheeks were quite red now. He didn't say anything, but the suspicion was there. Lewis cleared his throat. "Oh, don't exaggerate, Daniella. You make it sound like I'm just over the moon—"

When his eyes caught Beatrice's, he broke off. His little sister grinned at him slyly, but said nothing more on the subject. Instead, Mrs. Conlin offered a covered dish to Beatrice. "I hope you don't mind something extra for the table."

"Thank you, Mrs. Conlin. That's very gracious of you."

Grateful for the opportunity, Beatrice took the dish into the dining room and set it down with the rest of the food. The others followed in and took their seats: Mr. Foster at the head of the table, Beatrice on his left and Daniella on hers, then across the table sat Lewis and his mother. Before beginning, Mr. Foster took a moment to say grace.

"Thank you, Lord, for this generous meal on this most holy of days," he said in that gruff, deep voice of his. "And let us be grateful for the kind company we have the opportunity to share it with, by your grace."

They said "amen" in unison, then began to eat.

The meal was full of laughter and teasing, good food and high spirits. They sat at the table late into the evening it seemed, ignoring the howling of the snow outside, which had begun well after dark. Mr. Foster got up twice to stoke the fire, and Daniella insisted on singing several carols, each one charming—and very out of tune. Mrs. Conlin shared stories of her late husband and of the trouble of raising children.

It wasn't until the end of the meal that Beatrice started to notice it. "Mr. Conlin, is everything alright?" she asked gently, noticing that he'd grown unusually quiet—even for him—and had wiped his hands on his trousers at least three times in a very short amount of time.

At first, he seemed startled by her question, but then he forced a laugh. "Oh, yes. Merely thinking of what a lovely meal this has been."

Beatrice did not trust this as honesty, but not wanting to

cause a scene, she let his comment go. She smiled at him and thanked him.

"Beatrice, fetch the cider?" asked Mr. Foster, offering his glass.

Beatrice nodded and stood, taking the glass from him and turning to head into the kitchen. She didn't realize Lewis had followed her there until she turned to find him only a couple of steps away. Startled, she nearly dropped her glass, but just barely managed to keep hold of it. "Oh! You startled me! Did you need something?"

Taking a deep breath, he nodded his head. "Yes, I do, ma'am. I need something desperately, but I'm afraid I don't have any right to ask for it." His eyes sparked with intensity, full of hope and uncertainty.

Frowning a little, she asked, "And what is that you feel you have no right to ask for?"

He took a step forward. "Your hand."

She nearly dropped the glass again. This time, she set it on the counter before she risked it again. "My hand?" she asked breathlessly.

He nodded his head. "Yes. I must admit that I've fallen in love with you, Beatrice. And I was hoping that, if you might feel the same, you would consider to consenting to marrying me."

He eyes widened and her heart leapt within her breast. Then, without thinking of the impropriety of it or the complications of his question, she threw herself into his arms. She embraced him as tightly as she could, and after only a moment, he returned the embrace. It was awkward due to her rather large belly, but neither of them seemed to care in the slightest. Just as they began to pull apart, the answer "yes" shining in her eyes, the door pushed open and Mr. Foster walked in.

Everyone froze.

Mr. Fosters eyes widened, then narrowed into tiny slits as he approached Lewis. "You thieving, no good—"

The couple broke apart and Lewis urged Beatrice behind him, shielding her from Mr. Foster's anger. He held up one hand to suggest for the other man to calm down. "Now, Mr. Foster, let me explain."

"What could you possibly have to say that might explain *this*?" demanded the older man. "That woman you were so crudely embracing is to be my *wife*! Have you no shame?"

Lewis flinched at the man's words, but other than that, he held his ground. He would not give up so easily on winning Beatrice. "I want to tell you that we have done nothing wrong," he began, but Beatrice thought of the stolen moments out walking and talking in the fields. Was he wrong? Had they done something inappropriate?

"Nothing wrong? What do you call this!?"

Lewis straightened himself up as tall as he could and faced Mr. Foster like a man. "Begging your pardon, sir, it was not my aim to be improper. I wanted only to ask Beatrice first if she might feel as I do before making a fool of myself by talking to you."

Mr. Foster scoffed, but did not stop Lewis as he continued to explain.

"I was going to ask you tomorrow, should she say her feelings mirrored mine. I would have done nothing improper before speaking with you."

Mr. Foster didn't look appeased. His face was red with anger and his mustache twitched as his jaw clenched and unclenched several times. He looked ready to protest further, to tell them that he would not allow this, when Beatrice stepped around Lewis to be included again.

Her hands settled on her engorged belly and her voice came out soft, but strong. "Please, Mr. Foster, do not deny this. When I first answered your ad, I had every intention of fulfilling my end of our bargain. I came here expecting a marriage of convenience, because I thought I could have nothing else. My love had died; I could not love again. But from the moment I met Mr. Conlin, I felt that familiar spark of life within me again. I did my best to deny it, but one does not deny love—for it is a gift. A gift I *need*. And my baby will need it, too."

She smiled weakly at him and stepped forward, placing her hand on his arm. "I know that you are a decent man, but you have no love for me, nor I for you. It was the whole reason behind our bargain, but things have changed for me now. It would be unfair to everyone if I married one man while I loved another."

Mr. Foster frowned, but slowly the redness in his cheeks began to fade. His eyes darted between the two young people in his kitchen. He didn't look happy, but when he sighed, Beatrice knew they had won.

"Very well. For the sake of your baby," he waved at her stomach, "I will allow this."

It was the first time he'd referred to her baby; the first time it was not merely her *condition*.

She beamed at him and thanked him profusely. He mumbled something in response, then turned to exit the kitchen. The couple embraced once again.

After that, the evening went smoothly. Lewis announced to his mother and sister that they were to be married, and both were quite shocked by the news at first, to say the least, but very excited about it. They spent the rest of the evening singing carols and laughing over cider. Mr. Foster retired to his seat by the fire to read, unconcerned with the merriment and uninterested in joining in, but he held them no ill will.

When it was time for everyone to retire for the evening, Lewis escorted the three women to Beatrice's cottage, navigating through the whipping wind and snow as best he could. Upon arriving, he bid the women goodnight, lingering with Beatrice's hand in his. He smiled warmly at her, and returned to the house where he would be staying for the night.

The women settled in for what was expected to be a quiet night, but quiet, it was not. Not long after laying down, Beatrice's water broke, and suddenly, she was going into labor. If it were not for the two women there with her, she would have had a very difficult time. Throughout the night, they made her as comfortable as they could, propping her up with pillows and dabbing at her sweat-covered forehead with a damp cloth. They encouraged her, and soothed her, and eased her through the birth. She cried out several times, but the storm swallowed up her howling to join it with its own. By the time the baby was born, the storm outside went quiet. On Christmas Day, the sun was just beginning to rise from between the trees when Beatrice was handed her newborn baby boy.

"Thomas," she whispered to him, cooing softly as she cuddled her tiny miracle.

CHAPTER 13

It wasn't until the following spring that Beatrice and Lewis were married. They wanted to wait for both the snow to pass and to give baby Thomas time to adjust to this new world before making their vows.

In April, a year after the passing of her first love, Beatrice did something she never thought she would be capable of again. She donned a beautiful cream-colored gown, dressed Thomas in a carefully embroidered outfit, and walked down the aisle carrying him in her arms. She met Lewis there at the altar in front of the priest and knew that, somehow, she had found love again. She didn't know how, or even if she deserved such happiness a second time, but she felt blessed to have found it.

Lewis was a wonderful man; a kind, warm person who treated her with such love and care. He looked so fondly on little Thomas, unconcerned that the child was not his, because when he promised to love her until his death, he promised to love little Thomas, too.

Beatrice only wished that the Millers had been able to attend, but she had received several well-wishing letters from them. It was not the same as having them in attendance, but it took the last weight off her shoulders to know that they were not upset with her for finding happiness once more.

Little Thomas giggled in Beatrice's arms and she smiled down at him. Lewis did the same before leaning forward and pressing his lips to hers. The kiss was sweet, chaste, and spoke of a love that Beatrice felt so lucky to have found again.

Truly, she was blessed.

THE END

MILLIE'S CHRISTMAS SURPRISE

Brides Of Weber Valley

MILLIE'S CHRISTMAS SURPRISE

OGDEN, UTAH TERRITORY – 1875

Millie Saxton knows what she wants. Or, more accurately, she knows what she doesn't want. She left New York, the place of her birth and her successful job as a seamstress at a shirtwaist factory, to find love out West. She met a man named James O'Neill who placed an advertisement in the newspaper and, before long, sent for her. But when the train stops in Ogden, Utah and a nasty winter storm hits, Millie finds that her future as Mr. O'Neill's bride might not be what she wants.

A blacksmith by the name of Clyde Roberts hammers his way into her life and refuses to leave. What started out as a chance meeting on the main street of Ogden becomes something far more noteworthy for Millie.

Will she be forced to continue westward and keep her word to James, or can this handsome metalworker unlock her heart and let her dreams come alive?

CHAPTER 1

THE TRAIN JOSTLED MILLIE SAXTON AWAKE. HER HEAD was pressed up against the glass window and she didn't know how long she'd been asleep, but gazing out of the window she realized that her train had stopped. She had finally arrived at her destination – well, her first stop anyway.

Gathering her bags, she stepped off the train and onto the platform at the Ogden station. From here, Millie's plan was to continue on to California. She grinned a bit as the sun's warm rays touched her pale skin. She'd just arrived and already the West felt like home.

The sun couldn't quite ward off the wintry chill, however. As soon as she'd thought about how pleasant this place was, a gust hit her face and woke her up to the fact that it was indeed mid-November and it was no time to be standing outside without a coat on. Fortunately, Millie had packed along such a garment.

She brought her bags to a bench and set them down before rummaging through them for her handmade, black woolen jacket. Millie hadn't had much back home in New York, but she'd worked in a shirtwaist factory so she knew a thing or two about making clothing. Once she found the jacket in question, she threw it on and carefully buttoned it up. That would help keep her warm for the time being.

Collecting up her bags once again, Millie marched with purpose to the ticket counter. She smiled politely at the man sitting there. "Hello," she said. "What time is the train to Coloma arriving, please?"

The man at the ticket counter looked at his ledger and tutted a bit. "'Fraid the train is delayed three days. There's some nasty weather in Nevada."

Millie's smile folded into a frown. This was not the sort of news that she wanted to hear, nor was she prepared for it. "I see... Well, thank you, sir."

Collecting up her bags again, she approached a carriage driver who was parked outside of the train station, seemingly for the exact purpose that she needed him for. "Excuse me, sir?" she said, approaching him with another polite smile on her face which she somehow mustered even though she was feeling rather downtrodden at the news.

"Hello, little lady," the driver said, smiling back at her. "Do you need a lift somewhere?"

Millie nodded. "I sure do. The problem is, I'm not

entirely sure where... Is there a good inn or boarding house around here where I might be able to stay until my next train's departure?"

The driver rubbed his chin a bit, furrowing his bushy, graying black brows. "There's an inn nearby that often takes in people from these trains," he told her. "I reckon it's nicer than staying at the boarding house in town."

"Great," Millie said, a sigh of relief edging into her voice. "That will be perfect. Thank you."

The gentleman climbed out of the front seat of his carriage and took her baggage, organizing it in the trunk before helping Millie into the cushioned back seat. It was a black carriage, with a matching black upholstered interior. It wasn't fancy, but Millie couldn't remember the last time she had ridden in a carriage like it. She was used to walking, or at the very least riding in the small hansom cabs for a few blocks. This carriage made her feel like a princess.

Once she was all settled inside, the driver got back up on his seat at the front and they were off down the street. Millie looked out the windows and admired the small Utah town that she hadn't expected to really see much of before. It looked like a sweet little place.

The driver was correct about the inn being convenient for train riders, too. It felt like she had only just sat down when they arrived at the large farmhouse. Millie gaped out the window at it. "Why, this looks like a family's home!" she cried in her surprise. "I wouldn't want to intrude..."

The carriage driver chuckled as he helped her down

from her seat. "A lot of people say that when they first see this place. Mrs. Pratt does a mighty fine job of keeping her inn feeling like a home, too, I assure you." He retrieved the bags for Millie and walked with her to the back door, while she admired the exterior of the house the whole way. It was made of wood and stone, and painted white with blue shutters. The city didn't have houses like this; Millie was used to being surrounded by brick and concrete.

At the back of the house, there was an entrance with a sign above it that read *Mrs. Pratt's Inn*. While Millie stood looking at it, the carriage driver leaned forward and knocked on the door. After a few moments, the door opened up and a radiant blonde woman smiled out at the two of them. "Hello and welcome," she said brightly, holding the door wide so they could pass through and come inside the pleasantly warm house. There was a small counter to the right and the woman bustled there behind it, taking out a ledger book so she could take down her new guest's information. "What is your name, please?"

Millie blinked, amazed by the woman's efficiency. "Millie Saxton," she said. "From New York."

The woman scribbled that down into the notebook. "How many nights will you be staying with us, Miss Saxton?"

Millie blushed a bit. "I was told that the train was delayed and would be here within three days..."

"Lovely," the woman said, taking that down as well and giving a nod. When she was done writing, she looked back up and smiled at Millie again. "We're certainly glad to have you here with us, Miss Saxton. I am Mrs. Pratt, the owner of this residence. I can show you to your room now, if you'd like."

At that, she gave the driver a look as if she understood that the man didn't want to tarry there for too long. Besides, he was holding two fairly heavy suitcases.

Millie looked at him too and understood at once. "Oh, yes, please."

Mrs. Pratt smiled another delighted smile and led the way towards the staircase further inside the home. Millie continued to gaze at the place, admiring too the small crowd of people that were gathered in the spacious living room area. They were all chatting over tea and cakes. It seemed more like some kind of party than a group of strangers who all just happened to be staying at the same inn.

Yes, I could get quite used to staying here, Millie thought confidently with a smile of her own.

CHAPTER 2

AFTER BEING SHOWN TO HER ROOM, MILLIE FELL BACK onto the soft blankets and pillows and immediately drifted to sleep. She slept for only an hour or so, and when she awoke she felt more than a little embarrassed. *That is no way to make a good first impression on these kind people who are allowing me to dwell in their home!* she mentally chastised herself. She briskly got out of the bed and tidied up her appearance, using the large mirror on the room's beautiful cherry wood vanity. Her long, auburn-brown tresses were completely disheveled by her slumber, so she collected up some of her hair pins and ribbons from one of her suitcases and carefully styled her hair back into a fashionable, up and braided look.

For a brief moment, she thought about sitting down and writing her beau in Coloma a message, telling him how sorry she was about the delay, but then she realized that it would only lengthen her absence from the company of Mrs. Pratt and her other tenants. Mr. O'Neill didn't need to know about her silly train delay. It wasn't like it was going to be much longer until she was there with him. He'd been patient for so long already; surely, he could wait a few extra days.

Millie left her room and walked down the staircase, into the glowing light of the living room. She smiled once more when she saw all of the friendly faces that were gathered there. She didn't know any of them yet, but already she was happy to be one of them.

"Ah, there you are," a young woman said, stretching a hand out for her in greeting. "I'm Mrs. Hattie Ford. I'm Mrs. Pratt's assistant."

"It's wonderful to meet you," Millie replied, shaking her hand gently. "Gosh, everyone is so kind here. I can see why people come to the West."

Hattie laughed softly and gave a slight shrug. "It's at least why people stay in Ogden, I believe." She grinned a bit. "May I get you some tea or coffee, or a sandwich? You've been traveling for an awfully long time, surely."

After thinking for a moment, Millie nodded. "Some coffee and a sandwich, please?" Even though Hattie had offered, she still felt that asking was better than giving an order or something like that. She was a guest, not a boss.

Hattie gave a happy nod back. "Certainly. Please have a seat and I'll be back soon with your treats."

Before Millie could say anything else, the young woman was off on her new mission. She took a seat on a large sofa, not far from where two other ladies were sitting in wing chairs, gossiping over their sewing. She tried to guess at Hattie's age, but it didn't matter much to her. *She's a friendly girl,* she thought. *A friendly face is always good to see...*

Back home in New York, Millie had a small group of friends – many of whom she met at the shirtwaist factory – and many of them were clearly happy to be independent and not at all in the business of looking for a husband. This always struck her as interesting, and she wondered if perhaps she was one of the last remaining romantics. It gave her hope when she saw the young, married ladies here in this town. The women of the West didn't seem to be trying quite so hard to be independent, single ladies. There was value in being strong, steadfast farmer's wives... Mrs. Pratt clearly had things figured out, as she owned her own inn and business seemed to be booming for her.

"What're you smiling for?" Hattie asked, grinning at Millie as she stood nearby with a silver tray of coffee and fixings, as well as several vegetable and ham sandwiches.

Millie blinked at her, coming out of her reverie and embarrassed to be caught in a daydream. She laughed lightly. "Sorry, I was thinking about how different this place is compared to my old life back in New York."

"I hope you think it's a good kind of different," Hattie said with a smirk. She carefully set the tray of treats down on the table in front of Millie's place on the couch. "We are delighted that you're here with us."

"You probably say that to everyone who passes through your door," Millie replied. "But thank you."

Hattie laughed. "We do say it to everyone; but we mean it every time. I've made you some sandwiches and some coffee with sugar and fresh milk. Is there anything else I can fetch for you or help you with, perhaps? Just because it's snowy outside doesn't mean you have to stay locked indoors at all times. I know from experience that snow can make for some lovely walks, provided that you're careful and bundled up."

Millie gave a small grin. "This is precisely why I'm grateful that this place is different," she said. "Everyone so far has been so nice. It makes me happy about my decision to move out West."

"Well, I'm certainly glad to hear you say that," Hattie said. "Enjoy your luncheon and I'll be back soon to discuss things further. I would love to hear all about you, if you don't mind sharing."

With that, she swished away to attend to another task. Millie was tickled pink just to be in this home with such thoughtful, pleasant people. After living her whole life in the hustle and bustle of the city, in small and frankly dingy spaces, it was wonderful to finally feel like she could breathe.

CHAPTER 3

AFTER SHE FINISHED HER SANDWICH AND COFFEE, MILLIE decided to call it an early night so she could start exploring the inn and the surrounding town some more. She took Hattie's words to heart: a little snow on the ground didn't mean that she had to stay inside. After all, Millie Saxton from New York was used to snow!

She woke up the following morning, feeling well-rested and excited to experience new things. She hadn't decided to move out West simply because of the gentleman who had advertised in the newspaper for a bride. She wouldn't even have been looking at the newspaper listings if she hadn't been yearning for some kind of new and wonderful escape. Quickly, Millie dressed in a lovely pink frock and hastened down the staircase to see who was around and what might be going on that morning.

The crowd had thinned considerably from the late afternoon luncheon that she had been a part of the previous day. She figured that was the way of things in inns. Most people didn't stick around in this house, save the family who called it their permanent home. Millie was hoping to get to know those people most of all.

She knew how to make the most of a slightly unfortunate, spontaneous situation.

"Good morning, Miss Saxton," Mrs. Pratt said brightly as she came into the living room and saw her there. She was on her way to the staircase, but she stopped when she saw her guest had awakened. "Is there anything I can help you with?"

Millie tilted her head a bit as she smiled back at her. "Your assistant, Mrs. Ford, mentioned yesterday that it's safe to walk around the area... Is there anything you recommend?"

Diana chuckled. "I can understand not wanting to be holed up inside all winter. I recommend you eat something hot, first of all. Do you have a nice, thick coat?"

Millie looked down at the jacket she was wearing – the one she walked into the inn wearing in the first place – and smirked. "This is the warmest coat I have with me."

Blinking at her, it was Diana's turn to tilt her head a little. "Oh, I see... Would you like to borrow a thicker one?"

"Yes, please," Millie said. "If you think it will be that cold... Goodness, you are all so generous."

Diana smiled and waved that off playfully. "Not at all.

We simply like to take care of our guests. Don't move a muscle." She headed to the staircase and climbed quickly, as if she was absolutely thrilled to be lending someone some outerwear. Millie stood there, blushing a bit and feeling extremely fortunate to have stumbled upon this place. *Thank goodness for that carriage driver. He knew exactly where to bring me.*

She ended up moving a muscle, but only to sit down upon the arm of one of the sofas. She doubted that Mrs. Pratt would mind that; surely, she hadn't meant for her to stand there waiting. Nevertheless, it was only a few more moments before Diana Pratt reappeared, carrying a large, light gray coat with fur on the collar. It did indeed look warm.

"This is my mother's old coat, but it should fit you well," she said, opening it up so she could place it onto Millie.

Millie stood up and went to her, stepping into the coat and smiling as she instantly felt its warmth. "Well I certainly don't need to wear this by the fire, that's for sure. Thank you – and your mother – very much."

"You're very welcome," Diana replied. "If you just go out back, one of my husband's assistants can give you a lift into town. We keep our wagons and carriages back there with the horses."

Millie recalled walking past them when she first arrived. They had been shrouded in shadows and she'd been overcome just by the sight of the house, but she did remember the carriages being there. "I know precisely where to look," she said brightly. "Thank you again!"

Diana was true to her word about not letting Millie go out without some hot soup in her belly, though. Millie sat on the sofa, the thick coat hung up nearby, and ate some hot noodles and broth. She could tell that Diana had a real mother's intuition and nature. A less caring innkeeper would've just let her be off on her way. Millie was glad to have the former.

When she was finished eating her soup, she wrapped herself in the comfortable winter coat and strolled out the back door in search of the wagon and the helpful farmhand who might be able to take her into town for some independent sightseeing. The backyard of the inn was covered in dusty snow, and in the distance, Millie spotted row upon row of brown and black cattle.

"Can I help you, little lady?" a young man asked from her left. "You ain't lost, are you?"

Millie jumped a bit – not outwardly, she hoped – and turned to regard this man. He was lanky and he had a cute, impish sort of face. She had a feeling that he was a little younger than her, which made sense if she was a farmer's apprentice.

"Oh, thank you. I'm not lost. I'm trying to see about borrowing a cart to go into town. Mrs. Pratt said I might find someone who could help me out here..."

The young man rubbed his leather-gloved hands together and cupped them in front of his mouth, blowing into them to summon warmth. In her eagerness and her borrowed coat, she had quite forgotten just how cold it was outside. "I reckon I can help you out with that," he said after lowering his hands. "My name's Glenn Daniels." He tugged the glove of his right hand off and reached out to her.

Millie gladly took his hand and they shook. "Millie Saxton. It's a pleasure to meet you."

He smiled wryly at her and put his workman's glove back on. She appreciated that he didn't shake hands with her while wearing the dusty and dirty things. Not that she would've said anything about it; she didn't want to be rude or seem ungrateful.

"Wait right here a moment," Glenn said then, before rushing off into the fields beyond, towards the cattle.

Millie smiled and nodded a bit as he went, watching him find someone with whom he could share the news of this new task of his. She didn't have to wait long at all before he came hurrying back towards her, holding his gray-brown cowboy hat on his head so that it wouldn't fall off in the gust from his running.

"Where... would you like... to go, Miss Saxton?" he asked between gasps of breath.

She hadn't anticipated being so excited about taking a break from work in order to do this. "Town," she said with a shrug. "Wherever you think would be most interesting or helpful for me to know about."

He grinned then. "I know just the place."

CHAPTER 4

Millie was impressed that the ride into the center of Ogden was not very long at all. The folks that she'd talked to about the town hadn't been exaggerating when they said that everything there was relatively close to each other. It made sense to her; after all, it was a small Western town, still being developed and settled. That was something that she found so enthralling about the West. Everything there was still a work in progress. She was eager to see what it would develop into, but she also rather hoped that it would never stop developing. Sometimes, finished projects weren't as interesting as the process of working on them.

"Thank you, you can stop the wagon here, please," she told Glenn. She was admiring the central street in the town and noticed that there were several shop windows that interested her. Though the town mostly had a lot of businesses that were saloons or grocers, there did appear to be some novelty shops.

Glenn parked the wagon on the side of the dirt road and, after giving his horse a swift pat, he looked over at the places that Millie had noticed. He lowered his brow a bit and gave her a flummoxed sort of look. "There isn't much there of interest, Miss," he said. "I've hardly ever seen anyone shopping in those shops."

"That's because you're a man," Millie said with a smirk at him as she carefully alighted from the wagon. "Men are never interested in purchasing clothing. I know this from experience."

Glenn chuckled and shook his head slowly at her as she walked away from him and the wagon. Millie wasn't trying to buy any new clothing – she didn't really have extra room in her suitcases for that sort of thing and she didn't like to spend money on things she didn't need – but it would be fun to see what was available anyway. It was good simply to get out of the house for a bit and stretch her legs. She was used to walking all around the city. At least until she was too tired, and then she would take a cab. As she walked along the big and bustling street, she admired all of the shop fronts to decide which one deserved her attention first. She wasn't looking for anything to buy, so browsing would be strictly fun for her today.

She strolled leisurely toward the clothing shop, since it had caught her eye first. Along the way, she noticed a gentleman sitting outside one of the other shops. He had a large anvil and he was striking a metal hammer against it, causing some sparks to fly out. The sound of the hammer hitting the anvil was quite loud – loud enough to make Millie jump more than once as she walked by him.

The gentleman noticed and stopped his hammering, setting the tool down and smiling at her, wiping his brow with a lightly hairy arm. He was tall with muscles on his arms and a broad chest. He looked exactly like a metal-worker should. Millie smiled back at him and nodded her head slightly in appreciation. He had dark brown hair and a pair of sincere, trusting brown eyes. She thought he was handsome, despite being the complete opposite of the gentlemen she usually would fancy.

A blush colored her cheeks as she continued to smile at him. "You didn't have to stop. I'm just passing by," she told him kindly. "But it's very considerate of you."

"I'm not in the habit of startling passers-by," the blacksmith told her, still smiling back at her. "Especially not ones as lovely as you. I haven't seen you around these parts before."

Millie's blush deepened. "I'm not from around here. My train stopped in yesterday, and I'm afraid that I'm stuck here 'til my next scheduled train can continue onward..."

The handsome blacksmith whistled softly. "So, you really are just passing by," he said. "I'm Clyde Roberts. I was like you once. I suspect most people here were, unless they're children."

"It's a pleasure to make your acquaintance," Millie replied. "My name is Millie Saxton."

She realized that she was now standing on the sidewalk, engaged in conversation with a tradesman that she knew she wasn't going to do business with. She was enjoying herself, though, so why stop? As long as he continued to enjoy himself as well, of course.

"Millie," Clyde said, as if he was testing out the name and had never heard it before. "Is that short for anything?"

She reddened anew, but there was some embarrassment to it now. "Millicent," she said. "But no one ever calls me that. I think my mother thought it looked good on paper."

Clyde chuckled at that. "It's pretty. But I will call you Millie. Or Miss Saxton, if you prefer."

Millie smiled bashfully at him. "Please call me Millie. *Miss Saxton* makes me feel far more important than I actually am."

The blacksmith stood up from his chair and removed the black apron that he wore to protect his pants from sparks and grime. He placed it into the chair he'd been sitting in, leaving the metal project he'd been working on. "What brings you to Ogden?" he asked her. "And is there anything I can help you with?"

Millie held the coat tightly around herself, though she didn't feel cold. "I wanted a change," she told him honestly.

"Don't we all?" he replied with another kind and handsome smile. "Well, don't let me disrupt your shopping. I hope that we run into each other again sometime."

She beamed happily back at him and nodded a little. "I'd like that, too," she said. "I'll see you around."

Clyde gave her a wave and then strolled down the street towards one of the saloons. Millie realized that it must have been time for lunch. She hadn't realized how late it had gotten until now. Continuing on in her exploration, she went into the clothing store that she had first spied on the street, but she only stayed inside it for a few moments.

She couldn't think of anything other than the handsome new friend she had made.

CHAPTER 5

Once she had returned to the inn, Millie went back upstairs to her room. She didn't feel like talking to anyone else in town until she wrote to her betrothed in California. The conversation with Clyde had got her thinking and she found that she was unable to stop thinking about things that he had said to her. *What brings me here?* She thought. *A change.* Now that she was stopped in Ogden – unplanned – for a number of days, she knew that she must let Mr. O'Neill know. She wasn't going to be able to achieve her goal of change for herself until she continued on to Coloma.

Poor Mr. O'Neill must be worried sick about me! Here I've been, making the best of a bad situation, and I haven't even given him any notice of my whereabouts or my delay.

The more she thought on this subject, the more

wretched she felt. As soon as she sat down at her vanity in her bedroom, she got out some paper and a pen and set to writing to him.

My darling James,

It grieves me to have to write this to you, but I feel as though silence is not the answer. You must be dreadfully worried about me, so I want you to know first off that I'm okay. I'm actually not so very far away from you now. I'm in Ogden in the Utah Territory, where a winter storm has forced me to remain until the trains can make safe passage through the town's station. As soon as possible, I shall be on my way to you again, and I am looking ever so forward to making Coloma my home and you my husband!

I pray that you are well and that you aren't cross with me for being so long in my writing to you.

All my love and devotion,
Millie Saxton

She read it over and felt a growing worry in the pit of her stomach. What if James read this note from her and really was peeved at her delay, both in travels and in writing to him? She felt like such a ninny for thinking that she should be friendly and carry on as if everything was fine and dandy for her. She'd thought once of writing to him, but didn't want to be rude and keep her hosts waiting. *Well, wasn't it also rude to keep my beloved waiting? I wrote that I was devoted to him, but am I truly?*

Millie sat back in her chair, looked down at the letter on the desk and continued to feel sorry for herself. She hadn't planned any of this. She hadn't wanted to be delayed. But she also didn't want to feel guilty about it now that she was at the inn, surrounded by such nice people.

James wouldn't want her to be miserable where she was staying. He'd want her to come to him as soon as possible, but he wouldn't want her travels to be stressful or unpleasant. "This is all okay," she told herself, placing the letter into an envelope and carefully inscribing his address upon its front. He would be so happy to hear from her that he likely wouldn't be at all miffed about her slight delay in writing to him. Besides, the mail service had been rather slow between New York and California, so he'd probably be relieved to receive this letter faster due to her closer proximity to him now.

Millie bit her bottom lip and then licked the envelope closed. *Worrying myself into a tizzy won't do*, she thought. *I'll just have someone here send this off for me and then I shall see what James makes of it.*

At least now Millie had a few key friends in town. She knew that she could rely on Glenn to give her a ride into town if she needed it, and then there was that blacksmith...

She chuckled a bit. "What need do I have for a blacksmith? He's more a friend to me than a tradesman that I will require."

Suddenly, there was a light knock on the door that made Millie jump and drop her letter onto the floor. It landed softly on the blue rug at her feet. The door then opened and Hattie's face peeked in. "Sorry to bother you, Miss Saxton, but would you like some lunch or tea in your room this afternoon?"

Millie leaned down and scooped up her letter. She smiled a somewhat embarrassed smile at Hattie. "Yes please, and it's no intrusion. I was just about to go down and try and find you." She stood up from her chair and walked towards the door, outstretching the letter towards the assistant innkeeper. "I have a letter that must be mailed at once, to Coloma."

Hattie gave a nod and took the letter. "I shall see to it that this goes out at once. And I will find you downstairs for your luncheon?"

Millie smiled and nodded. "Yes, thank you."

She went down the stairs a few moments later, feeling a bit sheepish for hiding out in her room after her outing. The living room was busier than it was in the morning. Several people were sitting around, eating their varied luncheons. Millie took up residence at a small wooden table near the fire.

When Hattie returned with a tray of sandwiches and tea, she set it down on the table and then passed some generous helpings of each to Millie. "Did you enjoy your visit to town this morning?" she asked pleasantly.

"Yes," Millie replied. "The weather wasn't too bad, either. It's definitely cold, but I'm hoping that the trains will be working again soon. I believe I'm feeling a bit restless. And that's not to say that I don't appreciate you and Mrs. Pratt for all of your hospitality."

At that, Hattie gave her a sympathetic look, letting her usually-smiling mouth turn into more of a straight line. "I can understand being restless. Here you were, trying to start a new adventure, and now you're stuck in a small town, miles away from where you're supposed to be headed. I think anyone would feel restless if they were in your shoes."

Millie shrugged and sighed a bit. "My trip to town wasn't completely full of regret, though. I met a nice gentleman who works at the blacksmiths…"

Hattie's eyes lit up. "Mr. Roberts? Oh, he's such a sweet man."

"I thought so, too," Millie replied. "He offered to help me with anything I need, even though nothing I shall need requires a metalworker."

The two ladies giggled together.

This feels extremely nice, Millie thought to herself. *It feels as though I finally have friends with which I may gossip and giggle about handsome men. Almost as if I'm a girl again.*

Her delay in leaving Ogden began to concern her less and less and at the moment, that didn't bother her at all.

CHAPTER 6

THOUGH SHE HAD SENT OFF A LETTER TO JAMES O'NEILL in California, Millie didn't expect to receive a response from him. The times were unusual, because she was stuck in limbo between where she'd come from and where she was intended to go. It was more than likely that as soon as a letter arrived for her at the inn, she would be on the train to him. She thought that he would save the paper and save the time spent worrying over it.

What she also wasn't expecting was a visitor at the inn.

Right as she was setting down her drained teacup, there was a knock on the front door of the house. Diana Pratt rushed to it from seemingly nowhere. She opened it up and there stood Mr. Clyde Roberts. He grinned at her and tipped his hat – a brown, ten-gallon hat that Millie thought gave him a slightly comical look which somehow worked with his otherwise attractive appearance. It endeared him to Millie even more.

"Good afternoon, ma'am," Clyde said. "Do you happen to know if Miss Millie Saxton is in?"

He looked from Diana to Millie and winked.

Millie's face went pink. She smiled, baffled about why he could possibly be there to see her but touched just the same. She'd never received a gentleman caller before in her life.

Diana turned her head to cast a quick look at Millie. Finding her looking so happy, she turned back to Clyde and nodded. "Yes, she is right inside. I'll bring you to her." She opened the front door and let him pass through. She then led him over to Millie sitting at the fireplace, though she didn't really need to for Clyde strode over to her unaided. Diana looked from Millie to Clyde once they were together at the table. "Please let me know if you need anything," she said.

"Another cup of tea, Mrs. Pratt?" Millie asked, not taking her eyes off of Clyde. She didn't want to be rude to her visitor.

Diana nodded curtly and left them alone. Clyde sat in the chair across the small table from Millie. "You're probably wondering why I came to see you," he said. "So, I'll start out by explaining that. It's much too cold and snowy for me to expect to find you outdoors on Main Street again. You said that you were only here temporarily, so I figured, well, the inn is probably the place where I could find you. And here you are."

Millie blushed another pretty shade of pink. "I thank you for coming to visit me. But that doesn't explain *why* you wanted to see me…"

Diana returned and placed a cup of tea on the table in front of Clyde, as they continued to talk as if they were the only two people in the room. "Isn't it obvious?" he asked Millie with a smile. "I haven't been able to keep you from my mind ever since I saw you earlier. As soon as I closed up my shop for the day, I knew where I needed to go."

"But… Why?" Millie asked him. She felt that she knew the reason why, but she refused to believe it. It just seemed so silly and too good to be true. Anyway, it wasn't as if anything would come of this. "You only talked with me for a few moments today."

"Ah, but that was enough," Clyde said. "Besides, I knew from that brief encounter that I wanted to speak with you more. Because you captivated me, plain and simple."

Millie really wanted to ask 'why' again, but didn't want to keep going around in circles. "You flatter me, sir."

Finally, Clyde paid attention to his tea. He picked up the small cup and brought it to his lips, sipping quietly and slowly so he wouldn't burn his tongue. He then set the teacup back down carefully and gazed into her eyes. His brown eyes were so gentle and warm; Millie couldn't help but have faith in him that he was genuine in what he said. He wasn't putting her on or anything like that. But even if his intentions were as pure as the snow outside, there was one small problem that they had to consider.

"I'm engaged, sir," she told him honestly. "I cannot in good conscience allow your interest in me to go any further. I would've mentioned this to you sooner, but then I didn't think that it was a necessary conversation topic for two strangers passing on the street."

Clyde fixed her with a look that didn't appear to be disheartened so much as surprised. "Do you know this gentleman?" he asked her. "Why has he made you travel to him by yourself?"

She felt uncomfortable about the answer to his question. Though she had written to Mr. O'Neill for several months, could she really honestly say that she knew him? The letters had been ways for them to get to know each other, to break the ice as it were, but that was as far as they had gotten... "We met via the newspaper service," she admitted. "I haven't met him in person. Oh, but I will. That's the plan. He arranged for me to travel west and be his bride."

Clyde downed the remainder of his tea. He frowned a bit, looking thoughtful. "Plans can change," he said. "After all, it wasn't in your plan that you would stay here, was it?"

"No, but..."

"I'm not asking you to make any big decision about it right now," he said, standing. "I just want you to think about it... I know I can't offer you much. I'm a lowly blacksmith, and this gentleman of yours is probably raking in gold every day. I just think that you and I can be so good for one another, if we're given the chance to get to know each other better... in person. No letters."

Millie felt a lump in her throat. He made a good point, but she didn't necessarily like that. "But I've promised myself to Mr. O'Neill…"

"As I said," Clyde replied, gesturing a hand for emphasis, as if he was laying what he said out for her. "I don't expect you to make this decision today or even tomorrow. Though I do think it's rather telling that you refer to this fiancé of yours as *Mr. O'Neill*. And now I must bid you good evening, Millie."

With that, he bowed politely and left her sitting there to ponder what he had said and the position that she was faced with. He left the inn all together, and Millie was shocked to find that she felt much more alone than she had felt before. She was alone with her problems in a way that no one else who lived in Ogden could really understand. What had seemed like an adventure before now felt slightly like a trap.

CHAPTER 7

WHILE MILLIE WAS ASLEEP, THE SNOW AND WIND OUTSIDE picked up considerably. She slept fitfully the entire night because of the conversation she'd had with Clyde. He'd certainly made her think about things. He had a good point, a few good points, but she felt so torn. She didn't want to go back on her promise that she'd made to Mr. O'Neill – James. If there was one thing that she prided herself on, it was that she kept her promises.

But, as Clyde had said, things happened... Plans could change.

She had terrible nightmares all night, tossing and turning, and always imagining James' sad face looking at her. She was breaking his heart by tarrying; that was all that she kept dwelling on.

When Millie awoke and looked out her window to

discover the enormous amount of snow that blanketed the ground outside, she let out a low moan. "Just my luck, even fewer chances to go outside."

She threw off her blankets and dressed herself in a white dress with yellow daisies on it. She tied up her light brown hair with a ribbon and some pins, allowing for a bun and some loose tendrils of hair. Regarding herself in the mirror on the vanity, Millie thought that she looked pretty, not that it really mattered what she looked like. She was even more trapped in this town than she had been yesterday.

Clearly God is trying to punish one of us, James, she thought. *Probably me. You can keep on living your life whereas I'm in Limbo.*

She went down the staircase to see if there were any others paying attention to the state of the snow. Sure enough, many of the other inn guests were sitting, faces practically pressed against the glass of the windows. Millie shamed herself for being so cynical. Snow was nothing new to a girl from New York, but apparently it was magical to some people... She just wished it wasn't such a hindrance for her!

"How long has the snow been falling?" she asked Hattie when she caught her coming into the room from the desk in the back. "It wasn't this heavy when I went to sleep last night."

Hattie looked towards the windows and smirked almost apologetically. "It always seems to get worse before it goes away," she said. "I hate to tell you this, Miss Saxton, but you very well may be waiting 'til spring to leave Ogden."

Millie hung her head. Clyde's words to her yesterday were beginning to feel more and more accurate. She must be stuck there for a reason. *Plans can change.* She looked back at Hattie. "Please be ready for me to send out another letter," she said. "My... I have someone who will want to know that I've been delayed once again."

"The mail likely won't make its way out in these conditions," Hattie replied.

"As soon as you can, anyway," Millie said. She rushed to the nearest table and began looking for materials to draft a fresh letter.

The young assistant innkeeper turned on her heels and rushed to find some paper and a pen for Millie. As soon as she brought the items back for her, Millie got to writing.

"I can't help feeling that I'm a horrible person," she said mournfully as she wrote.

My darling James,

I pray that you received my last letter and that you are not broken-hearted at the news of my delay. I must inform you, alas, that the snow here has gotten worse and I shan't be able to join you in Coloma until perhaps the springtime. It is too dangerous to go out of doors when the snow is falling as thick and fast as it has begun to. The trains surely are unable to run in these conditions. I count myself fortunate that I am not stuck somewhere on the rails, unable to keep warm and fed. I am staying at quite a nice inn here in Ogden and the people here have cared for me most kindly.

All of my love and comfort to you in this trying time. Please do not lose faith in me, my love!

EVER YOURS,
Millie Saxton

SHE LOOKED DOWN AT THE LETTER SHE'D JUST WRITTEN, feverishly as if the words were flowing out of her very soul. It felt odd that she should sign her name 'Millie Saxton' when she used her given name with total strangers in this town. Surely Mr. O'Neill knew her well enough to call her by her first name, but still she faltered when it came to it. Much in the same way she still thought of him as 'Mr. O'Neill.'

Oh, curse that Clyde! She thought, frowning. *He's given me way too much to worry about in this time when I'm so helpless to change anything!*

She handed off the letter to Hattie, who likely wasn't going to be able to do anything with it for a good number of days. As Hattie walked away with the note and a promise of coffee and breakfast cakes, Mrs. Pratt appeared from the opposite direction. She'd been checking on the state of affairs from the front porch.

"I know that this must put a damper on your plans for

traveling to California," she said sympathetically. "But I want you to know that you are very welcome to stay and celebrate Thanksgiving with us. It's almost here, after all."

Millie hadn't even been thinking about the holidays that were indeed fast approaching. Up until this point, she'd only had one concern, and now that that concern wasn't going to be able to be tended to for quite a long while, she supposed that she really must try and make the best of things. She smiled at Diana. "That's very kind of you," she said. "I'd love to celebrate the season with you. And I promise to help out as much as possible, as well. I don't expect you to make the entire meal yourself. I've got two hands and enough skills to be of at least some use to you."

Diana laughed gaily. "Oh, I'm certain you have plenty of skills. I don't normally allow guests to strain themselves in such a way, but if you insist, I won't complain about the extra help."

Millie giggled. "I don't mean to argue with you, Mrs. Pratt, but I do insist."

She wondered how many people would be there for this Thanksgiving feast that they were now planning. Surely all of the people who were currently lodging in the inn. That wasn't as many as it had been when Millie first arrived, but it was still a rather large number of mouths to feed! Instead of feeling stressed or anxious about it, she was absolutely excited about this new challenge. She hadn't cooked a big Thanksgiving meal in a long time; not since it had been her turn to help her mother out when she was eleven years old. She knew that she could do it, and do it well!

"I hope you don't mind, but several other people from town will likely come by for this fete," Diana added. "It's my custom to invite all the shopkeepers, etcetera so that no one has to dine all alone."

Millie knew that she was telling her this because of Clyde. "That's very sweet of you. And also sweet of you to let me know. I don't begrudge Mr. Roberts a good, hot meal for Thanksgiving. Or for Christmas, for that matter."

She hoped that her words sounded sincere. Even if she wasn't exactly looking forward to being around him again after the mixed-up way he had made her feel, she didn't want him to be alone during the holidays. What kind of person would she be if she did? Certainly not one worthy of all the generosity that she had received from everyone in the town of Ogden, including Mr. Clyde Roberts.

"The more the merrier," she added.

Diana smiled at her and nodded. "Lovely. Thank you, Miss Saxton. I didn't think that it would be a problem, but I wanted to give you a heads up in case it made you want to change your mind."

She left her there with the coffee and cakes which Hattie brought to her from the kitchen. Millie ruminated as she ate. *I suppose it's possible to spend more time with Clyde and be friendly towards him, so long as he understands that I must continue on my way once the ice melts and the snow clears from the ground.*

CHAPTER 8

MILLIE TOOK TO HER DUTIES AS THANKSGIVING HELPER with great aplomb. She found that she could be just as excited about cooking as she was about making garments. This feeling only grew when she was at last introduced to Diana's mother, Mrs. Cooke.

"Oh, my dear, you are a natural," the older woman enthused upon meeting her in the midst of the younger ladies baking their fourth pie.

Millie beamed proudly at Mrs. Cooke, a smudge of flour on her right cheek making her look even more like that of a professional in the field of cookery. "That's awfully nice of you to say, but I must admit, I haven't actually cooked in a long while. Especially not like this."

"Well just your enthusiasm alone could have fooled me," Mrs. Cooke replied merrily. She jumped right in to help them with their latest pie – a mixed berry concoction that Millie had suggested after noting how many berry bushes had grown in the yard out back.

"They don't all need to be apple, after all," she had pointed out.

"Too right," Diana had agreed.

Besides Mrs. Cooke, Diana and Millie, Hattie was there in the kitchen to help out, along with her sister Zelda. The kitchen wasn't the biggest, but it was full of smiles and teamwork so it never felt cramped.

"I can't explain to you ladies adequately how happy this makes me," Millie said once the fourth pie was in the oven. "Growing up, I was the only girl in a family with five children. In New York, I only had a few friends that I would consider close and we never participated in activities like this. We mostly saw each other at work in the factory."

"I could never imagine not cooking with my sisters," Hattie said. "Even when I was very young, we bonded over times like this."

Zelda made a face at her. "Well, not when you were very young," she teased. "When you were very young, you would dip a spoon in things and then run around the house with a spoon full of chocolate and the like!"

They all giggled together.

"She helped keep you on our toes," Mrs. Cooke said with a wink.

"It's not good to be on your toes when carrying hot dishes!" Zelda replied with another laugh.

Millie smiled at Zelda and Hattie. "Still, I *am* envious. Please don't take those times for granted. This shall always be a treasured memory of mine now, no matter where life takes me next."

"Aww!" Diana cooed. They all came together, wrapping their arms around each other in a big group hug.

This was exactly how Millie had always wanted her Thanksgivings as an independent adult lady to be: warm and surrounded by good friends.

It was just a shame, to think about how this was all going to have to end at some point. She surely couldn't stay in Ogden forever. She was needed elsewhere, by someone who needed her cooking skills, too.

Cooking the entire meal took over a day, when they factored in all of the things that had to sit out overnight to cool, such as the pies. By the time Thanksgiving actually arrived, Millie was exhausted but looking forward to seeing the reaction on people's faces when they tasted the food that she played a part in cooking.

The living room was converted into what was essentially a restaurant. The sofas and wing chairs were all replaced with wooden tables like the one Millie found herself occupying in front of the fireplace on more than one occasion. She sat at a table of high honor, with Hattie and Diana. She knew that this was largely because she had played a hand in cooking the meal, but it still gave her a warm and fuzzy feeling to feel like an honored member of the family. Diana hadn't been kidding when she told her that she wanted her to be included in their holiday festivities but this was even better than Millie could ever have imagined.

As they were just sitting down at their head table and Mr. Aaron Pratt was about to make a toast, the front door burst open. Wind and snow flew into the house, along with one Mr. Clyde Roberts. There was tension at first, but it soon dissipated as people realized that this visitor was none other than the town's most trusted metalsmith.

"I beg your pardon for my intrusion," he told the waiting crowd of people, hurriedly closing the door behind him and stopping the rush of cold air and ice. "I closed up shop this morning and had quite a time getting here for this fine-smelling feast." He took off his hat and coat, placing them on the nearby wooden rack.

"No need to apologize, Mr. Roberts," Diana said kindly. "We are glad to have you here and I'm so sorry to hear that you were caught up in the snow."

"We can help you get back tonight, if you would like?" Hattie offered.

"Don't be silly," Aaron Pratt said. "We have more than enough spare room in this house, Mr. Roberts. Please stay here, at least until this latest storm has passed. The holidays are no time to send anyone out in the cold."

Millie felt something form at the pit of her stomach. At first, it seemed like it might be ire at seeing the man again, but then she realized that it was something else. Could it be pleasure at seeing him, and learning that he would be staying for a while? This would give them the time to get to know each other that he – and, she now admitted, she – had been hoping for.

"I wouldn't want to intrude further," Clyde said gallantly, smiling a sheepish sort of smile. "I've interrupted your Thanksgiving enough as it is..."

Millie rose from her chair, feeling bolstered by the good will of the others in the room. "Nonsense," she said, noticing Diana's approving smile out of the corner of her eye. "You were invited here. We want you to be here with us."

This was met with shouts of "here here" and gentle pounding of mugs on tables.

Clyde laughed. "Well, all right then, if you insist. But might I request a seat at your table, Miss Saxton?"

She blushed. "Only if you call me Millie instead."

Smiling in his appealing and intriguing sort of way, he came into the room and met her at her table, bowing when he was beside her before sitting down in the unoccupied chair at her side.

Millie didn't think that it would quite matter to Clyde what she was wearing, but she was pleased all the same that she had chosen to wear a pretty deep green, velvet dress. The bodice of it really showed off her curves in a way that a lot of her cotton frocks could never achieve. She'd chosen only the best gown for this special occasion. Of course, now she was wondering what she was supposed to do about her Christmas attire! *You're being silly now*, she told herself.

Behaving like such a girl when he doesn't seem to care one fig what you're wearing so long as you look pleasant.

Clyde hadn't quite bothered to dress for the occasion the way she had taken pains to. He was dressed in black pants and white shirt, and outfit that was similar, if not exactly the same, to the one he had worn the day they met. Nevertheless, he wasn't wearing the black apron and for that Millie was glad. She thought she might be confused if he had shown up wearing a three-piece suit. Such a look would do nicely on him, but it didn't seem to match his Western character. It was this very character that Millie found especially appealing about him. He was unlike any gentleman she had ever met.

Well, she thought, not including Glenn. *But he's more a gentleman-in-training.* She smiled at the teenaged boy. He was sitting a ways across the room from her, at a table occupied by all of the younger farmhands and other such assistants.

"So, how have you been since we last crossed paths?" Clyde asked her, smiling before taking a careful sip of his water. "You didn't seem to like me much when I last saw you."

Millie blushed, embarrassed about that last meeting still. "A lot of things were said in that meeting that I wish hadn't been, or had at least been phrased differently. I'd been feeling so stuck and unsure about things, as you are well aware."

"Sure," he conceded. "And how are you feeling now? You seem to be enjoying the part of partial-hostess."

She was quite glad that the room was buzzing with many conversations. Glancing over at Diana, she found her lost in chatter with her husband and her brother-in-law. No one was paying any attention to Miss Saxton and the good blacksmith. All of the perceived intrigue into her personal life was imagined, and Millie felt both relieved and as if she must be so conceited to have ever thought…

"I hope I do not offend you," he went on when she didn't say anything. "I know that sometimes my wording can be a bit harsher than I intend."

"You don't offend me," Millie replied. "Your words may have been difficult to hear at first, but I think it was more because they struck me as perhaps being too on the nose for me to handle at the time."

Clyde blinked at her, startled to hear her say this. Startled but not displeased. He smiled. "I never intended to hurt you. Please forgive me for any upset that I might have caused. I only meant… Well, you know. I think I made my opinion known already."

Millie looked down at the bit of turkey, carrots and potatoes on her plate. She sighed a little, hoping to perhaps clear away this subject with his apology. "I forgive you," she said, giving him a small but sincere smile. "I've since written to inform my would-be groom of my delay here. I have yet to mention any further thoughts on the matter to him, and I plan to keep it that way. This town is lovely and I enjoy spending time with all of you, but I cannot go back on my promise to James. He trusted me. We made an arrangement and he paid for me to come be with him in California. As much as I don't want to leave this place and travel to yet another small town to which I must grow accustomed, I am not the sort of person to break an agreement. Do you understand?"

Clyde appeared startled to hear this. "I had hoped that your zeal this evening might be due to a change of heart on the matter. Now I see that I was wrong to think that... Just answer me one thing."

Millie took a bite of her turkey and swallowed it down with some water. She was regretting their proximity now. Would he not take no for an answer?! "Yes? What is it?"

Clyde looked into her eyes and then leaned in closer to her, so no one would eavesdrop on their delicate conversation. "Do you love that man?"

She reddened. "I already told you, I promised myself to him."

"But do you love him?" he persisted. "It's all well and good to make a promise in a letter on paper, but do you *actually* love him? Or is this more an obligation than something you are passionate about?"

Millie pouted at him. She felt more than a little scandalized. Were they not amongst friendly, joyous company she might have worked up the nerve to throw her water in his face. And yet...

She didn't have a good answer to his question. She wasn't in the habit of lying just to try and save face. "I don't know," she said after some time. "He wrote an advertisement professing to be in desperate need of a wife, and I answered his plea. Surely, he cares about me, because he has been writing to me for all this time. And he paid for this trip, which has been one of the most momentous events of my life so far."

Clyde nodded slowly. "But if you do not love him, might you be entering into an agreement falsely? And, putting aside his feelings, how do you feel about being married to a gentleman whom you might feel nothing for?"

Millie's cheeks still burned with both frustration and indignation. "And you think I would instead feel something for you?"

"Can you honestly tell me, that even at this early juncture, you don't?"

If she had been feeling stuck before, she was completely lost now. Setting down her silverware on the table beside her plate, Millie rose from the table. She turned to look at Diana and Hattie. "It seems that I have become rather dizzy," she fibbed. "If you'll please excuse me, I'm going to step out onto the porch for some air."

Diana looked deeply concerned. "Are you sure that's the best idea right now? It's frightfully cold outside."

"I'll put on the cozy coat that you've lent me," Millie said. She went to the rack by the door and pulled out the fur-lined coat. Mrs. Cooke gave it a look of recognition, but said nothing.

Millie didn't care if it was cold outside. Being in that house right now, with that man, was absolutely stifling.

CHAPTER 9

STANDING ON THE WIDE FRONT PORCH OF THE PRATTS' residence, Millie wrapped the fur coat around herself. Though the coat was warm, the velvet dress she wore wasn't helping her fend off the cold very well. She gazed over into the distance, watching as white flecks of ice blew around in all directions. There didn't appear to be any grass or road to speak of. All outside was white.

There really wasn't any purpose to her being outside and now that Millie was there, shivering away, she wondered what her point had been. All she had intended to do was to get away from Clyde Roberts. But she could have just as well escaped to her bedroom.

Perhaps I should have just stayed inside and told him 'no' right to his face. That would have shown him. But even the thought of telling him 'no' didn't ring true to her. The question had been a bold one, and of course she didn't know Clyde Roberts well enough to think of him in that way, but she couldn't deny that she *was* captivated by him. She didn't want to lie to him about something as important as this felt to her. *Ugh, what does it matter?* She thought miserably. *It's not as if I'm staying here. Why should I settle for this town when California is the place that I have been dreaming about for months?*

She looked out at the swirling snowdrifts in the center of what used to be the street, as if it might give her the answer she was looking for.

"Pardon me," an all too familiar voice said behind her. "Would you mind some company on this beautiful night?"

Millie rolled her eyes and turned around to meet Clyde's warm gaze. He was smiling at her and holding out a small plate of berry pie. "They recommended this flavor to me when I mentioned that some dessert might be just what you needed."

"It was my idea," she said, carefully taking the plate of pie from him. "The pie flavor, I mean. They were going to make one pumpkin pie and three apple pies. Can you imagine how boring that would have been?"

Clyde chuckled a bit. "It sounds like you know how to throw a party," he said jocularly.

Millie was just relieved that he'd made no mention of their awkward conversation from earlier. She wasn't about to bring it up now, either. "I actually haven't ever thrown a proper party in my life before," she admitted. "My mother and father used to throw lavish ones, but I was a child back then. It hardly counts."

He tilted his head a bit as he looked at her. She noticed then that he had stayed mostly near the doorway, not venturing to move closer to her. Maybe he worried about her pushing him away or something. It was if he somehow understood that he had overstepped at least a few boundaries beforehand and had finally learned his lesson. "You never played party hostess with friends in New York?" he asked her. "I thought that all the young ladies liked to do that sort of thing. Isn't that why men want wives so badly, so they have someone to be sociable for them?"

Millie had to smile a little at that. "I think that must be part of it, yes. But I didn't really have that much of a social life once I grew up and moved out on my own. I was told that working in the shirtwaist factory was going to be the way to make so many friends and have so many wonderful, life-changing experiences. But in reality, I had only a few coworker friends and I quickly realized that I'm much too shy to really get that close to people."

Clyde gave her a look of mock surprise. "No, really?"

She smiled at him and then neatly cut into her piece of berry pie. "I suppose that's why finding James via the newspaper service was good for me. I was able to make a connection with him that I probably wouldn't have if we had met in person right away. I'm not very talkative with strangers."

"Well you could've fooled me," he said to her, waving a slightly dismissive hand. "You were quite friendly towards me... when we first met, anyway. You told me all about where you'd come from, where you were headed. You stopped and looked at me first. Don't forget. You called attention to yourself."

Millie blushed. "I won't forget," she said. "I wasn't trying to draw attention to myself, though. I was surprised when I heard your hammer come down. Startled isn't the same as attracting attention."

"I see," Clyde said. "I suppose it's just how pretty you happened to be while you were startled, then."

She ate her pie for a few moments in near-silence. The whirring wind around them made complete silence impossible. "You make it all seem like it's just supposed to be easy," she said finally. "Even if I wanted to stay here and spend my days with you, you infuriating man, the fact of the matter is, I made a promise."

He finally moved slightly closer to her, still careful to keep his distance and remain entirely proper, even though his brown eyes had taken on a romantic, far off sort of look. "I think that the question of love came up," he said. "I think that the promise you made to this *Mr. O'Neill* includes the promise of love. And that if you can't give that to him, then you may as well have stolen the ticket that brought you here."

Millie wanted to throw her pie at him, to strike him, anything to wipe that expression off of his face, but she was too flustered by his words to do anything. "I think you're a lot of talk," she said slowly and softly, looking down at her plate as if it was suddenly the most interesting thing in the world. "But it's not as if you've really done anything to earn the things you want from me. You've made me feel like a fool and embarrassed me right out of that party. And why? I don't understand what you hope to get out of treating me this way."

"I thought that was obvious," Clyde replied. "I want you to stay here in Ogden. It's where you belong; it's where you've made friends. I want you to stay here and marry me instead."

Millie sat frozen, staring at him with widening eyes and a slowly gaping mouth. "Marry you after you've criticized me for marrying someone I never met in person? I hardly know you."

"Ah, but you'll get to know me," Clyde replied. "We can start tonight, if you promise me that you'll stop with the O'Neill fantasies and stay here with me."

She furrowed her brows as she looked at him. "I don't know why I took this pie from you," she said. "I'm not hungry. In fact, I just feel sick. Every time we talk, I end up feeling sick."

"Some might call that love..." He gave her a hopeful sort of look as he smiled at her. "Look. I'm not asking you to do anything that you haven't already been doing. I just want you to stick to where you are and who you know here, instead of running off to live with someone who is a complete gamble."

I've made a terrible mistake. Actually several. I never even saw his picture and I was going to give my life to him... Frowning, Millie handed the plate of pie back to Clyde. "But what happens to poor James? He would be brokenhearted if I write to him and tell him that I'm not coming to be with him. He spent so much money on me."

Clyde appeared thoughtful. "Here," he said at last. "I'll make you a deal. If the storm clears out and you still want to continue on because you can't bear to break poor James's heart, I won't stop you. But if the storm clears and you do want to stay here and marry me, I will pay poor James the amount he paid to get you westward. Is that fair?"

Millie bit her lip. *That means several more weeks of spending time around him,* she thought. *Several more weeks of him trying to convince me to leave James. He really wants to ruin my honor, doesn't me?*

"Very well," she replied. "Let's say that I have until Christmas, though. I might be able to leave earlier than we think."

Clyde held out his hand and they firmly shook on it.

Why do I feel like I've made another promise I shouldn't have?

CHAPTER 10

MILLIE AND CLYDE RETURNED TO THE PARTY TO FIND that it was time to clean up. Many of the inn's guests had gone upstairs to their bedrooms, leaving Diana, Hattie and Mrs. Cooke to tend to the dishes and the laundry. "There's plenty of leftovers if you were wanting something that you missed," Diana informed Millie with a knowing smile.

"Maybe for lunch tomorrow, Mrs. Pratt," Millie said. "Thank you. Let me help with that." She rushed away from Clyde so she could work on cleaning some of the dirty plates and silverware. Clyde didn't linger too long, leaving the ladies to finish up the housework for the night.

As soon as he was gone, Diana and Hattie moved closer to Millie so they could gossip with her. "What went on out there?" Hattie asked.

"I was about to send out a chaperone," Diana said,

mostly joking. "We didn't know what you two might've been up to."

Millie felt her face grow warm with a fresh blush. "It was nothing, really. Mr. Roberts asked me to stay in Ogden because he seems to believe that I don't actually want to marry my beau in Coloma." She kept her eyes and hands focused on her work, though she wondered if they could hear the pounding of her heart.

Hattie and Diana looked at each other. "Ooohh," Hattie said, grinning.

Millie chuckled. "Oh hush," she replied. "More than anything, I think Mr. Roberts fancies getting to know me better to see if I'm worth keeping around."

Diana nodded a little. "That's known as courting..."

"I *suppose* so," Millie replied, feigning surprise. "But it's not quite as romantic as all that. He told me that I don't love Mr. O'Neill so I might as well stay in Ogden where I knew people and could be happy. Not quite his words, but just about."

"He wants to get to know you," Diana said. "He's trying to win your love. I think that's plenty romantic!"

"Well, do you?" Hattie asked.

Millie looked up from the soapy glasses at her. "Do I what?"

"Do you love Mr. O'Neill?"

Sighing, Millie shook her head a bit. "I never said that I did. I thought that was just something that would come."

"Oh, Millie," Diana said, giving her a sympathetic look.

"Sometimes it works out that way, but there's no guarantee and it really should come more naturally. That's the real way you know for sure if a fellow is the one for you. This is precisely why I could never get into this whole mail order business. It seems far too risky."

Hattie was thoughtful. "I suppose that I could've enjoyed it," she said. "But then, I love writing letters to people."

Millie finished up the washing with the other ladies of the house, and then made her way upstairs to her bedroom to try and clear her mind. She caught herself wondering more than once which room Clyde was staying in. The number of bedrooms in this house was seemingly endless. She undressed, carefully hanging up her crushed velvet dress in the bureau and changing into her white cotton nightgown. She took her hair down and gently ran a comb through her shiny brown tresses. Looking at her reflection in the vanity, she tried to imagine herself as a bride. The white nightgown made it somewhat easy. But when she imagined her groom, all she could think about was Clyde Roberts.

He was staying in the inn as well now, which meant that he would have ample opportunities to see her and wind her up, depending on how he was feeling. She was grateful for a chance to try and learn more about him, but she wasn't looking forward to the way he made her stomach feel whenever they met. She wanted him to help her uncover some answers for herself, rather than overwhelming her with questions!

Somehow, Millie managed to fall asleep. The following morning was much more relaxed. The crowd in the inn had died down quite a bit, and everyone was going about things at a more leisurely pace. When she came downstairs, dressed in a simple blue frock with little birds sewn into the fabric, she looked around at the change and couldn't believe it. *Does this mean the trains are running again?* She thought hopefully.

"Where did everyone go?" she asked Hattie at the desk in the back entryway.

"Oh, some people decided to move to different lodgings in nearby towns, some took wagon trains west or east. People are always coming and going from here," Hattie said. "But he's still here, if you're wondering."

Millie was a bit frantic now. "And the trains?" she asked. "Are the trains running again?"

She had promised him that she would tell him her answer by the time the trains were up and running again. She hadn't expected them to be ready so soon!

"No," Hattie said, popping that bubble before Millie had a chance to worry herself into an early grave. "The trains are still not coming into Ogden. There may have been some melting going on, but not enough to run trains through. To tell you the truth, I feel bad for any horse that's forced to walk through all of this ice, too."

For some reason, Millie felt a wave of relief wash over

her. She wasn't ready to make a big decision. After all, she needed more time to get to know Mr. Roberts.

"You said that Mr. Roberts is still in here?" she asked Hattie awkwardly. "Do you happen to remember where you squeezed him in last night?"

Hattie chuckled. "We didn't squeeze him in. He was quite happy to sleep in the cellar, provided we gave him enough pillows and blankets."

Millie was amazed. "He slept in the cellar?"

"Sure," Hattie replied. "He says that he's used to sleeping in places like that. His home is the blacksmith shop, you know. I've never seen him go anywhere else, until you came into town." She winked at Millie.

"Oh, I'm sure you're just pulling my leg about that. There's no way that the only place he ever goes is to his shop. I don't think a man can live here without going to the grocers, the saloons, and everywhere else. Don't be silly." Millie smiled at the very idea that Clyde would have been a shut-in until now. "He certainly doesn't talk like a man who stays in and works all day every day."

Hattie shrugged a bit. "Well, you know him better than me."

"Who knows who?" Clyde's voice suddenly asked behind Millie. She made a show of being surprised to see him, which clearly tickled him a great deal. "Is this the gossip desk? I thought this was the reception desk."

Hattie blushed and Millie just rolled her eyes at him.

"Ignore him," she said. "He's just picking on us because we have things to keep us occupied here and he doesn't."

"Oh yeah?" he asked Millie. "And what do you have here to keep you occupied? A bunch of unsent letters to your *beau?*"

She glared at him a little. "That's just mean. No mail is going out in this weather. You ought to know what."

"I know," he said. "I was just kidding. My, you sure are still sensitive about him."

"You'd be sensitive, too, if you cared about other people's feelings."

For a moment, Millie thought that Hattie was embarrassed to be witness to their sniping at each other, but then Hattie smiled a conspiratorial smile at her.

"Be that as it may," Clyde said, letting her words fall from him like water off a duck's back. "Would you care to sit with me in the living room and pass the time over a lovely breakfast?"

Millie tittered at the way he'd phrased it. "Really, you can be so silly. Yes, I'll eat with you. But if you mention James O'Neill again, I'll put you out."

They walked through the hall together, past the kitchen and into the spacious living room which was even more spacious now that several of the winter travelers were gone.

"On whose authority are you going to put me out?" he asked her with a wry smile. "You're not the innkeeper here. Mrs. Pratt's too nice to kick me out on nothing but your word."

He held a chair out for her at one of the vacant tables and Millie graciously sat down. He sat in the chair opposite her, giving her space again. *He really is learning his lesson,* she thought. *At least about personal space.*

"So," Millie began as soon as they were both situated at the table. "I have it on good authority that you don't leave the confines of your blacksmithing very often."

Clyde smirked at her. "Oh, who told you that? Little Miss Gossip back there?" he asked, gesturing a thumb towards the back door of the house. "Just cos some people never buy from me, they want to start rumors about me never going outside." He tisked. "Well, you know. You saw me sitting outside my shop the day we met."

"I think it's a sign that people don't know what you do with yourself outside of work, is all," Millie said. "You said that you wanted us to get to know each other. What do you do when you're not working?"

Clyde smiled at her. "A lot of things. I go for walks or rides. I like to make things for fun, too. It's not doing work if it's purely for the sake of enjoyment."

"What do you like to make?" Millie asked him, leaning her chin against her hand as she looked across the table and right into his eyes.

He suddenly gave her a shy kind of look. She wasn't expecting that response from him. "Musical instruments," he told her, keeping his voice down as if he was afraid of getting made fun of for such a thing.

Millie gaped at him. "What?" she asked, incredulously. "That's amazing!"

"Yeah, yeah," Clyde said, still smiling embarrassedly. "Please, keep it down. Not everyone will find that so amazing. Besides, I never said I was any *good* at it."

She had enough faith in him to believe that he was just being modest. "I bet you are," she said. "Why don't you want anyone to know about this hobby of yours?"

"It's more than a hobby, first of all," he said. "And second of all... Because people don't expect the hammer-wielding blacksmith to make and play the flute in his spare time."

"Awwwww!" Millie cooed without being able to stop herself.

"And then there's that reaction." Clyde didn't seem to be able to stop smiling at her. "So now that you know more about me. Why don't you tell me an interesting fact or embarrassing anecdote about yourself?"

She was just so taken by the idea of him playing the flute that she could hardly think of anything else at the moment. "Umm, well I already told you about the no friends and no parties thing," she said, thinking. "I was probably the only young woman in New York who didn't relish being a single working woman there for the rest of my life."

Clyde leaned forward in his chair a little bit. "Why's that?" he asked. "Didn't you like working in the factory making... What was it again?"

"Shirtwaists," she answered readily. "I enjoyed the work well enough, but I didn't exactly love the atmosphere. It was always so stuffy. The whole city was like that, really. Stifling. Smelly."

"So, you wanted to move out West where there's space and you can breathe again," he said. It was a statement of understanding, not a question.

Millie smiled at him and nodded. "Precisely. Not a lot of gentlemen are understanding about that either. They figure, oh, I was a working girl and all I really need in my life is to get married and start making a family with someone. When that's not really it at all."

"Isn't it?"

She shook her head. "No. I don't need a man. I want a man. A little-known fact about me – well, out here anyway. My friends back in New York used to tease me relentlessly about it... I'm a hopeless romantic. I didn't crave independence like they all did. I want to find that special gentleman and start a family with him. I sure as sugar wanted that man to be Mr. O'Neill – James."

Clyde raised an eyebrow. "I thought that subject was off limits."

"I've decided to change the rule, since we're being so honest and everything." Millie raised an eyebrow back at him.

"Have you made up your mind about him then?" Clyde asked her.

She rubbed the tip of her tongue against the tops of her front teeth inside her mouth, mulling that over. There still was nothing easy about this situation. "I think I've made up my mind about him anyway. It remains to be seen how I feel about living permanently in Ogden, though. Or your proposition."

"*Proposal*," Clyde said with a laugh. "It was a proposal. And it still stands, if you'll have me. Flute and all."

She smiled at him, letting the tip of her tongue stick out a bit between her rows of white teeth. He was giving her such a trusting look, a look that said, *I know you're not going to turn me away...*

CHAPTER 11

Staring down at the blank piece of paper before her, Millie was at a loss for what to write. She didn't know how she was meant to go about this. Surely this was going to ruin everything. James might be so angered by what she had to say perhaps he'd come all the way to Ogden to drag her to Coloma himself. Of course, such a thing would be rather crazy, but she wasn't sure that it was completely outside the realm of possibility. Men could be awfully hot-headed and possessive... She'd been told.

There was a great deal to be said for being honest, however. He had appreciated her candor so far, in her letters. Though she worried that this would break his heart, why should she be any more afraid to be honest now than all of the previous times? When she'd written about her hopes and dreams? When she'd written the promise to come to California and be his bride?

Oh, she felt wretched.

M*y dearest James*,

I'm afraid that I haven't been keeping you as abreast of the situation as I indeed should have. I have been in Ogden for a little over a week now and I feel as though a startling and welcome transformation has come over me. I like it here. So much so, that I am not sure that I want to leave. And even more importantly... In the time since my last letter to you was written, I have met a gentleman who dearly wishes to marry me.

Naturally, I told him that I was engaged to be married to you and that I was only in Ogden in the first place because you provided the means for a ticket and transit. I greatly appreciate that. You are the one who has helped me see more of the world and start on the adventure that I had craved for so long. Alas, my darling, I feel that I cannot in good conscience continue on my trek across the country. I've decided to stay here now, not only for myself and my own dreams but for this gentleman who loves me and inspires me every time we meet.

I shall not send this letter to you right away, for I have a few more plans for you. Please do not let it ever be said that I was not thinking of your best interests, even when I knew they would hurt you to learn about.

. . .

Forever your friend,
   Millie

Even though she had managed to complete the letter, it didn't exactly make her feel better about things. Of course, the letter was only the first part of her plan. She had an idea in her head; she just needed to talk about it with Clyde. After all, he was the cause of all of this.

She safely tucked the letter into its envelope, keeping it open so that she might add to it at a later date, as she promised. Poor, unsuspecting James…

Swinging her legs around, Millie climbed off of the chair in front of her desk in her room. She made her way down the stairs, keeping an eye out for her co-conspirator the whole time. She didn't see him on the stairs, but then she remembered that he was lodging in the cellar. *That still makes little sense to me,* she thought. *It must be terribly cold down there. And there seem to be plenty of empty rooms here, now that so many people have moved on.*

Millie wondered what James would say if he knew that people had indeed been able to leave during the storm. They didn't rely on the train the way she did, but perhaps she hadn't needed to either. She wondered if she might have been a great ninny about all of this.

"Is Mr. Roberts about?" Millie asked Diana as the innkeeper poured her a full cup of coffee.

Diana nodded vaguely. "He's downstairs in the cellar,"

she replied. "Doing whatever it is that keeps him occupied most days."

It was then that Millie realized that the reason Hattie had spoken about him in such mysterious ways was because he was simply a private person. And now that Millie knew why, she had to smile. It was thrilling to be privy to something like that; the story of what made a man tick.

"Say," she said then to Diana. "Do you happen to know any young, single ladies of about my age?"

Diana didn't even have to think for too long. "There's a girl who works with me in the schoolhouse most days," she said at once. "She's quite a skilled teacher. Her name's Suzy Church. ...Why do you ask?"

Millie grinned back at her. "Do you think she might be willing to move to Coloma?" she asked. "I think I've got a fellow for her to marry."

"Who's getting married?" came Clyde's voice as he opened the cellar door and came out from downstairs.

Giggling a little, Millie shook her head at him. "You're always coming in at the tail end of conversations. I was just telling Diana that I think I have a good way to appease Mr. O'Neill."

"You mean besides me paying him back for the railway ticket?"

Millie was floored by that. "Oh!" she cried, shocked. "That might be a better idea, though money won't mend his broken heart."

Diana was tilting her head at the two of them now.

"You're not going to Coloma?" she asked, this bit of information finally being new to her.

"Reimbursement for the train ticket is the same as a wedding ring, right, darling?" he asked Millie, getting down on one knee in front of her and taking her hand.

She smiled down at him. "I'll marry you on Christmas if we can pull this off," she said, surprising herself by just how excited she sounded.

Diana looked from Millie to Clyde, not quite sure what to think but nevertheless enthusiastic about the proposal that was happening right in front of her very eyes. "I will go and fetch Miss Church!" she said, rushing from the house and nearly forgetting to grab her coat in the process.

Millie watched in amazement as she ran from the house. "I see it's all well and good to go out into the snow if you're the innkeeper."

Clyde laughed. "Do you think you can answer me? My knees might not be what they used to be."

Millie looked down at him on his knee at her feet. "Oh, you're still here," she quipped. "Well, I've already written my letter telling James that I intend to stay put here in Ogden. I guess if you really are open to paying him back, and Diana has a girl to introduce him to… There's no reason for me to say no."

"Aww, come on, woman!" Clyde said, smiling though his posture deflated a little. He wasn't going to be pleased with that non-answer, teasing though it was.

"Yes," Millie replied with a smile. "Yes, of course. Now

get up before you hurt yourself."

Chuckling, Clyde bounded back up to his feet again, seemingly much more nimble now that he had the answer he'd been looking for. He opened his arms to hug Millie and she calmly walked into them, embracing him and feeling a strong sense of ease pour over her. This felt right in a way that nothing ever had in her life before. She didn't know how she was ever supposed to explain it, but there it was.

She knew and felt to the very core, that she had made the right decision for herself at long last.

CHAPTER 12

"I'D NEVER REALLY GIVEN MUCH THOUGHT TO continuing onward to California," Suzy Church told Millie in what felt like a job interview but was actually a *bride* interview.

"It helps if you don't think of it so much as moving somewhere new as much as meeting someone new. I'm sure that your skills as a teacher will be quite important and valuable in Coloma, as well." Millie didn't want to put too much pressure on this young woman, but she was, in a way, depending on her. Sure, James would survive if all he was given was the money back for her journey, but she didn't know how she was meant to live with herself if she just left him essentially at the altar.

Diana smoothed Millie's hair back and out of her face,

pinning it up in the back and making her look like a princess in her white gown. It had been a simple nightgown before, but the skilled ladies had worked together and repurposed it into a wedding dress. Millie found that she didn't feel too picky about what she was wearing when she married Clyde Roberts, as long as she married him.

"What is this gentleman like?" Suzy asked Millie as the ladies continued to get ready in Millie's bedroom.

Clyde and some of the other gentlemen had already headed off to the small chapel that thankfully wasn't very far from Diana's inn. As some kind of sign from God surely, the snow had melted quite a bit and the temperature outside felt much more hospitable. *Now I'm definitely not just staying here on account of the snowstorm,* Millie thought to herself. *This is me completely staying because I want to live here with Mr. Roberts – Clyde.*

She blushed a bit. *Now that we're getting married, I'm having a harder time thinking of him as just 'Clyde.'*

After hemming and hawing quite a bit – the former literally – Millie had made plans with Clyde to wed at the chapel on Christmas Eve. That gave the ladies plenty of time to finish her gown and the ground plenty of time to thaw and warm up. And it had worked wonders.

"Mr. O'Neill is a very kind man," Millie told the concerned Suzy. Now that she wasn't going to marry him, she found it easier to describe him to other people without feeling quite so guilty. "He's a miner and he's made quite a bit of money, so you'll certainly be comfortable. He's generous and caring, and he's never judged me for even my most embarrassing confessions." She smiled at the young teacher. "He never laid eyes on me, but he made me feel so pretty and so special. Surely, he'll treat you with as much revere, because he seems to be an incredibly honorable man and it's not in his character to treat a woman any other way."

Suzy smiled and looked down, bashful.

Just then, the music started and it was their cue to take their places to walk up the aisle. Diana and Hattie were Millie's bridesmaids; Suzy had been given the honor of being her train attendant, making sure it didn't get dirty as she walked along the aisle.

Millie walked confidently up the aisle, looking to her left and her right as she went and smiling at all of the friendly well-wishers who were in attendance. Then she looked ahead of her and saw Clyde there next to the minister, looking nervous as all get out but also smiling away like this was the best moment of his life, just looking at her in that dress, coming towards him.

The music stopped when Millie reached the front of the congregation, and Clyde stepped forward to stand at her side. The minister stepped towards them, at the center of their oak wedding arch which was topped by a large, gleaming and golden cross.

"Dearly beloved," the minister intoned in a kindly voice.

"We are gathered here today to celebrate and share in the love and devotion of these two souls who have made the decision before you, myself, and Jesus Christ to join together in holy matrimony. I ask at this time that if there is anyone here who sees a reason why these two shall not be wed, let him speak now or forever hold his piece."

For a brief moment, Millie wondered if someone might say something, someone who knew the story of how she'd come to Ogden in the first place. But no one spoke. No one made a sound.

"Then we shall proceed," the minister said approvingly after that moment passed. He looked from Millie to Clyde. "Millicent Elaine Saxton and Clyde Byron Roberts, I pray on this day that you will find peace and strength within each other as well as in yourselves. As it says in Philippians 1:9, *I pray that your love for each other will overflow more and more, and that you will keep on growing in your knowledge and understanding.*"

The minister now turned to Millie. "Millicent Elaine Saxton, do you take this gentleman, Clyde Byron Roberts, to be your lawfully wedded husband? To have and to hold, to love and to cherish, to honor and obey, forsaking all others, in sickness and in health, for richer or poorer, as long as you both shall live and until death do you part?"

There was a lot to that vow, but Millie intended to stay true to every word of it. "I do," she said confidently, turning her head a bit to look into Clyde's eyes and smiling at him.

The minister turned his attention next to Clyde. "Clyde

Byron Roberts, do you take this woman, Millicent Elaine Saxton, to be your lawfully wedded wife? To have and to hold, to love and to cherish, to protect and to treasure, forsaking all others, in sickness and in health, for richer or poorer, as long as you both shall live and until death do you part?"

Clyde gulped audibly, which made Millie's smile only grow bigger. The fact that he was this nervous really amused her because he had been so adamant about marrying her. Now that it was a reality, he was practically beside himself. She supposed that it wasn't every day that a gentleman out West found himself a bride without some sort of assistance...or at the very least, the help of a newspaper advertisement.

"I do," Clyde finally said, breaking the silence that was deafening to everyone other than Millie.

The minister smiled at the both of them. "Then, by the powers vested in me by the great town of Ogden and our Lord and Savior Jesus Christ, I now proudly pronounce you husband and wife. You may kiss the bride."

The applause began as soon as the minister had finished speaking. Clyde finally got some of his usual bravado back once the minister had pronounced them officially married. He took Millie into his arms and kissed her deeply.

She kissed him back enthusiastically, overcome with joy that she had been able to have some say in her life for a change.

There would be time for more merriment later. Clyde

and Millie held hands as they ran back down the aisle, followed by her three ladies in waiting. They all climbed aboard the carriage – driven by Glenn, who had volunteered for the privilege – and they rode off to a destination that few couples immediately ventured to: the train station.

CHAPTER 13

THE TRAIN STATION WAS FAIRLY EMPTY WHEN THEY arrived. All of the bothersome snow was gone for the time being, which made it the perfect day to get on the train and get out of Ogden before the next storm hit. Millie knew that winter could be unpredictable, but the sound of trains in the distance proved that she was correct when she made this plan.

She turned to Suzy Church and handed her a stack of letters to Mr. O'Neill. "He'll understand when you hand him these. We don't have time to wait for the mail service to deliver these to him. You'll be able to provide some solace to him right away, when he finds out that I'm not coming."

"You could pretend to be Miss Saxton if you want," Clyde offered, winking at Millie. "After all, Millie Saxton doesn't actually exist anymore."

"No," Millie said, shaking her head but smiling slightly at his ridiculousness. "No lies. I want you to tell him the truth. That way whatever happens there for you will be based in honesty from here on out."

Suzy held the letters to her, nodding and nervous-looking. "Suppose he turns me away?" she asked.

It was a fair question, but Millie knew him better than that. "He won't. He may not take you straight to the altar as he would have done with me, but he will not abandon you."

The large, black beast of a train came into the station. Millie gave Suzy a tight hug to assure her that everything was going to work out. "I feel sort of sisterly towards you, you know," she added. "I know that I am in your debt now. Please write to me if ever you need anything that you think I can provide for you. At the very least, I'd love it if we were pen-pals."

Before long, the time came for boarding the train. Clyde helped Suzy with her bags, handing them off to the conductor. He and Millie stood and waved on the platform until the train was rolling steadily away from Ogden.

"I hope this was the right thing to do," she said to him as they walked back to their carriage. "Are you sure the money we enclosed was enough?"

Clyde took her hand as they walked, smiling at her sweetly. "It was more than enough," he promised her. "It was enough for him and his new bride to spend on a pretty nice dress, like the one you wore for me."

Millie blushed. She thought about her final letter to

James O'Neill and hoped that that, too, might be more than enough.

Dearest James,

I have no doubt that it is clear to you by now that I am not coming to Coloma to be with you. I hope that you will accept the hand of Miss Suzy Church in my stead. My husband Mr. Roberts has also provided you with the equal amount of funds that you gave me for the journey to California. I only used half of it, but it was money well spent in my case, I promise you.

I pray that you and Miss Church will be most happy together and that you can forgive me for my change of heart. I never meant to cause you any sorrow; I only know that my own heart would have broken if I had been forced to leave Ogden and this wonderful man who I now call husband.

I wish you every happiness that God may grant you.

Always your friend,
  Millie Roberts

She hoped that those words to him would suffice. There wasn't anything else that she could think of that would make it any better for him, but Clyde had a point when he emphasized that she had to think about her own feelings, hopes and dreams, as well.

"I guess that's that," she said at last, as they met up with Diana and Hattie in the carriage. "I've been here with a sort of mental tether to California this whole time. It'll be nice to be able to enjoy my new life without worrying about the things that were simply never meant to be."

Clyde smiled and put his arm around her as they rode off towards the inn. "It's...hard to find the right words. I'm so completely overjoyed. I'm so grateful that you had the courage to give me a chance," he said as his eyes welled up a bit.

The wedding reception was to be held at the inn. It was a part wedding fete, part Christmas party for all those who were staying in the inn. It hadn't struck Millie until now that she and Clyde would be needing their own place to stay instead of living in a room and the cellar in Diana's home for the rest of their lives. But that could wait until after Christmas, surely.

Everyone cheered as they entered the house. Millie hadn't anticipated that the throngs of people there would be so big. Aaron Pratt, Matthew Ford and Mrs. Cooke had all gone ahead of the bridal caravan and set everything up. Now that Diana was back in her element, she resumed her hostess duties.

"We have punch and pie if anybody wants some," she announced. "And of course, later on we will have a Christmas feast to welcome the holiday."

Mr. Pratt rolled in a small upright piano from somewhere in the recesses in the back of the large house. He sat down himself and began to play a bouncy tune. Everyone around started dancing. Millie danced with Clyde, smiling up as she gazed into his face.

"I'm glad I finally allowed you to sweep me off my feet," she told him. "I could get used to feeling special like this."

Clyde chuckled at her. "I'm going to hold you to that when, in the future, you're feeling cross with me."

After a while of dancing in which Millie felt that time slowed and allowed her to relish the moments, everyone finally sat down at the various tables that had been set out exactly like they had been on Thanksgiving. The newlyweds were given their own private table at the front of the room.

Hattie and Diana went around, placing plates of pie and glasses of purplish punch in front of every guest and partygoer. They started at Millie's and Clyde's table, of course.

Once the passing out of refreshments was done, Hattie held up her glass. "A toast to the groom and the bride," she announced. "May they have a wonderful and fruitful life together."

"To the groom and bride!" everyone echoed and sipped their punch.

After everyone ate their pie and drank their punch, Aaron went back to his piano playing, pounding out practically every Christmas song that he could think of. Everyone returned to dancing. That's when Millie realized something.

She sidled up to Diana. "There's no Christmas tree

here," she pointed out, as if no one else had noticed the lack of spruce in the room.

"I thought that we might do some decorating later this evening, whilst the revelers are resting before dinner. Not that I expect you to do anything other than rest and be blissfully happy." Diana smiled and raised her eyebrows a bit at Millie. "You are happy, right?"

Millie blushed and nodded. "Exceedingly," she admitted. "But that doesn't mean I don't want to help you decorate for Christmas. Besides, how else am I supposed to show off for my husband further?" She winked.

It dawned on Diana then that Millie was hoping to give off more impressions of herself as a skillful housewife. She had first proved it to Clyde by helping to make the Thanksgiving dinner and dessert.

"You're crafty," Diana said to her with an impressed smile. "I won't refuse you then. But do get some rest before we get started. You've had a long and busy day."

When the celebrations came to an end, Millie took her leave so she could indeed get some rest from the day's events. She went up to her bedroom and Hattie helped her out of the cotton and lace wedding gown. Lying on her bed, she drifted peacefully off to sleep thinking about her new husband and what the future held for them.

She startled herself awake about an hour later, when she heard the sound of activity going on downstairs in the living room without her. *Oh goodness,* she thought. *They've started without me.*

Millie supposed that she should have asked for Diana to wake her up when they were ready to decorate, but that didn't much matter now. She threw on her crushed velvet dress and came quickly down the stairs.

Mr. Pratt and Mr. Ford were carefully standing a tall fir tree up in the corner of the living room while Diana and Hattie looked on, giving them suggestions about where it should lean and planning out which colored candle should go where.

"Well now, there's a tree that's guaranteed to make our Christmas morning merry and bright."

They all turned to look at her as she came to the bottom of the staircase. They were all smiles, including Millie. As soon as she came into the room, she set to work on sewing a nice blanket to go under the tall, green Christmas tree. It was made of white tablecloths, making the tree appear as though it was standing in snow; like it had never left the wintry forest where it had come from.

"I wish I hadn't just slept for so long," Millie said, frowning a bit. "Now that I've seen this, I surely won't be able to sleep tonight!"

Even though the anticipation would likely keep her up for hours, Millie couldn't remember the last time she'd been this excited about Christmas. In New York, it had been a fairly solitary affair for her. But in Ogden, she knew deep down, that she'd never have to worry about being lonely again.

CHAPTER 14

THE MORNING OF CHRISTMAS ARRIVED AND MILLIE WAS out of her room and down the stairs before she heard anyone else stirring from their beds. She was relieved to see that she wasn't the only one awake at such an early hour. Other guests smiled at her and she smiled back. When she got to the bottom of the staircase, she looked up at the tall tree, decorated with lights and vivid colors. The white blanket she'd made for the occasion was now covered with beautifully wrapped gifts of every size, shape and color. She didn't anticipate receiving anything from below the tree. *My gift was already given to me*, she thought gladly. *My gift is getting to live here with all of these lovely people, and marrying a gentleman who truly understands me.*

Just as she was thinking it, Clyde appeared from his bedroom down below the rest of the house. He was dressed in a smart suit; the kind that she had once had a difficult time imagining him wearing. He smiled and came over to Millie at once. She was wearing her crushed velvet dress again, not having adequate time to make another dress for herself what with the wedding and the holiday season. As he gazed upon her, she could see that it didn't matter to him what she wore.

"Merry Christmas, Mrs. Roberts," he said, bringing her into a warm hug.

"Merry Christmas, Mr. Roberts," she replied, hugging him back. It felt heavenly to be held by him. "Did you sleep well down in your dungeon?" she asked him, teasing.

Clyde let out a laugh and nodded. "As a matter of fact, I did. Did you enjoy your slumbers up in your princess tower?"

Millie smiled at him. "I did," she said. "Although I slept about as well as a child does on Christmas Eve. I couldn't stop thinking about everything that this day might bring."

This pleased him greatly. She could tell by his expression. His brown eyes seemed to sparkle in the colorful candlelight. "That's good, because I have a Christmas gift for you that's worthy of anticipation," he boasted, placing his fingertips into the tops of his pants pockets.

She knew that he was trying to get her to ask what her present was, but she wasn't going to take the bait that easily. She smiled wryly at him. "Oh? I thought our exchange of presents happened yesterday."

Another big smile stretched across Clyde's face. "Vows

don't quite count as gifts," he countered. "Though I will accept them graciously from you, since they weren't easily given by you."

Millie looked at him curiously. Then she looked up at the Christmas tree. "I haven't really had time to think of anything other than marrying you. That's been my priority."

Moving towards her, Clyde planted a kiss on her forehead. "That's it. That shall be my Christmas gift: the nicest thing you've ever said to me."

Laughing softly, Millie smiled at him. "I can put it into a needlepoint, if you'd like."

They held hands and took in the majesty of the tree for a while longer. She was pleasantly surprised to see how well they went together. He had been right all along. He had always been right. Even their playful jabs at each other had a certain unique sweetness to them. She could see now that his words had never been meant to demean her or make her feel foolish in her decision-making. He had been looking out for her and keeping her best interests at heart always. She might not ever know how he knew her soul so well, but she was deeply grateful that he did.

"Would you like to see your present now?" Clyde asked her then, looking around and noting that more one by one, more guests were making their way out of their beds and down the stairs. "It requires leaving the inn, but we can always come back for Christmas dinner tonight, if that's what you prefer."

Now Millie was intrigued. "Oh? You didn't intend to give me one of these presents under the tree?"

He shook his head at her. "What I've got for you won't fit into a box or under a tree."

She blinked at him, giving him a skeptical sort of look. They walked hand in hand out of the room and out the front door of the house. Clyde acted as though they wouldn't be missed, but Millie had a feeling that Diana and Hattie would ask about her whereabouts. The three ladies had become friends almost overnight, and Millie didn't want that to be taken for granted now that she was married to this man.

"Where are you taking me?" she asked him as they strolled along the wintry road. A few small remnants of ice were there along the sides of the street, but they were easily avoidable if one knew where not to step.

"First of all, I thought a short walk might do us both some good. I know that you're fond of getting air when you have been cooped up inside for days."

She looked at him expectantly. "And? Where are we walking to?"

Clyde chuckled. "You're not very fond of surprises, are you? I'm taking you somewhere that, I hope, will be the start of the new life that you've always wanted."

Millie's breath caught in her chest. He was taking her *home*.

The walk to Clyde's house wasn't actually very long. He didn't even live that far from Diana! She wondered now what Hattie had been talking about; filling her head with all kinds of silly stories. Though she had to admit that Hattie had succeeded. Her interest in Clyde had only grown after that discussion with the assistant innkeeper.

His house was similar in style to Mrs. Pratt's, although perhaps not quite as big. It was made of wood and stone, painted the same white color that she noticed a lot of the homes on the street had. The front door was painted a bright red. "Beautiful," she said earnestly.

"I think so too," Clyde replied.

Millie smiled as she gazed up at her new home, and then she blushed a bit when she realized that Clyde was gazing at her instead of the house.

"This isn't your only gift, of course. This is just the first one. The next one should come as a complete surprise." His eyes lit up with excitement. He enjoyed giving her things, clearly. Even more than he enjoyed receiving things, it seemed.

He let her by the hand up onto the front porch and then inside the sweet little home. Millie admired the décor of the interior. It wasn't fancy. In fact, she could see that there had been some truth to what Hattie had said actually. There was some simple wooden furniture – chairs and tables – and one low couch in the living room, but it didn't appear to be a house that was well lived in. At least not yet. Millie had plans for it now that she knew that this was her home, too.

"We can host our own parties here," she said joyously,

sitting gently down on one of the chairs. "Once we get some more decorations and a bit more furniture."

"If you like," Clyde agreed. "But this still isn't the surprise. Wait here."

Millie didn't know what to expect anymore. A new home for her to decorate and live in with him was more than enough. She would no longer have to while away the hours during the afternoons. She knew that she was going to miss him when he went to work in his blacksmith shop, but being able to work on this house would help her feel accomplished and make the time they were apart go faster.

Clyde smiled lovingly at her once more and then left her sitting there in the living room, contemplating all of this. When he returned, Millie could see that he was holding something small in his hands but she couldn't, for the life of her, guess what it could possibly be.

She smiled playfully at him. "Wait," she said. "I thought you said that you were giving me something that didn't fit in a box or under a Christmas tree. That looks like it could."

Clyde grinned at her. "It's not the object itself. Listen."

He came towards where she sat and held the gleaming object up to his lips. Now that he was closer to her and more in the light, Millie was delighted to see that what he was holding was an instrument – some kind of pennywhistle that she had no doubt in her mind that he made.

Clyde began to lightly blow into the pennywhistle, tooting out a pretty little ditty for her. It sounded like the playful tweeting of birds during a sun shower. Millie was absolutely mesmerized by everything about this. She smiled and clapped as soon as his song was done. "That's marvelous! Did you make that yourself?"

"I sure did," he said with a nod. "It's perhaps not my best craftsmanship, but it's the first instrument I completed. I wanted to show you what I can do with it."

"How did you learn to play?" Millie asked him.

Clyde shrugged and smiled. "I practiced," he answered. "I have more like this downstairs, if you would like to see."

Of course he made these instruments in his basement. A blacksmith was simply the most comfortable in a dark, cool place. Millie understood more of the rumors now, and why he chose to sleep in the cellar at Diana Pratt's house. *I hope that he doesn't intend for me to sleep in the basement with him*, she thought jokingly to herself.

He offered his hand to her and she took it. She took hold of his pennywhistle, too, examining it and feeling surprised by the lightness of it. "You could easily sell things like this, alongside the tools you make."

Clyde laughed lightly. "Maybe. Though I don't think there's much call for musical instruments around here."

"Oh no," Millie said, shaking her head emphatically at that. "There's always a call for music. It aids in keeping life bearable."

He led her down the long, slanting staircase and into his basement cellar. It was about what Millie had expected, dark and cold and filled with mostly rundown old furniture and other forgotten things. However, upon further exploration, she happened upon what looked like a bookshelf but was holding nothing but silver and brass colored instruments. She gasped a bit when she saw how many there were. It was enough to supply a whole band with instruments!

"Clyde! You have been busy." She turned her face to look at him, smiling in her wonderment. "You just keep all of this to yourself?"

He stepped over towards her and took the pennywhistle back from her, gingerly touching it with his fingertips. "Not anymore," he said. "This is my passion and I am sharing it with you." He gave a short toot from the whistle again.

Millie smiled and rested her head against his shoulder. She supposed that everyone had a passion that they carried close inside them. Not everyone's passion needed to be shared with the world. The fact that Clyde was sharing his music and his beautiful instruments with her made them all the more special in her eyes.

"Now that you're here with me, I reckon I don't need to spend all my time in this cellar," he said to her as they cuddled. "I want to make things together with you. Things that'll make this drafty little house feel like home."

Millie beamed at that. "I did rather hope that I'd be seeing more of you now that we're married and we'll be living here together..."

Clyde pulled away from her just enough to give her a kiss. It was sweet and warm. She knew that he was content because he hadn't stopped smiling since bringing her to his home and showing her his collection of instruments. "What do you say we decorate this ol' house some?" he asked her then. "I know it's already Christmas, but since we're going to be here and all, why not make the place merry to go along with our happy new life?"

Millie let out a laugh and nodded her head. "That sounds like a lovely idea to me."

Before long, they'd bundled themselves up in coats and scarves and they strolled out together in search of a worthy tree for Christmas. As they were approaching a promising fir, she slipped on some snow and fell. Clyde rushed to help her and found that she was laughing.

"Are you all right?" he asked her, smiling now that he could see she was more amused than shocked or harmed.

Millie nodded and stood up with the help of his offered arm. "It's cold," she told him. "You should see." She brought a hand from behind her back and gently mushed some snow into his face.

"Ahh!" he shouted, and then he was laughing too. "So cold!"

Soon they were chasing each other around in the snow, tossing it about and laughing 'til they cried a little. Millie had never experienced such fun in all her life. This was indeed going to be a first Christmas to remember for many joyous years to come.

THE END

AMELIA'S BLESSED CHRISTMAS

Brides Of Weber Valley

AMELIA'S BLESSED CHRISTMAS

OGDEN, UTAH TERRITORY – 1876

A recent widow, young Amelia Hawkins leaves behind her life of bereavement and bad memories to travel west to live with Mr. Percy Andrews, a friendly and caring general store owner who is well-liked by everyone in the town of Ogden. From their very first meeting at the railway station, she is taken by his kindness and gentle nature and knows that God has blessed her with a second chance at happiness. That calm and peaceful feeling doesn't last very long, as the horrors of her past begin to creep back into her life in the form of bad dreams. Her fears and anxieties begin to consume her and Amelia begins to doubt herself and, in turn, begins to doubt her future with Mr. Andrews.

When Christmas arrives, she feels increasingly out of sorts and ill. Her good-natured friend Mrs. Tabitha Hughes implores her to go visit the doctor in town who informs her of the cause of her symptoms and Amelia is then convinced that she must leave at once and stop wasting Percy's time.

Will Amelia become consumed by the memories of the past? Or will Percy's tender warmth and kindness be enough to calm the fears that have been haunting her once and for all?

CHAPTER 1

"You're mine now, you ungrateful girl!"

Amelia jolted awake. She'd nodded off on the train and the nightmare about her late husband was all too real. In life, Luther Hawkins had been a nightmare even in her waking moments. Still shaken, she looked out of the window and admired the western countryside. Amelia had lived on the east coast, in New York, all of her life. The only west that she had known were things she'd heard about in stories. But as she looked out of the train window and gazed at the view, she knew that she had never seen such golden fields before. She'd seen nothing like this in her whole life.

Admittedly, twenty-two years was not so very long of a life thus far, but still this emphasized to Amelia that she'd needed this change. She'd been miserable as Mrs. Hawkins and now that she was a widow she felt that she had a new opportunity for happiness. She hadn't been able to run away from her husband, but now she was free!

She hoped that that didn't make her a terrible person.

Now that she had been so disturbingly awakened, Amelia looked around for a passing conductor. "Excuse me?" she said when she spied one nearby. "Can you please tell me where we are?"

The conductor – a vaguely portly gentleman with rosy cheeks – smiled at her. "Sure I can, Miss. We're coming up on Ogden station now. We shall be there within the hour."

"Oh, splendid! Thank you very much." Amelia sat back in her cushioned train seat, pleased to know that she was close to her new home and her new husband-to-be. *Perhaps it's a good thing that I nodded off,* she thought. *Even if my dreams were scary, at least they helped me pass some of the time.*

In truth, she'd been riding on that train for days on end. Getting to the west from the east wasn't as quick and easy as she would have liked. That was why she counted her blessings that she was finally arriving at her destination!

The only thing she knew about Ogden was that it was a small town near where the railway had been joined, bringing the east and the west together. As a city girl, Amelia rather liked the idea of living in a small town where she might be able to know everybody, in time. She hoped that the place was as friendly and welcoming as it sounded.

The folks here are used to people stopping in on their way to somewhere else, Amelia's beau had written to her. *I think that's part of what makes this town so friendly and such a good place to call home. Everyone is a friend here, even the people who don't stick around.*

Of course, Amelia hoped to stick around. She'd written a letter in response to an advertisement in the newspaper. A gentleman by the name of Percy Andrews had placed an ad that sounded so sweet and full of promise that Amelia couldn't stop thinking about him until she'd written to him. He was the owner of the general store in Ogden. She didn't imagine that he made quite as much money as her late husband, but then he was the owner of the store and she figured that had to count for something.

When the train pulled into the station, Amelia was almost too giddy to sit still. As soon as she could, she rose up from her seat in her compartment and called for the conductor to help her with her bags. Carefully, she climbed down from the train and strolled towards the center of the platform there, looking every which way for any sign of the sweet shop-owner with whom she'd been exchanging letters. They hadn't exchanged photographs, which Amelia was now kicking herself over.

The conductor placed her suitcases at her feet and was gone a moment later to assist someone else. Amelia held her coat around herself. She hadn't thought it would be so cold before, but then it was December. Anything less than chilly would have been even more of a shock to the system, in her opinion. After all, she came from New York which nearly always had a white Christmas.

As she was scanning the distance for any sign of the man

she'd come to meet, she realized that a gentleman was slowly walking towards her. Like Amelia, he was holding tightly to the coat he wore, keeping its collar over his face in order to protect himself from the bitter cold. This of course meant that Amelia couldn't see much of his face, apart from his kind brown eyes.

He appeared almost nervous as he reached out a bare hand to her. In so doing, his coat's collar fell away to reveal his face. His cheeks were red – from the cold and perhaps also from shyness – and he had a scruffy brown beard over them that almost hid the redness but not fully. Bits of silver were also there in his beard, which Amelia found attractive for reasons she couldn't quite explain. She knew that he was a widower and that he was thirty-eight years old, but as she gazed upon him she felt as though she could learn a lot from him. All because of a few gray hairs on his chin.

Gingerly, she took his hand in her lavender-gloved one.

"Mrs. Hawkins?" he asked her, looking directly into her eyes and causing her to blush a little herself.

Amelia suddenly feared that this might not actually be the gentleman with whom she'd been writing. What if he was a hired valet or something similar? And she'd been thinking him handsome already. Oh! What embarrassment that would be!

"Mr. Andrews?" she asked back, raising an eyebrow slightly in order to convey her slight skepticism now. One could never be too sure when meeting a stranger on a train platform...

The man smiled at her and nodded his head ever so slightly. "Indeed," he said. "Thank you for doing me the extreme honor of meeting me all the way here. Please, let me escort you to my carriage so we can get out of this frightful cold."

He didn't waste time and collected her things right away. Then he offered his arm to her and they walked across the way to a horse-drawn buggy. Mr. Andrews assisted her into the seat of the carriage before climbing in himself.

They rode in silence towards his home. She smiled shyly at him, as butterflies flooded her stomach and indeed her mind, as well. She hoped that she was making a good impression. It was always too difficult to know for sure. She certainly hoped she would have better luck with this gentleman than she'd had with Luther.

CHAPTER 2

Mr. Percy Andrews didn't live in a mansion. Amelia hadn't imagined or assumed that he would, but it did take her by surprise when the carriage stopped outside of the small wood and cement house. It appeared to be the home of a bachelor, not the sort of place that a family would reside.

He could see the baffled disappointment in her eyes no matter how much she tried to hide it. "It isn't much, but I'm planning to expand. I was hoping that, now that you're here, we could work together to build a dream home for the both of us."

As surprised as she was at the sight of the house, she did like the idea of making something new together. "A household project!" she said enthusiastically, though her voice didn't raise much above a whisper. The brown-haired, doe-eyed girl was a wisp of a thing, her voice included.

Mr. Andrews smiled as he alighted from the carriage, giving her a hand as he assisted her out after him. "I hoped that you would like the idea. I'm a humble man of simple means, as you know. But I've been saving up for such a venture. My late wife and I didn't get far enough into our marriage to really warrant additional space..."

They never got to have children, he means, Amelia thought sympathetically. She could tell by the look on his face that he carried a sadness about that. To be sure, most men who set out to marry hoped to start a family.

Luther Hawkins hadn't been that way, but he hadn't been a gentleman or a normal sort of husband, either. He'd been gruff, violent, and forceful, and he'd hated children and never neglected to remind poor Amelia of that.

Smiling to Percy Andrews, she placed a hand on his arm. "I understand what you mean," she said. "I hope to be a good wife and partner to you, sir. If that is what you still want."

He took her hand and kissed it. "Darling, that is all I shall ever want in this world."

In his letters, he asked her to be his wife which hadn't come as a surprise to her because that was indeed what the advertisement service was meant for. Yet Amelia still held onto the hope and desire for a real, in person proposal. Her heart soared a little at the mere mention now.

Percy guided her into the home and she looked around.

Though it was small, it did have a cozy living room and a kitchen, and a staircase going up which surely led to the bedrooms. She blanched suddenly. Perhaps it didn't have more than one bedroom...

"I know what you're thinking. I will sleep on the couch here in the living room," Percy explained. "And you may sleep in the bed upstairs."

This was a great comfort to her for a number of reasons.

"Please make yourself comfortable while I take these bags upstairs," he said then, carrying her two suitcases with him as he went.

Amelia sat at once on the living room's large blue couch. There was a solitary cedar table nearby, in an alcove of the room. Two chairs were placed there, and she knew at once that this was where they were going to take their meals. A wide space had been left empty in the room, between the couch and the home's front door. As the holidays were coming up, she believed that this space was meant for their Christmas tree. She wondered what the holidays were like in this small town, and the possibilities excited her in her quiet, unassuming way.

When Percy came back down the stairs, he was rubbing his hands together a bit nervously. "Now that I've got you all settled here, I've got to get back to my store, I'm afraid. You're welcome to come with me, if you want. Otherwise, you may rest up from your travels while I'm gone."

Amelia of course liked having a choice, but she didn't know which one would be the better one to make. She didn't want to be rude to her new fiancé, but she was pretty tired from her trip to the west. She was also a bit shy about going to see his place of work so soon after arriving, even though she was intrigued by it and hoped to help him with it in the future. "If you don't mind terribly, I think that I should rest here today. But I would so like to accompany you another day."

Percy smiled at her. "Certainly, my dear. The room is yours, and you may help yourself to anything in my kitchen should you get hungry."

Smiling back at him, Amelia nodded her head. He wrapped his dark coat and gray hat around himself and then exited the house, carefully locking it as he went. The sound of the key in the lock made her feel momentarily nervous. It was almost as if he was locking her inside a cage.

Don't be silly, Amelia told herself. *He's only locking up to prevent a break-in. You're free to explore outside if you want to, surely."*

She went to the door and gingerly touched the doorknob, about to open it in order to prove her freedom to herself, but then she thought better of it. *Suppose I unlock the door and then I can't lock it again.* This home wasn't really hers yet, and besides she was in an altogether new place where she didn't know anyone outside of Mr. Andrews.

Her ability to leave decided, Amelia turned and climbed the stairs. There was a short, nondescript hallway with one bedroom. The door to the room was already open and she could glance the bed from the doorway. It had been made up nicely, with a downy-looking comforter. Simply looking at it made her sleepy, so she walked into the room and threw herself upon the bed.

It took a while for her restless thoughts to catch up with her tired body, but eventually sleep overcame her and she finally stopped worrying about every little thing.

CHAPTER 3

ANOTHER NIGHTMARE FORCED AMELIA AWAKE. SHE looked around for a moment, confused by the unfamiliar room but then she relaxed as she remembered where she was, and that she was indeed, safe. The sky outside her window was dark and she sat up, rubbing her eyes and wondering what time it was. If Percy was going to work late every day, then surely, she was in for some very lonely nights.

She tightened and adjusted her gray-blue dress and headed downstairs. Her coat was still there on the rack by the front door, where she'd left it, and she was about to put it on to protect her from the draft she felt when she realized that Percy's coat was back on the rack as well. It was only then that she noticed the smell of butter and garlic coming from the back room.

Amelia smiled and walked to the kitchen, where she did indeed find her intended. Percy was standing over the hot stove, stirring at a pot of some kind of stew. She inhaled the smell now that she was closer. "Mmm, that smells wonderful," she enthused.

"I don't know if you've ever had rabbit stew before, but I thought it might be the perfect dinner to welcome you here." Percy gave her a sweet, happy look.

Now that his winter attire was off, she could see his slightly graying brown hair. It went well with his similarly-shaded beard. Amelia thought he was a handsome man, in a soft-spoken sort of way. Percy Andrews wasn't the flashy sort of attractive, and that drew him to her more. She would have to get to know him better before she could marry him, and learn his personality before she would be fully comfortable in his presence. Fortunately for her, she'd told him in her letters about her life and her marriage to her late husband, so Percy wasn't entering into any of this without knowing about her idiosyncrasies and the like. She didn't feel that she could be honest without letting him know about everything right away.

She made a slightly shocked face at him. "I never thought about rabbits being eaten before," she told him. "I've mostly eaten things like beef or hens."

"See?" he said back merrily. "Perfect."

While he cooked, Amelia helped by setting the table. He had to tell her where the silverware and linens were located, but she knew that she would be able to commit such things to memory in no time. After all, though it was different from her previous dwellings, this was not the first house she'd ever lived in. What kind of housewife would she be otherwise?

Once the table was set to their liking and the stew was finished cooking, Percy served the wonderfully aromatic concoction into two bowls and placed them on the cedar table. Amelia took a seat and he sat across from her there. For a while they ate in silence, enjoying each other's company and neither of them wanting to perhaps ruin it by talking. At last Percy cleared his throat a bit. "I hope you rested well," he said, wiping at his mouth with the off-white napkin she had placed in front of his chair. "When I arrived home from work, I didn't see you about so I thought you must be still sleeping. I didn't want to disturb you."

Amelia smiled at him appreciatively. "You didn't," she replied. "How were things when you returned to the store? I hope my arrival didn't disrupt your business."

"Oh, not at all. It's customary for me to take a break or two. Especially for a special occasion such as this."

She noted that the way he referred to her arrival in Ogden was still in the present tense. He still thought of spending time with her as a special occasion. Amelia smiled softly, her cheeks going a bit pink as she thought about it. She wished to always be special to him. She couldn't think of a time before when she had felt like anybody's special anything.

"I'm looking forward to going to your store tomorrow,"

she told him. "I've never run a business before. I'm afraid I don't know the first thing about it."

Percy smiled supportively at her. "That's all right. I can show you a few things, if you like, but you don't have to work in my store if you'd rather not. The hours can be long, and at times they feel even longer. Plus, you're a shy and sweet little thing. I wouldn't want to overwhelm you with all of the customers that come into the place."

Amelia nodded vaguely. He made a good point there. "I suspect I shall have plenty to keep me busy here in this house anyway, if I'm to help you make it into a proper household like you mentioned."

They finished eating their meal and then worked together to clean up. She was amazed that Percy was so adept in the kitchen. All of the men she'd been around previously – admittedly only a few – had been fairly useless at household chores. Her father was a businessman, as were her brothers and her late husband. They didn't bother themselves with menial tasks such as washing dishes and cleaning counters. Amelia wondered if this should be a sign to her. Everything else about him had been.

"You're probably wondering about the giant space here," Percy said, gesturing with a nod toward the front area of the living room. "I was hoping to decorate for Christmas, now that the holiday is fast approaching, but I didn't want to do it before you arrived, in case you would like to help me?"

Amelia couldn't get enough of his kind inclusiveness.

He'd evidently made all kinds of interesting and friendly plans for things to do with her. A sure sign of the anticipation that he felt about being with her.

"I'd like that very much," she said with a shy, small smile.

CHAPTER 4

GOING TO SLEEP IN THE NEW BEDROOM WASN'T AS EASY for Amelia the second time, but that was largely because she'd already slept for several hours in the afternoon. Also she was restless with the giddy excitement of knowing that the following day was going to be filled with new and – she hoped – amazing experiences. She was an introverted girl, but that didn't mean that she hated the idea of being around people. To the contrary, she really did want meet and make friends with the people of this town.

In the morning, she awoke feeling sleepy but raring to go because she was so excited. She'd been like this when she first set off for the train on the morning that she left New York, too. She loved the feeling of buzzing as she threw off her covers and put on a fresh dress. For her first impression for the town, she chose a quite pretty yellow gown that she had made herself. She combed her long brown tresses and then carefully braided them and pinned them up onto the back of her head. She felt like a princess as she came down the stairs to find the prince who had saved her.

Percy grinned as he looked up and saw her descending the stairs. Though it was early in the morning, he felt fully awake and alive. The coffee in his hand helped with that for sure, but even more so did the sight of his darling bride-to-be. He bowed to her when she reached the bottom of the stairs, and offered his hand to her.

Amelia graciously took his hand. "I hope I haven't kept you waiting," she said sincerely.

He shook his head. "No, not at all. You've arrived just in time."

She knew that he wasn't only talking about this morning when he said that.

They took time to put on their coats and he finished sipping his coffee, placing the emptied mug onto the table to be taken care of later. Taking her hand again, Percy walked Amelia out to the carriage that was waiting for them outside.

"Do you always hire carriages?" she asked him curiously as they rode together.

Percy chuckled. "Until I have my own stables, I don't exactly have a choice in the matter. I'd love to build up our house and purchase a horse or two, and eventually hire a driver... But those things take time. We'll get there. I'm confident of that."

Amelia smiled at him. "I'm confident that you will get everything that you've been hoping for," she said. She was also confident that they were really going to be married now! She'd had her nervous doubts at first, of course, but they did seem to be hitting it off incredibly well so far. It helped that they'd been writing letters back and forth to each other for months. They were already becoming great friends.

The ride to Percy's general store didn't take very long at all, which Amelia believed to be a good thing since he had to be in charge of the business all the time. It also made her feel better to know that, when he was at work and she was at home, he wasn't really far away from her. The distance between them was never again going to be so painfully vast.

The carriage stopped and Percy climbed out, going swiftly around the other side so that he could assist Amelia. She felt a warm kind of electricity whenever he held her hand. It was a happiness she'd never experienced before. They were both smiling as they entered the store. At once, she marveled at the size of it. From the rather plain exterior – *Percy's General Store* in white lettering on a brown façade – she never could've guessed at how much would be contained within the store's walls. There were aisles upon aisles of goods, organized in such a way as to be both easy to locate items as well as to follow along as new necessities come to mind.

Percy went around and lit lanterns on the walls, illuminating things further for her. Amelia beamed as she turned to look at him. "I love it!" she said excitedly, clapping her hands a bit in her inability to hide her joy at all.

"I'm so glad!" he replied, smiling back to her. "It would make me so happy if we were able to work side-by-side in here sometimes. Of course, you may take your time getting to know this place. I don't expect you to memorize the products for sale today. I also don't want you to commit right away, or feel as though by saying you want to help that I expect you to always work here. We've a home to build as well, you know." He winked at her as he smiled.

Amelia felt her cheeks grow hot as she continued to smile merrily at him.

Once all of the lanterns were lit in the store, Percy went to the front door and pulled it open, propping the door with an old anvil that he kept right outside for that purpose. Now people could start coming in and shopping. Amelia was thrilled to be able to witness him at work.

Customers started billowing in through the doors. Amelia stood back and watched Percy work, doing her best to stay out of the way and learn by watching and listening. *I quite think I could handle this*, she thought. *And enjoy it, too!*

CHAPTER 5

AMELIA DIDN'T STAY AT THE GENERAL STORE THE WHOLE day. When it was time for Percy's lunch break, he closed up and looked at her with another friendly smile. "Now's when I usually go to the saloon and have a bit of lunch. It's not much, but their tasty meals get me through the rest of the day. I reckon you probably want to head back to the house, though. A saloon isn't really the place for a fine lady like you."

She blushed at him. She didn't think that she was too good for any place that he might want to go, but she didn't argue with him. "I think perhaps you're right. I'd like to learn my way around your home and your kitchen, if I'm to get any progress made there for you."

He shook his head at her a little. "Not for me, darling. For *us*. I don't want you to be burdened by housework or feel like you have to do anything to please me. I want my wife to be my partner in life."

Amelia wasn't used to that attitude. From her experience, a wife was supposed to be the homemaker and the one who made sure hot meals were on the table at dinnertime. That was how her late husband had made things out to be for her, anyway. "I'm afraid this is going to be a bit of an adjustment for me," she confided. "Being your partner instead of things being my duty to you."

Percy reached out and gently cupped his hand against her cheek, stroking it with his thumb as he gazed into her large brown eyes. "I understand. I'll be patient and help you adjust. I want you to be happy here, with me."

"I am," she said truthfully, looking deeply into his eyes. "That's not something that I have to adjust to. I'm already so happy with you in this sweet little town."

They parted ways not long afterwards, but not before Percy gave her some bread and meat from his store. "A perk of being the general store owner's wife is free groceries," he said with a wink. He sent her on her way with the items and she took a hired carriage back to the small house.

Opening the door with the key he'd given her, Amelia stepped inside. She took her coat off and looked around, feeling a good kind of strange about having the house to herself. This was her new home, and she fully intended on making it feel so. Right away, she brought the bread and meat into the kitchen and set to work making some sandwiches. They weren't anything fancy, but they would tide her over until Percy came home. She hadn't intended to be too adventurous in the unfamiliar kitchen anyway. She figured she could learn where everything was and get used to cooking before she set out to make more advanced meals.

That being said, it would be nice to surprise him with a nice supper... After eating a sandwich, she carefully stored the rest away on the kitchen counter and looked around in Percy's cabinets for some ingredients and ideas for their supper together later. There was still some rabbit in the root cellar. *Perhaps I can season it with some of these spices and we could have rabbit and potatoes tonight. Nothing too fancy, but certainly better than just left-over sandwiches!*

Amelia was more confident about rabbit now that she'd eaten some of it the night before. It was different, but it didn't taste too different from venison, a meat which she did love whenever she had the opportunity to eat it back in New York. She supposed that rabbits were much more plentiful out west than they were in the big city, where the noises and large amounts of people would scare them away.

Amelia decided to wait a bit and begin cooking closer to when Percy would return home so she could serve him a nice warm meal. She went out into the living room and admired the space more closely. The roof was high up enough that they could decorate with quite a tall tree, and such a Christmas tree would be needing some kind of a skirt underneath, so that the presents would have something nice to rest on. She smiled to herself. "I have just the idea," she said. She climbed the staircase at once and went into her room, opening up her suitcase and bringing out a few rolls of red and white yarn and her knitting needles. She'd brought her tools along with her, though she hadn't come up with anything to knit in quite some time.

Bringing her knitting kit back downstairs with her, Amelia sat upon the couch and began creating a Christmas tree skirt. She was in her element now, knitting away and thinking about the festivities that were soon approaching. The holidays were sure to be much brighter now that she would be spending them with someone who would truly enjoy spending time with her – someone who would truly appreciate her efforts.

After a while, she realized that she felt a bit chilly, so she set her knitting aside and went to the rack by the door, retrieving her coat and throwing it onto herself. She noticed that there was a fireplace in the living room, but it wasn't lit and she didn't want to presume that she knew how to light it. She didn't want to set the house on fire. *As with the kitchen and the store, I shall wait until I'm more familiar before messing with that.* She decided that it would be best if she just stayed snuggled up on the couch in her coat and waited for Percy to return home. Amelia had gotten through far colder winters than this one, surely.

She wondered if she could complete the main bits of the Christmas tree skirt before Percy came home.

CHAPTER 6

When Percy finally arrived at home, he found Amelia sitting on the wooden floor of his house, carefully laying out a knitted red and white blanket of some kind. He smiled at her. "Why, hello," he said, taking off his coat and hat. He hung the outerwear on the rack by the door and then noticed that she was wearing her coat as she sat there on the floor. "Oh dear, it's absolutely frigid in here! I knew I forgot to do something before I left for work."

He rushed to the fireplace. Meanwhile Amelia laughed and stood up from the floor, wiping her hands together, proud of her progress on the tree skirt. "It's quite all right," she said. "I wasn't here all day and there's no sense in risking a fire for my sake. I'm used to chilly winters."

Percy struck a match and set the stack of logs ablaze before turning to look at her, his smile returning to his face.

"I know that you're tougher than may seem, but I still want to be a good host and provider for you."

Amelia went to him, ignoring the tree skirt on the floor for the moment. She hugged Percy. "You are a wonderful host and provider. I appreciate how hard you work, not just for me but to keep this home the way that it is."

"Ah, but I want it to be better," Percy said, taking her hands. "And you will surely help with that. I want us to decorate for Christmas, and then for our life together."

"I made a skirt for the tree," she said with a smile, gesturing her head a bit in the direction of the unfinished skirt on the floor. "It isn't much yet, but it's certainly a start."

Percy looked over at it and then chuckled a little. "You're something," he said, returning his eyes to meet her gaze. Suddenly, he lowered himself down onto the floor in front of her. His movement was slower than it might've been for a younger gentleman, but that just made the gesture that much sweeter in Amelia's eyes.

She knew what was coming before he even said anything.

"Amelia," he said in a steady voice, looking up at her now. "Would you do me the immeasurable honor of becoming my wife?" He produced a sparkling gold wedding band from the front pocket on his gray shopkeeper's vest.

She could feel her eyes well up a bit with tears. Though she wasn't surprised by this question – indeed, he had asked it in a letter some weeks back – she was quite emotional about the fact that it was really happening now. It no longer felt like just a wonderful, far-off dream. "Yes," she said happily, beaming down at him. "Yes, yes, a thousand times yes!"

Percy rose back up and placed the ring onto her finger. He threw his arms gently around her and pulled her in for yet another wonderful and warm hug. She could never get enough of his hugs.

When at last they broke apart, remaining close to each other because they both wanted to forever be close to each other, Amelia stretched out her arm and admired the way her new ring sparkled on her finger. She'd had an engagement ring before, but it had never been as important as this one was to her. She wished that she could marry Percy tomorrow, but she knew that these things took time. It also wasn't as though marrying him right away was going to fully heal the wounds that had been inflicted on her by her late husband. She certainly didn't want marrying Percy to seem like something she only wanted to do because of Luther, either.

With the magical proposal and the tree skirt being well on its way to completion, Amelia went into the kitchen to begin cooking their supper. Percy was amused that she decided upon finishing the rabbit, and it was absolutely delicious the way she prepared it.

"My darling, you amaze me," he told her over supper, taking a sip of water. "Yesterday you'd never had rabbit and you seemed so unsure of it, and today you went ahead and perfected it tenfold."

Amelia blushed. In that moment, she felt like the strong and competent woman she had always dreamed of becoming. Once she was free to be herself and reach her potential.

"Tomorrow, as payment, I shall find and chop down the tallest and prettiest tree for our Christmas."

She laughed lightly at that. "Perhaps not quite the tallest," she mused. "The roof will not allow that."

Percy laughed along with her, nodding. "Quite true. The tallest that will fit, then."

Amelia would be sad to send him off to the store the next day without going to see more of him at work, but she was very excited to experience a full day in her new home. There were all kinds of things that she hoped to accomplish here at the house, from cleaning things up a bit to even doing a bit of decorating herself. A tree was only the beginning of Christmas decorating. One thing she was surely going to need to do as soon as possible was to set out plans for Christmas dinner! That would involve Percy as well, for he sold the items that she would need in order to cook things.

As anxious as she was to get started on everything, Amelia slept like an angel that night. She finally felt at home, here, with her loving husband to be.

CHAPTER 7

BREAKFAST THE NEXT MORNING WAS A MORE TALKATIVE affair. Now that Amelia had a task to focus on and some things ahead to look forward to, she became quite the chatterbox. Percy was enamored with the way she talked about things, her little voice barely pausing for breath. He was sad to leave for work and she was sad to see him go, but he left with the promise of a Christmas tree when he came back.

She worked on the tree skirt for the rest of the morning and then laid it out once more on the floor. "All it needs now is a tree and some presents nestled on top of it," she said out loud with a smile.

Looking out the window, Amelia saw the bright blue sky gently dotted with white, fluffy clouds. She didn't want to spend all of this beautiful day cooped up inside. Many of the tasks that she hoped to accomplish couldn't be done alone anyhow. And there was the matter of needing a few things from Percy's store... *Wouldn't it be wonderful to surprise him at work?*

She took off her white apron and hung it on a hook in the kitchen. She was wearing a fairly modest blue dress that a worker might wear. That was indeed what she was doing on this day, but she hoped that she would still appear pretty for her future husband.

Thinking quickly, she decided to put a deep crimson bodice on over the dress so that it had a little bit more flair while still being modest and tasteful. Amelia placed a fingertip on the gold band on her finger and smiled as she stroked it a bit. She was going to be the general store owner's wife! It still felt like such a dream come true. Throwing her coat on, she stepped outside and then realized that there wasn't a carriage waiting for her. Percy would've hired a carriage if she'd mentioned this visit to him earlier, but she'd only thought to do this now. She bit her lip in her frustration with herself.

Looking around and assessing the landscape, Amelia decided that she could surely walk to the store. It was close to home, after all. There wasn't snow or ice on the ground, though the bite in the air indicated that it was nigh. As she walked along the road, careful to watch out for passing buggies as well as any tree roots or rocks that might obstruct her path in this new-to-her terrain, she noticed that there were quite a few other ladies and gentlemen out and about. She was eager to get to know her neighbors.

Amelia held her coat tightly around herself and walked briskly, not wanting to stay out too long in the cold air. She arrived at the general store and found it to be quite crowded. The impending holiday meant that everyone was in search of food, spices and other essentials, just like Amelia. Surprising Percy would be made easier by this throng of people, but on the other hand, Amelia was terribly nervous due to the boisterous crowd. She waited in line by the cash register so that she could meet Percy and tell him what she needed. When at last she reached the front of the line, her hands were trembling and she had a lost, fearful look in her large eyes.

"Amelia!" Percy said delightedly as soon as he saw her standing there. "What a pleasant surprise. I didn't expect you to come in today, or I would've called for a carriage."

He could see right away that she was out of sorts. She was biting her lip deeply and keeping her eyes downcast. She also appeared to be flushed on her cheeks, as if she had run the whole way there.

"Are you alright?" he asked her as he came around the counter and brought her into his arms. "Darling, you're shaking."

A sudden clap of laughter erupted from some of the people in one of the nearby aisles, which made Amelia noticeably jump.

"I just... I'm afraid that I forgot myself a little, in coming here," she said vacantly. "I need some things for Christmas dinner, but I should have waited. I should have just asked for you to bring them home for me."

Getting ahead of yourself, she scolded herself. *You're never thinking, you're just too excitable, too quick to do things without proper planning!*

Percy continued to hold her there, ignoring the stares and questioning looks from the shoppers in the store. He lovingly pet her back. He knew that she had experienced verbal abuse and all kinds of horrors at the hand of her late husband, so it didn't come as a surprise to him to see her reacting this way to unexpected yelling and carrying on. "You're safe here with me," he whispered to her. "Now that you're here, I'll help you find what you're looking for."

Amelia trusted Percy. His words were soothing to her, even if they didn't completely erase the sudden things she was afraid of, the experiences that had been called back to her mind with the sound of those gentlemen's raised voices. They'd been laughing. Luther had laughed some of the time, too. Loudly and darkly, but still laughter.

She knew in that moment that working in the general store was something that she may not ever be able to do. She knew, too, that Percy would be perfectly fine with that. He hadn't been looking for a wife who wanted to work in the store. But still, she felt weakened by this condition of hers. In her mind, she felt like a less-worthy wife for him. *He could do better* she thought.

She started to cry.

Just then, Amelia heard the sound of a woman's voice.

"Oh dear, what seems to be the matter? Is there anything I can do?"

"She got a bit startled by the rowdy men in the store a moment ago," Percy said, his voice instantly letting Amelia know that he knew this woman.

Peeking out from behind his shoulder, she saw the statuesque beauty standing there talking to Percy. They spoke together as friends, and Amelia wished at once to be her friend, too. At last, another kind face in this town!

"Hello, dear," the woman said. "My name is Mrs. Tabitha Hughes, but you may call me Tabitha. Percy here is a good friend of mine who helped me get my start in Ogden, so if you're with him I know you're in good company. Might I invite you to join me at my home for some hot tea and some friendly conversation?"

It was clear at once that this Tabitha was far more gregarious than Amelia could ever hope to be. She looked from Tabitha to Percy, her heart sinking. She did need to get out of the store and away from the loud groups of people, but she'd been so excited with the idea of seeing her beloved fiancé.

"I suppose I could use some air and a bit of quiet..." Amelia looked at Percy. "I will tell you next time I'm planning a visit here. Please forgive me for this outburst of mine."

Percy gently wiped the now-drying tears from her face. "There's nothing to forgive, darling. I understand if you choose not to come here when the store is busy."

It was a comfort to know that he understood. But then, he had been remarkably understanding thus far. She smiled at him. "God has blessed me with you," she said, crying a bit now for a different reason.

After another hug from him, Amelia cleaned her face with his handkerchief and then allowed Tabitha to lead her out of the store. Amelia admired the way the other woman carried herself. She wished that she could exude that much friendly confidence. It really pained her to know that such a thing as the sound of gentlemen having a good time could render her so scared and sensitive. *If Luther could see me now, he'd probably be glad that he has left such an impression on me...*

CHAPTER 8

THERE WAS A CARRIAGE WAITING OUTSIDE FOR TABITHA. Amelia wasn't at all surprised, given the way the other woman was smartly dressed. "Do you live on one of the farms in town?" she asked Tabitha.

"Yes," Tabitha replied with a pearly white smile. "My husband comes from one of the largest and most prosperous families in Ogden. He recently inherited the farm from his father, who has gotten on in age and can't manage things himself any longer."

The two ladies got into the carriage and rode off down the slightly rocky dirt road. Amelia noted at once that they were going the opposite direction from where she and Percy were lodged. She looked out of the carriage's window and saw all of the elegant farm houses coming into view. They weren't at all like Albany mansions, but instead were sweet-looking homes attached to nearby barns and stables on sprawling pieces of land. Much like what Percy wanted for their home.

The carriage pulled up in front of a large farm house – it did in fact resemble a mansion – and Amelia gaped in wonder as she got out of the cart and walked towards it, following Tabitha's lead. Despite its grandeur and the fact that it supposedly held a large family within its walls, the house was quiet and tranquil as the two ladies stepped inside together.

"Please make yourself comfortable," Tabitha said, gesturing to the wide plush couch in the center of the living room. "I will go start the tea."

She was gone before Amelia could argue with her – not that she would have. Sitting on the couch as directed, Amelia looked around and admired the tall Christmas tree that took up more than half of the room on her right, near the front door. Already there were stacks of colorfully-wrapped gifts underneath it. Amelia found herself feeling rather envious, not that she wished this family any ill fortune but because she didn't know how she and Percy were ever supposed to have a Christmas so fine. They didn't even have a tree yet.

It doesn't do any good to think about what you don't have or what Christmas might be like for someone else. You're being ridiculous again. Amelia wished that she could simply think the way that normal people did. She was fairly certain that normal people didn't worry quite so much about every last little thing. She also knew that being envious of other people's Christmases went against everything that the holiday stood for. *Good will toward men,* she reminded herself with a wistful sigh.

Tabitha returned after just a few moments, sitting down on the couch, close to, but not immediately next to Amelia, giving the woman space to breathe and relax after the ordeal she'd been through. "Let me just say right at the start how glad I am to know that you are here to be with Percy. He is a dear friend to me. He deserves every happiness, which I'm sure you already know for yourself. How did you two meet, if you don't mind my asking?"

This Tabitha was quite a chatterbox. It made Amelia smile. A shy girl sometimes needed a talkative friend to help her feel comfortable enough to come out of her shell. She wished that she could be more like her.

"We exchanged letters for months on end," Amelia replied, her voice soft but nonetheless happy. "He really is a lovely man. Ever since we first met at the station, he's been so very kind to me."

Tabitha nodded along to everything that Amelia said. "I believe you two will be tremendously happy together," she replied with a smile. "And I don't imagine that Percy wants or expects you to get over your anxiety around loud groups, either. I know you must feel embarrassed about that, but I don't want you to waste another moment putting yourself down about it. I can tell that you're feeling poorly about it, but trust me, it's nothing to be ashamed of. Not everyone is cut out for the type of work he does. That's why we're so grateful that he does it."

At that, Tabitha rose from the couch again. The tea kettle was singing its high-pitched song. She rushed off as before and was back in but a moment. *Speaking of not being cut out for things,* Amelia thought in her amazement. *I don't know if I shall ever be as good a hostess as she is.*

Tabitha would likely tell her that no one expected her to host parties either. Amelia felt rather sad about that, even if it was just an imagined summation. "I just am so dreadfully unsure," she said as Tabitha poured the tea into two perfect little teal mugs. "It isn't anything that Percy has done, of course. It's also nothing about this new town. Not really. It's all in my head. I suspect my late husband put a great deal of fear and doubt into my mind."

Tabitha gave her a sympathetic glance before handing her a mug of tea. "Well, no time like the present for you to start over, right? Stop thinking about what happened in the past and what some gentleman said or did to you. It's in the past. He's no longer around to torment you." She reached over, hesitated a moment, then rubbed Amelia's back a little bit in an effort to console her.

Amelia blew gently on her tea before taking a small sip. She smiled appreciatively at Tabitha. She didn't think that it was quite as easy as Mrs. Hughes made it out to be, but she knew that the other woman was doing her best to help her feel better and more at home in town. "There is truth to what you say. It doesn't matter what he thought of me, or did to me, anymore. He can't get to me now."

She said this more for herself – and to perhaps scare the ghost of her past away – than for Tabitha to hear.

Nevertheless, Tabitha nodded. "That's right." She picked up her own mug and carefully hit it against Amelia's in 'cheers.' She then relayed her own tale of woe, all about how she and her ill sister had ridden across the country to get away from a horrible old suitor who she'd been forced to wed. "I left before they could make me walk down that aisle. I knew what was good for me and it certainly wasn't that man."

Amelia wished that she could be that strong. She wasn't even running from anyone. Not anymore. But it still felt so relatable to her. "It is truly divine providence that you were in the store today," she told Tabitha, taking her hand and looking into her eyes as she smiled at her. A genuine smile. "I hope that we might become the best of friends."

Tabitha grinned, clearly complimented and touched by her words. "I would like nothing more!"

Setting their mugs safely down on the table, the two ladies hugged each other. Amelia didn't think that her problems were behind her, or that they would be behind her so soon, but it did feel good to know that she had a compatriot with whom she could confide her painful stories. Owing to her shy and anxious nature, she'd never had a large friend group before. Perhaps it was a possibility in Ogden. Tabitha Hughes certainly seemed like the kind of lady who could introduce her to new people and experiences.

After finishing up their tea, Amelia stood up and smoothed out her pale blue skirt. "Thank you so much for this," she said. "I hope our paths will cross again soon."

"Oh, indeed they shall," Tabitha replied, standing up and giving her another good-natured hug. "I'll make sure of it."

She was kind enough to let Amelia borrow her carriage. Tabitha's husband was working in the fields beyond the house, but once Tabitha opened up the back door and called to him, he was there in a moment. Amelia blushed, keeping her eyes downcast when she saw the handsome, young farmer. She wasn't quite prepared to meet another new person on this day, particularly a new *gentleman*.

"Neil, this is Mrs. Hawkins," Tabitha introduced. "She's engaged to our dear friend Mr. Percy Andrews."

Mr. Neil Hughes smiled delightedly and bowed. "It's a pleasure to make your acquaintance, Mrs. Hawkins," he said, offering his hand and then kissing hers politely.

Amelia continued to blush away. "I'm delighted to meet you, Mr. Hughes. I was just speaking with Mrs. Hughes about how she came to know you. It's truly a remarkable and memorable story."

Neil was pleased to hear that. He continued to smile. "Would you like me to drive you back to your home?" he asked then, surmising the reason for Tabitha calling him inside.

"That would be splendid," Tabitha replied readily. "I

think she would like to get home before its dark and her betrothed begins to worry about her whereabouts." She joked, but Amelia did indeed think that Percy would worry if he didn't see her when he got home. After all, she hadn't been in the best state when they'd last parted company.

"Well, then," Neil said, smiling politely from his wife to Amelia. "I'd be more than happy to."

The two ladies bade each other farewell and then Amelia followed Neil out to his carriage, which was currently parked near the stables of the farm. He helped her inside and then sat atop the tall driver's chair. On the way home, Amelia imagined what it might be like to one day have a carriage and some horses on a farm with Percy.

CHAPTER 9

Thanks to Mr. Hughes's carriage driving, Amelia was home before it got dark and before Percy arrived from the store. She hadn't been able to start work on the Christmas dinner she'd planned, but she knew that it could wait. They had two more full days before it would be Christmas. She could send him off to work the next day with her list of necessary items.

While she waited for him to come home, she worked on tidying up the living room. He slept on the couch each night with a pillow, so she fluffed it up nicely and set it aside in an armchair so that it wouldn't get dirtied while they sat upon the couch that night. She was still looking forward to decorating with Percy, even after all of that drama at the store. She hoped that he was still excited about it, too. She hoped that she hadn't ruined everything.

The front door opened and Percy came inside, removing his coat and hat before coming all the way in and giving Amelia a big hug. "Hello, sweetheart," he said to her in his gentle, comforting voice. "How was your day?"

Amelia smiled and closed her eyes, so happy to be back in his warm embrace. He didn't seem angry at all with her. He seemed exactly like he always was. She was so relieved. "I had a wonderful chat with Mrs. Hughes at her home. They have a lovely farmhouse. And of course she has only the best to say about you."

Percy laughed softly. "She flatters me. Mrs. Hughes is a good woman. And a good friend to anyone who is lucky enough to meet her." Amelia knew she meant her. "I intend to put on my workman's gloves and fetch my ax now. We're in need of a tree, are we not?" He grinned at her. "You may join me if you like, but I must say, it's awfully cold outside."

"Oh no," Amelia said, slowly shaking her head but smiling at him. "I think I've had my fill of getting in the way today. It's best if you take care of chopping down a tree and I take care of supper."

Percy smiled and nodded. "Fair enough." He moved to go to the back door of the house, but not before kissing her on the cheek as he passed.

Amelia let out a soft laugh and touched her cheek where he had planted his soft lips. Her cheeks were hot again. She didn't know why she had ever felt that she should be scared amongst the kind people of this town. Everyone she'd met in Ogden had shown her such generosity and pleasantness. Especially her sweet new fiancé.

Now that he was off to cut down a tree, she went to the kitchen to prepare a delicious supper for them, thinking of what might be the perfect gift for him while she cooked.

The front door burst open for the second time and Amelia gasped, jumping a bit at the sound. But then she cautiously went out of the kitchen to find Percy making his way inside, pulling a thick, green tree behind him by its trunk.

"Oh, perfect!" she said, clapping and grinning with delight.

Percy stood the tree up and leaned it a bit against the wall so that it wouldn't topple down. While he held it there, Amelia came over and knelt under it, bringing the red knit tree skirt into position. He marveled at her. She was socially anxious but yet she had no problem messing about underneath a giant tree that could easily fall atop her.

"You're braver than you think," he pointed out to her.

Amelia stood up, admiring her handiwork. "I just want to help make it look its best."

They both stood together and admired their Christmas tree set-up. There weren't any candles or colored ribbons on its branches yet, but it was still beautiful. Suddenly, Percy closed his eyes and sniffled a little. "Supper smells delicious," he said, opening his eyes back up to gaze appreciatively at her. "What is it?"

"A ham tart," she said. "I found some leftovers in the root cellar from the sandwiches I made before."

Percy smiled a half-surprised sort of smile. "How clever," he enthused. "I don't know if I've ever had a ham tart before."

Amelia smiled proudly at that.

They ate their supper together that night and she kept happily glancing over at their Christmas tree. She could hardly wait to decorate it, though she knew it was the sort of task that took time. After all, if one rushed it, it wouldn't turn out quite as well as one hoped.

The next morning, after Percy set out to work, she began her preparations for his Christmas present. She'd stayed up half the night wondering what she should give to the man who had given her so much in such a short time. She knew that she could knit him something, but the trouble was that none of her ideas seemed to be good enough. *I could knit him a scarf, but that would only be good in the winter time. I could knit him a sweater, but he'd never wear it out. He only goes about in his work shirts and his apron.*

Then it dawned on her. He wore an old knit cap whenever he was outdoors. She had a feeling that he wore it even when it wasn't cold. It was one of his fashion statements, surely. And one thing that he could likely use two of.

Hustling out of the house like she had an appointment to make, Amelia walked into the town proper as she had before on that awful day. This time, she avoided the crowded general store. There was a small dress shop near it, and that place wasn't crowded at all, what with the town not having nearly as many women as men. She went inside and purchased some new, colorful yarn. When she exited the shop, Amelia decided that she didn't need to hire a carriage to take her back home either. The air was crisp with cold outside, but the sky was a bright blue and birds were singing. The brown and gold leaves were filling the ground now. It was a beautiful day and Amelia decided that she wasn't going to spend it indoors. Why, she wasn't even going to rush back home. A pleasant walk would do her good, she thought.

As she set out on her walk, Amelia decided to stroll past the cute farm houses that Tabitha had introduced her to. She longed to get to know more of the farmers and their families. Percy could no doubt introduce her around because he knew everyone in town, but there was something to be said for meeting them on her own. Happening upon them and striking up a conversation. *If only I wasn't so shy...*

As it turned out, Tabitha was in the front yard of her farm house. Amelia hadn't recognized the home because she wasn't really staring at each home specifically, but she grinned and waved as soon as she recognized her friend. "I promise you, I was only going for a stroll," she said jovially. "This is simply good fortune."

Tabitha giggled and came over to her. She was holding a bundle of holly and had been in the process of hanging it up all over her front porch when Amelia came along. Holding it all together in one hand like a bouquet, she hugged Amelia closely, rubbing her back with soothing affection. "How have you been, darling? You look quite happy today."

"Oh, I feel much better about things, Tabitha," Amelia replied, unable to hide her feeling of elation in her voice even if she'd wanted to. "I think I just got overwhelmed by all of the newness, but Percy and I have been decorating for Christmas and it makes me feel so much more at home. I see that you're decorating, too." She gestured to the holly in Mrs. Hughes's hand.

"It's hard to feel anything but happy around here at Christmas," Tabitha agreed. "I'm so happy for you. And I shall be looking forward to your wedding day. I know it's going to happen soon." She winked knowingly.

Amelia blushed. "Do you know something I don't know?"

"It's less knowing and more... intuition, I suspect," Tabitha said. "Winter is a lovely time for a wedding."

"Well, if that's the case I better get to work on my gift for Percy right away," she said, holding up her bag of purchases from the dress shop. "He won't want to marry me without this."

Tabitha giggled again and they gave each other another quick hug before they parted ways. Amelia didn't want to distract her friend from decorating, and she did indeed wish to get started on her knitting. Making a whole new hat for Percy was going to take up most if not all of her time while he was gone!

AMELIA'S BLESSED CHRISTMAS

By the time Percy came home that night, Amelia had made a good start on her gift for him. She squirreled it away in her bedroom shortly before his usual arrival so he wouldn't happen upon it, and that proved to be a wise decision. He surprised her with a basketful of candles, which they set to work placing into the branches of the trees.

"I never used to be this interested in Christmas," she confessed to him as they worked alongside each other at decorating. "I suppose I simply wasn't happy enough for such a joyful holiday." She gave a sad shrug.

Percy placed a gentle hand on her shoulder and looked into her eyes. "We shall make this the most joyful holiday ever," he told her. "I promise you. I plan to make the rest of your life as happy as you deserve. I don't like to speak ill of the dead, but your late husband clearly didn't deserve to have you."

Instead of lowering her gaze to the floor, Amelia lifted her chin a bit. She was done feeling sorry for herself and as if Luther still had power over her. He hadn't deserved her. After everything she'd given up to please him – her friends and family, her way of life, her freedom – he'd treated her like garbage. Now she knew a kind and decent man. She vowed to never look back again. "I do believe that you're right," she said to Percy. "It wasn't a surprise to me that he was killed while committing a robbery. He wasn't liked by anyone in town, and for good reason, it turned out. I never knew he was thieving around town, but it wasn't a great shock to me when I found out. And I can say to you now that when he died, I wasn't sad. I was actually... relieved."

Percy's hand never left her shoulder. If anything, his grip became a gentle massage there. A comforting sort of clutch. "Let's only look forward to our future now. That will hopefully bring you as much endless joy as it does me."

At that, they carefully lit the candles on the tree, then they cuddled together there underneath the lights. Amelia couldn't be sure, but she felt that this was what bliss felt like. "I can't imagine how Christmas can top this night," she said to him softly. "But I'm looking forward to seeing if it does."

Tabitha had predicted a winter wedding for them. Amelia decided, in her heart of hearts, that this would be her greatest wish this Christmas. She wouldn't voice it, of course, but she would keep it close there in her heart.

CHAPTER 10

THE MORNING OF CHRISTMAS ARRIVED BRIGHT AND glorious. Amelia rose with the sun, grinning even before she was out of her bed. This day was going to be different. Percy wasn't going to go to work at the store, meaning that she'd be able to spend all day with him. Though they'd gotten to know each other quite well through their letters and their time together thus far, it would be even more wonderful to spend a full day with him. And not just any day – Christmas! She put on a red skirt and a lovely green shirtwaist, looking like a jolly elf. She brushed her long red hair and then carefully braided a plait into it. Just because Amelia hadn't had a lot of luck with Christmas in the past didn't mean that she wouldn't put her all into it for Percy.

She came downstairs carrying a small, wrapped parcel which she placed under the Christmas tree. Percy was already there, in the kitchen, making some special, sweet-smelling hot cider for the start of the festivities.

"I love that your skills are seemingly never-ending," she complimented, approaching him in the kitchen and giving him a kiss on his cheek.

He poured a cup of cider for her and she held it up to give it a sniff. Shockingly, Amelia's stomach turned as she whiffed the spiced apple smell. She didn't want to say anything about it and hurt Percy's feelings, though. "My," she said, smiling a small smile even as her brain told her that the drink wouldn't sit well in her stomach. "This smells lovely."

Percy smiled at her. "You learn a lot, living amongst the great farmers of the west," he said as he poured himself a cupful of the cider. He took a sip and looked at her, clearly waiting to see her reaction to its taste as well.

Amelia raised her cup and, closing her eyes, took a small sip of the hot, apple drink. It didn't taste as bad as it smelled to her. In fact, it tasted quite nice. *What is going on? I've always loved cider...* "It's delicious," she said, her voice not betraying the strange relief she felt.

Together, they carried their cups to the living room and sat on the couch by the Christmas tree. "I see you've put a present there for me," he said, his voice laughing all on its own. "I've got something for you, too, but it's not there. I'll take you to it, later on."

"Oh?" Amelia asked, her large eyes brightening. She loved a good surprise. Anticipation filled her with warmth.

She was still feeling a bit out of sorts about the cider, though. Otherwise she would've been a great deal more excited.

"I thought we might spend this morning together, just the two of us getting to know each other a little better, and then the Hughes family – chiefly Mrs. Tabitha Hughes, which should come as no surprise to you – have invited us to spend the evening with them."

Now Amelia allowed herself to express full relief. "I must confess that the thought of cooking a full Christmas dinner was quite daunting. Especially after... Well, you know."

He fixed her with another loving, understanding smile. "I know," he replied. "I thought you would rather get to know some more people in the town, at a calm and pleasant setting that you're somewhat familiar with, as opposed to staying cooped up here with me or going to something even bigger. People in Ogden do love a good party."

Amelia's face reddened a bit. She couldn't help but imagine the kind of party that their wedding might elicit, given that everyone liked Percy Andrews. She knelt down beside the tree and took her gift for him off of the red tree skirt where she'd left it. Standing back up, she went and sat down beside him on the couch again. "Let's not delay in the gift-giving, then. I think you may need this later, when we go out."

Percy raised an eyebrow at her. "Hmm?" He took the offered gift into his hands and made a show of weighing it to try and guess at what it could be. "It feels like it might be something... soft."

Amelia giggled, smiling brightly. "Just open it," she said gaily. "I know you'll like it."

Taking her cue, he carefully ripped at the brown paper and pulled out the knitted blue cap she'd made for him. His old cap was gray. She spied it there in its usual place on the coat rack. "I wasn't sure what color to make it. Which color would best suit you? But I think blue will look lovely with your eyes and hair." She smiled sweetly at him.

Percy was giving the hat in his hands such an appreciative, touched look. He placed it onto his head at once, grinning handsomely at her. "I love it!" he declared. "Thank you so very much. You made it for me? It's just what I needed. My old hat has been with me for years and years. It came with me to Ogden, I'll have you know."

Amelia continued to smile sweetly at him. "This by no means needs to replace your old hat. I just think you might like to have options."

She hoped that he wouldn't notice that she wasn't touching her cider. In fact, she had placed it far from her on the coffee table in front of them, and she intended to keep it there. Hopefully the treats and drinks at the Hughes residence wouldn't also make her feel so ill just to smell them...

She also prayed that Percy's gift for her was not edible or drinkable.

"Now it's my turn," he said to her. He kept the hat comfortably there on his head as he stood up from the couch. "Wait right here." He walked to the back door of their house and went all the way outside. She was glad that he didn't expect her to follow, for it was frightfully cold outside. As she knew it would be for likely the remainder of winter.

When Percy came back into the house, he wasn't carrying a wrapped parcel like she'd imagined. He was carrying a fluffy, white puppy. Amelia leapt off the couch at once. "Aww!" she cried, smiling in her surprise and delight.

The small dog had short, floppy ears and a black, button nose. His stubby tail started wagging at the sound of her excitement.

"I thought it might be good for you to have a companion to keep you company while I'm spending long hours at work," Percy said with a grin.

He placed the dog on the wood floor and the puppy scurried right over to Amelia as she crouched down to greet him.

"He also could be a good guard dog for you," Percy added. "I haven't tested that theory, though."

Amelia laughed softly as she patted the puppy and let him gently nip at her fingers. The little dog yapped happily at her, wagging his tail away. "Well then, I think I shall call him Ami, for 'friend.'" She didn't boast to speak it well, but Amelia had studied French in school. Most ladies learnt it when they were growing up; she supposed it was meant to make them seem cultured and ladylike.

Percy grinned another pearly-white smile at that. "Amelia and Ami. I like it!"

Amelia really was transfixed by how handsome he was. She was grateful that they hadn't exchanged photographs because it made the sight of him now that much more special. She doubted that she could ever tire of looking at him, though, even if she had memorized every crease and line of his face.

"I will feel so sad to leave him when we go to the Hughes' party," she said, standing up with the white puppy in her arms. He'd settled down now that he'd been invited indoors and had met the nice lady who was to be his mistress. He was falling asleep in her arms as they spoke.

"Oh, there's no need to leave him here," Percy said with a laugh. "In fact, I wouldn't dream of it, seeing as he's not properly house trained yet. And I likewise wouldn't dream of separating you from your friend. Bring him along. I'm sure that Tabitha will adore him as well."

Amelia rushed over and hugged Percy. "I feel so spoiled. This is the best Christmas I've ever had!"

Aside from the mysterious ill feeling she'd felt earlier, that was. *I shall have to take Tabitha aside while we're playing with the pup and tell her about it,* she thought. *Hopefully she might know what caused it, and what I should do, if anything.*

CHAPTER 11

Percy and Amelia took a hired carriage to the Hughes' farm. Ami continued to sleep on her lap throughout the journey, which Amelia thought was good because it meant the little pup would have energy for the festivities. The home was all decorated with holly and colorful ribbons of red, green and gold. "Tabitha's really done a beautiful job, hasn't she?" Amelia said with a smile and a look of awe.

"She really has taken to living in this farm house," Percy replied. "Which isn't surprising, given where she came from and where she was living before, in the abandoned stable."

Amelia well remembered the tale that Percy had relayed to her, all about Tabitha Church's flight westward. "I suppose it means that she doesn't take much for granted," she agreed, sympathy rising within her for the lady who wasn't yet with them.

They carefully alit from the carriage and walked arm-in-arm to the front door of the farm house. Percy knocked. They could hear music and the sounds of laughter and talking from within. Amelia briefly considered just how many people might be in there, but she told herself to relax and do her best to have a good time. *Percy will be with you the whole time. As will Tabitha.*

When the door opened, she and Percy could take in the scene. There were indeed a lot of people inside the home, but many of them were recognizable people from town, and many of them also looked a great deal like Mr. Hughes. He did come from a large family! That was certainly no lie.

Mr. Hughes himself stood before them, holding the door open for them to enter. He smiled a big, wide-open smile at them. "Welcome, Percy! Hello again, Ms. Hawkins. Please come in, come in. Warm yourselves by our Christmas tree."

Percy and Amelia walked in, hand-in-hand, as they were greeted by nearly everyone in attendance on their way to the tall tree near the fireplace in the living room. She felt overwhelmed, but she told herself to ignore it and focus on how nice the people and party were.

"Darling!" Tabitha exclaimed, coming forth to give her a hug and hand her a mug of cocoa. She then hugged Percy and looked from him to Amelia. "You both look so well together. It brings me so much joy. Merry Christmas, to the both of you."

"Merry Christmas, Tabitha," Amelia said back, in a much softer voice though just as sincerely.

"God bless us, everyone," Percy said enthusiastically.

The party was soon singing carols together and the small string trio that Mr. Hughes, Sr. had hired played music that got them all dancing. For an hour, Amelia was so caught up in the festivities that she quite forgot about her little issue that she'd wanted to discuss with Tabitha. But then sipping the cocoa got her remembering.

"Would you like to meet my new puppy someplace quieter?" she asked Tabitha, sidling up to her friend and thinking herself mighty clever for coming up with that segue.

Tabitha looked at little Ami in Amelia's arms, enchanted with his innocent little face and brown eyes. "Yes, please," she said at once. The two ladies – and the puppy – went out of the living room and into the much more spacious back parlor of the house. The farmhouse was practically a mansion in size, but there was a gentler, homier feel to the place. It was the west's answer to a mansion, to be sure. Amelia longed to have one of her own, with Percy.

"So, tell me about this little fellow," Tabitha said. She sat down on the smooth, polished hardwood floor of the parlor and patted her lap.

Amelia placed Ami down on the floor and he toddled right over to Tabitha, jumping into her thick skirt-covered lap. "Percy gave him to me this morning as my Christmas present. I've never had a puppy before. I can't remember the last time I had a dog, for that matter. But he's already made me feel much better today."

Tabitha smiled as she stroked the white, fluffy puppy between his ears. She looked up, concerned, after Amelia finished speaking. "Why did you need to feel better? Did something unpleasant happen this morning?"

She of course knew by now about Amelia's difficulties in social situations as well as her cemented fears about her past. It was likely that it was going to take Amelia years to recover from the effects of living with her tormentor for so long.

"It was the strangest thing," Amelia explained to her friend. "Percy made hot apple cider and I normally love the scent of it, but this morning I simply couldn't abide it. The smell was awful and the taste didn't sit well in my stomach. I'm sure that he isn't to blame. I think the problem is me. I wonder if it's caused by nerves, though I've never been so nervous as to have to pass up food or drink before."

Tabitha arched an eyebrow at her. She stood up from the floor, holding the puppy between elbow and waist. He wagged his tail and lolled his head this way and that, clearly loving this brand new world full of attention. "I noticed that you were artfully avoiding your cocoa as well. Did the same thing happen then?"

Amelia nodded her head sadly. It pained her to think that she might not be able to enjoy the tasty treats of the season. "Something's off with me. I thought that I was feeling better, but now it seems as though my stomach doesn't agree with my mind."

Tabitha was giving her a thoughtful look now. She came over to Amelia and gently placed a cool hand onto her forehead. "You don't feel feverish," she remarked, more to herself as if she was dictating notes for her to recall later. "I think perhaps you ought to see the doctor. But obviously not today... Tomorrow morning, right away. My husband will take you. Don't argue, please."

Amelia smiled a bit. "I wasn't going to. Thank you, Tabitha. I was worried that you'd think that I've finally completely lost my mind."

"It's a friend's job to think that," Tabitha said with a smile. "But it takes a special friend to know when it's actually something serious."

The two friends returned to the party and Amelia was able to enjoy herself. Everyone got a chance to cuddle or play with Ami, depending on his particular needs at the moment, and it was great fun for all involved. She was very grateful to have him there with her, as it took some of the pressure of attention off of her. *I should bring him everywhere with me. He makes me much less awkward.*

When the music truly got going again, she danced with Percy and, later, everyone in the large room went in for the Virginia reel, which had her guffawing and carrying on as if she was the sort of girl who always went to parties. Amelia wasn't out of her element here, not really. She only had to believe in herself and let her confidence guide her.

"It was wonderful to meet you," a handsome, tall gentleman named Tom said to her before she and Percy made their exit for the night.

"I hope that we shall continue to meet," Amelia said, smiling as Tom Cooke politely kissed her hand. "My fiancé was right. This is a great little town you've all got here."

"We do our best," Mr. Cooke's wife Zelda said with a big grin of her own. She gave Amelia a friendly hug before Amelia and Percy parted from the party to climb aboard their carriage.

"Oh, I hope this is the start of something wonderful," she said to him as they rode home. "This surely was my best Christmas ever!"

CHAPTER 12

Amelia slept well the night after Christmas, feeling the joy of the festivities and the elation at having at last met the large group of people in town who were likely to be her friends. She went to sleep hopeful, and her new puppy slept on her bed at her feet.

When she woke up, she knew that she must now heed her friend Tabitha's advice and see the doctor. She dressed quickly, in a simple white and pink frock, and waited for Mr. Neil Hughes to arrive to escort her to the doctor. When he arrived, she was a bucket of nerves. Percy was already gone to work and he had no idea that anything could be wrong with her, apart from the fact that she'd been neglecting to drink the traditional beverages of Christmas. She'd stomached all of the food she'd been able to, but anything sweet or too aromatic had to be avoided for the time being, until she knew what was going on and how to stop it.

"If it should be something rather bad," she said to Neil before she got out of the carriage in front of the doctor's, "Please will you send for Percy?"

Neil nodded at her as he helped her down from her carriage seat. "I certainly shall. But I don't think it will come to that, Mrs. Hawkins. Surely this is just a little upset. Perhaps you ate something that you shouldn't have. Some meats and things can be awfully deceptive."

As a farmer, he certainly knew what he was talking about. But Amelia wasn't so sure that that was all this was...

She went into the doctor's office and told him all of the symptoms she could think of. Any little thing that had struck her as odd or off lately. Amelia wasn't sure that everything was important to mention, but the doctor requested that she be as thorough as possible. "My senses seem a bit heightened," she explained. "I don't know how else to describe it. Everything smells off somehow, and certain foods do not entice me like they would have before this change."

"I see," the doctor said, writing this all down. He then asked her some rather personal questions, about her lady habits and things of that nature. Amelia blushed but answered him honestly and to the best of her knowledge. She wasn't sure if the problem really did lie with one of her habits, and she was wondering what on earth could be the cause. "I haven't consumed anything out of the ordinary,

Doctor. The most unusual thing I've eaten since coming to Ogden was rabbit, and I don't suppose that has anything to do with this. It hadn't gone bad before we ate it, and even if it had that was so very long ago now. The most recent things I ate were ham and pheasant, and fresh vegetables from my fiancé, Mr. Andrews', store."

The doctor could see that she was very distraught. He didn't imagine that what he had to tell her was going to make her feel any better. "Mrs. Hawkins, do you think that there's any chance that you are with child?"

She went absolutely crimson. Casting her eyes downward, she nodded solemnly. "Yes... There is a chance."

Her late husband had been dead for two months by now, but that didn't erase things that had happened while he was alive, shortly before the robbery, when he lost his head as well as his life.

"Well, Mrs. Hawkins," the doctor said brightly, not fully grasping the implications and severity of what he was suggesting, but thinking of it as simply a happy bit of news for her. "I believe we've found the cause of your malady."

After telling her to be sure to get rest and continue eating as she normally would – even if she detested the very smell – the doctor sent her on her way. Amelia didn't know what to say to Neil as she climbed back into the carriage. She was embarrassed and no less distraught than she had been when she first arrived there. *What am I supposed to tell Percy now?*

She of course was going to tell him as soon as possible.

She couldn't keep something like a pregnancy a secret from the gentleman she was going to marry. She'd never dream of that. It certainly wouldn't make any of this easy on her, if she was going it alone without being able to share her fear and torment with any other soul.

The carriage ride was a silent affair, with Amelia keeping her eyes fixed out of the window for if she looked at Neil Hughes right then she surely would've begun to cry. *I need to speak with Tabitha right away,* she thought miserably. *Before Percy gets home. Before I disclose this news to him, because... There's a chance now that...* She would allow her mind to think no further on it. She couldn't think about what might come next, what Percy might do when he found out this new information.

Amelia felt dirty and sick to her stomach.

"Please," she said to Neil. "If you don't mind, may I accompany you to your home instead of going directly to my own house? I need to speak with your wife about what the doctor suggested and what we can... do now." She avoided his gaze as she said so.

Neil made sure to turn onto the correct road and rather than continuing straight on. He assisted Amelia out of the carriage, noticing the difference in her usually more cheerful demeanor. He knew that the woman was of a rather delicate disposition, having heard the tale of the general store from his wife, but she'd never been so distant and detached before. She didn't thank him as profusely as usual, and he chalked that up to nervousness about whatever the doctor had told her.

"I hope you are well, Mrs. Hawkins," he said to her before they parted ways and she went into the front door of the farmhouse in search of her friend.

It didn't take long to find Tabitha. She was in the living room of the large home, with a baby in her lap. She had many in-laws now, and in-laws brought more children into her life. She seemed quite at home with a baby there, and Amelia couldn't help but smile a bit at the coincidence. "Amelia!" she cried, smiling at her. "What brings you here? How did your meeting with the doctor go?"

Amelia found that she couldn't take her eyes off the baby in Tabitha's arms. She was a little girl with golden locks and saucer-like eyes. As soon as the baby noticed that Amelia was staring at her, she smiled and let out a little "ah!" sound like the coo of a dove.

Sitting down gently on the edge of the settee, Amelia didn't quite know how to lead into this conversation. It was shocking and it would likely be even more so to people who'd never laid eyes on, or let alone met the awful fiend who had done this to her. She sighed a little. "The doctor tells me that I am with child."

It was Tabitha's turn to stare. "This is a surprise," she said in a voice that was a great deal softer than her usual gregarious tone.

"It is to me too," Amelia said. She let out a sob and threw her face against her friend's shoulder in anguish. "I thought he was out of my life at last, but he's torturing me from beyond the grave now."

At first, she thought that Tabitha might be in agreement with her, the way her friend had gone rigid on the settee, with the baby burbling on her lap as if nothing was wrong. But then suddenly Tabitha turned to face Amelia and placed a free arm around her. Amelia cried against her chest, feeling like a small child herself.

"A person would have to be truly heartless to blame you for something your husband caused. But it doesn't have to be a torture to you. I promise you. This could be a blessing. Think of it this way: you're here now. You're away from him. And you have more love surrounding you here in Ogden than you ever had back in New York, clearly."

Amelia sniffled and sat up a smidge so she could look into Tabitha's honest eyes. "Do you honestly think that people will accept this? Will accept *me*? I think they're going to run me out of town, as they should…"

"Why?" Tabitha asked her. "Because you were married once? They know that. Things happen in marriage, whether we plan them or not." She shrugged a bit. "You were doing your wifely duty. No matter how your late husband behaved, you stood by him and did your best. That's no reason at all to judge you or run you out of town." She smirked a bit. "Silly Amelia, things are not quite as dramatic as they are in your head." She petted her head a bit, which Amelia found soothing even as she still clung to sorrow and worry.

"You should tell Percy right away," Tabitha then said.

"Chiefly because he deserves to know as soon as possible, but also because it will make you feel so much better to have it out in the open. He won't want you to distrust him or feel ashamed."

I know that trust is important for a successful marriage, Amelia thought. *But might this not ruin his trust in me?* "I just feel so dirty," she said sadly.

"You're not, darling," Tabitha said. "You're beautiful. And soon, that handsome, kind general store owner is going to make you his bride."

Amelia did her best to take her friend's words to heart. Tabitha knew Percy better and for a long time now, so she surely knew more about how he would react. Amelia told herself to trust in him. He wouldn't turn on her now, when she needed him the most. He just couldn't!

CHAPTER 13

THE CARRIAGE RIDE TO PERCY'S HOUSE WAS EQUALLY done in silence, though Amelia didn't spend the whole time looking out the window like last time. She even had a small smile on her face, the kind of smile that was plainly meant just for her. Neil was satisfied enough for their happier silence so he wasn't going to try to change it with uncomfortable conversation. Mrs. Hawkins had evidently had a good chat with Tabitha, and Neil wasn't at all surprised about that. The friendship between the two ladies made him happy because he remembered a time not too long ago when Tabitha was the new lady in town in need of comfort and compassion.

When the carriage stopped outside of the correct home, Amelia alit with the helping hand of Mr. Hughes. She smiled at him and gave a little nod. "Thank you kindly, sir. I'm sure we'll be seeing each other again soon."

He smiled back at her at that. "I'd like that very much, and I'm sure Tabitha would as well."

Amelia used her key to carefully open up the small house and step inside. The tree was still standing there in the living room; the first thing she could see now that she was inside, and it made the worry inch back into her mind just a little at a time. Now that she was there alone, all she could do was think about Percy and the baby and what she was going to have to say to him. It seemed so much easier when she was with Tabitha but now that she was back in her own home, she felt meek and afraid.

This is exactly how he'd want you to feel, she told herself, trying her best to be confident. *Don't give him any more power over you. He's not worth it. He never earned any of your care.*

It was difficult for a sweet, sensitive girl like Amelia to think in such a way, but Tabitha had instilled in her the feeling that she must take her own life back into her hands now that she'd been given a chance to start over out west. And she meant to do just that.

Percy arrived home at his usual time. Amelia could always depend on that. He was wearing his nice, new blue hat that she had knitted for him, and the sight of it on his head made her eyes fill up with tears. She didn't know if they were happy tears or sad tears and she didn't stop to wonder which before she was walking over to him and throwing her arms around his abdomen. "You're wearing the hat," she cried out, her voice breaking on the word 'hat.'

"Of course I am, darling," he replied, rubbing and gently patting her back as he returned her hug. "I had to show off my beautiful new present. How were you today? Did you miss me?"

He pulled back enough to look into her eyes and he could see the tears there. She knew he could. She smiled a little and felt like even that looked more pained than happy. "I did," she told him sincerely. "I'm afraid that there is something that we must talk about, something important. I know that we're planning to be wed soon, and I can't, in good conscience go through with that without telling you this…"

Percy blinked at her, still gazing into her eyes but his gaze was now concerned and less loving. "All right," he said. "I have a feeling that I should sit down first."

He stepped over to the couch and sat down upon it, staying on the edge of his seat in case the need arose for him to stand back up. He didn't know what she was going to talk to him about. *How could he? This is such a… a terrible situation.*

At first, she thought that maybe she didn't need to tell him right away. After all, she'd only just found out this morning. But then, her better judgment prevailed. *He'll want to know,* she reminded herself. *Just like Tabitha told you. He deserves to know, if you love him and trust him.*

"I went to the doctor this morning," Amelia confessed,

lowering herself to sit beside him. "Tabitha was concerned when I shared with her that I was feeling a bit queasy with all of the Christmas treats. That wasn't like me. So I went to the doctor's office in town this morning..."

Percy's eyes widened. "Are you alright?" he asked her, his voice itself seeming to plead with her to be alright. "You never told me that you were feeling unwell."

"I know," she said sadly, looking down at her hands in her lap. "And I should have. I'm so sorry... I didn't want you to worry. But I see now that you would've had every right to be concerned about me. I'm okay. But I'm... I'm with child. I've apparently been with child since right before Luther passed away."

She hated to say the words. She hated to confess to something so horrifying. The memory of being with her late husband didn't leave a pleasant feeling within her, even though Tabitha had described it as performing her *wifely duty*.

Percy was looking at her in a way that was difficult for her to read or figure out at all. He was staring almost vacantly and she could tell at once that he was feeling overwhelmed. *With rage towards me, no doubt. He's changing his mind. At this very moment, I can see the love dying in his eyes.*

Amelia brought her hands to her face and covered it, crying a more steady rain of tears now that she felt certain of his reaction to her news. They weren't going to be married now. It had been foolish to even imagine otherwise.

What man wanted to marry a woman who was carrying another man's child?

Percy brought his arms around her in a hug, but it was a lose hug. She told herself over and over again that she had lost him. *You can't unring that bell,* she thought, the words stinging even as she thought them. *Even his hugs will never be as warm and wonderful. There will always be this impenetrable space between us.*

What was it that Tabitha had told her? That things weren't quite as dramatic as she imagined them to be? Ha! Amelia wished that she hadn't so heartily believed that now.

"I think it's best if you get some rest, then," Percy said after some time of sitting in silence, only broken by her ardent tears. "I doubt very much that the doctor would recommend that you sit up all night, crying yourself into a tizzy."

There was truth in that, though it pained Amelia to think about some of the other implications. She told herself not to think of it as Percy not wanting to spend time with her or have her cook his meals. It was out of genuine concern for her well-being and the safety of her unborn baby that he wanted her to go get some rest. And indeed, Amelia was rather tired from her mentally trying day. She just wished that her mind wasn't always so at odds with her heart and how she truly wanted to approach things and feel about them.

She didn't want to feel as though everyone around her thought she was crazy.

Amelia did as she was told, seeing reason in what he said despite her misgivings, and she retired upstairs to bed. Ami the puppy was very pleased to see her. He wasn't so prepared for being left to his own devices and had done a number on the bottom of one of the room's cream-colored curtains. There was slobber and teeth marks all over it.

As soon as she got into her room and closed the door, noticing the state of the curtains and the guilty, lonely look on the pup's face, she began to cry anew. Things had seemed to fall into place at last and had been going so well. Why must Luther continue to torment her from beyond the grave? He'd always got the last laugh and the last word in life, and now his death was just no different.

"I wish I'd never met you!" she cried aloud. "I wish that things had been so very different!" She fell upon the bed and pounded her small fists into one of the soft, downy pillows. Her sobbing slowed after a short while and she was soon fast – but uneasily – asleep.

When the sun rose in the morning, Amelia was awake. She'd tossed and turned the whole night and could only have visions of babies and her horrible, evil late husband who cackled and bore himself into every facet of her life. She frowned as she looked out of the window and saw the sun. It was sure to be the most upsetting day in Ogden for her.

She'd resolved that she was going to speak with Percy about the baby and what it meant for their future, even if surely it was going to hurt.

CHAPTER 14

SHE FOUND PERCY IN THE SMALL, TWO-PERSON DINING room that he'd set up for them, sipping his morning coffee and acting like nothing at all had happened or changed from the day before. She approached him there but didn't immediately sit down. "Good morning, darling," he said to her. She noticed that he didn't look at her the way he had always used to. The love that had shown plainly in his eyes before had been replaced with a look of uncertainty and perhaps even frustration.

Frustration at having to keep me in his home...

"I just wanted to let you know that I'll... I'll understand if you don't wish to keep our engagement," she said to him, working hard to keep her tone even and unaffected, even as her heart within was breaking. "You shouldn't be forced to marry a woman who brings along another man's burden."

Percy stared at her wordlessly.

"I've packed up my belongings and I'm prepared to hail my own carriage so you needn't accompany me to the station if you'd rather not."

He blinked at her and suddenly she realized that he'd only been quiet because he was shocked. "What on earth are you talking about?" he asked her, starting from his seat. "I don't want you to go. I'm marrying you tomorrow!"

Amelia was so confused. She didn't think that she could believe him so easily, even though his words sounded marvelous to her after all of her internal turmoil last night. "But the baby..." she began.

Percy took her face gently into his hands and held her there, gazing into her eyes. She could see the love there once more, melting away any looks of doubt that may have been lurking there before. "I don't blame you for performing the actions of a married woman. I don't fault you for having a late husband. This is something I knew about you from the moment we began corresponding. My late wife and I... We always dreamed of having a family together. You well know that we began building this house with a family in mind. But she died not long after arriving here and I thought I'd never have a chance at having a family ever again. I don't see this baby as a bad thing. In truth... I see it as a tremendous blessing."

Amelia gazed upon him with tears in her eyes. She didn't have to wonder whether or not they were happy tears this time. She knew they were.

"But you acted so silent towards me all of a sudden," she pointed out. "You seemed to grow distant."

He smiled slightly at her, stroking her cheek. "I was overwhelmed, yes, but it was because I was thinking that I'd finally have what I wanted: a beautiful young bride and a perfect, adorable child to love and spoil for the rest of my life. I was worried, too, about how I'd support you both. But I think that, as long as we work together, we'll be okay. I also have it on good authority that a certain Mrs. Hughes will help us if we should need it."

Amelia was completely floored. Tabitha had been right all along. There'd been no reason to worry or be so dramatic. Things weren't as bad as they seemed in her head. It was time she started believing her heart.

She smiled at Percy and kissed his cheek. "Oh!" she exclaimed. "Oh, this is much better news than I thought I would receive this morning!"

Suddenly there came a little bark and she looked down to discover Ami sitting there at her feet, playing with a lace on one of her brown, leather shoes.

"Ami likes this news as well," Percy said with a laugh. "I suppose this means he wants to be a part of the wedding."

Amelia's eyes lit up and she picked up the puppy, cuddling him in her arms. "I think that will make this the cutest wedding the world has ever seen," she said with a smile and a laugh. She was almost too relieved to know what to do with herself. "I suppose that I should go upstairs and unpack. I'll be staying her a while now…"

She rushed upstairs, laughing as she carried the puppy along with her. She pulled her belongings back out of the suitcase and arranged them in the closet and the bureau to her liking. After all, the room was intended for Percy as well; this was her room for good now. She intended to make it feel more that way.

"Shall I go and inform Tabitha that we're to be married tomorrow?" Amelia asked Percy after coming back downstairs a short while later.

He chuckled at her. "Tabitha already knows, my love. She's known nearly since the beginning that I intended to marry you very shortly after Christmas."

So that was why Tabitha had said that winter weddings were the loveliest. She *knew* that Percy intended for them to be married before the year was out! Amelia smiled and blushed a bit. "I really have been such a ninny," she said.

"Oh, no," Percy told her, giving her a hug. She could feel the warmth and strength in his hug again and it made her feel as though she could achieve anything she set her mind to in life now. She could trust this gentleman. He had all the faith in the world in her. "You're a sensitive soul. I love that about you."

Amelia looked into his eyes. She was compelled enough now; she had to say it. "I love you."

He wrapped his arms around her again and held her close, petting her long, auburn locks. "I love you. I've always loved you."

When at last the hug ended, he pulled back just enough

and then gingerly placed his hands onto Amelia's belly. He looked into her face as he grinned. "Just think," he said. "Before long, we'll have a little one all our own to take care of and love. A child. An Andrews for the future."

Amelia distinctly noticed the glint of a tear in his eye. She loved a man who could be emotional like that. Luther had only ever seemed to have one emotion and that was anger. She pushed the thought of him from her mind.

He wasn't worth her time. She had a wedding to prepare for.

She wondered at first where in Heaven's name she was supposed to find a wedding gown in a day, until she realized that Tabitha had that all figured out.

"I've taken the liberty of repurposing my wedding gown," she explained. "My gown had a white fur coat sort of attached to it, and I think for you we can make it a bit more understated. After all, sweetheart, you are rather shy and reserved."

Amelia blushed. That was true. Tabitha produced the white wedding gown from the recesses of her closet and held it out in front of Amelia to make sure that the shape and cut of it would look well on her smaller frame. The white fur coat had been replaced with some lovely, light pink lace which was more in tune with Amelia's delicate nature. Tabitha had looked like a snow queen in her wedding gown and now her good friend Amelia would get to look like her sweet princess protégé.

"I hope you like it," she said as they admired the dress together.

Amelia quickly took the dress and rushed from the room to go change into it in the vacant guest room. When she came back into the bedroom where Tabitha waited for her, her friend gasped. "Oh, you look perfect!"

She blushed and smiled demurely. She gave a small twirl and let the lace fabric slide against her body. Amelia felt like she was going to float away any moment, and it wasn't even her wedding day yet.

Tabitha placed a few pins in places and promised to do some quick tailoring to make sure that the dress fit Amelia to a T. Then the two friends hugged. Because the wedding was the following day, it was decided that Amelia should spend the night with her friend, so she and Ami took up residence in the guest room at the Hughes farm that night. She missed Percy, though she was used to sleeping soundly in her own bed.

That's one thing that shall be an adjustment all over again, she thought. Sharing a bed with someone was not something that was comfortable right away. She knew though that, as with everything else, this time would be different. This time would be better.

The following morning arrived with all of the splendor and peacefulness that Amelia hoped for in a wedding day. She'd enjoyed her visit with the Hughes family, of course, but she was eager to get home to Percy. And even more eager to be married to him. Tabitha greeted her in the hallway when she was on her way to the kitchen for a quick breakfast. She could hear the sound of clattering dishes and conversation. But she stopped and gave a smile as Tabitha showed her the altered dress. It was just as lovely as before, and it had clearly been taken in and shortened just a smidge here and there.

"I'll go ahead and leave this in your room for you," Tabitha said brightly. "We must leave in about an hour."

Amelia nodded excitedly. "Okay. I'll only be a moment!" She rushed carefully down the stairs and got herself a pastry and some coffee. She ate her breakfast in record time and was back up in her room, ready to go.

Tabitha helped Amelia get into her wedding gown and then carefully braided her long tresses, plaiting them and pinning the braids up on her head so that her neck and shoulders could be on display a bit, which was a significant change from her usual appearance. "You look absolutely stunning," Tabitha told her. "Percy will be wowed, to be sure."

Ami the puppy would be traveling to the chapel along with Percy, so that he could surprise Amelia with the puppy's ceremonial attire. She was excited to see her two favorite boys. Once she was finished getting dressed and ready, Amelia climbed into Neil's carriage along with Tabitha and they were off to the chapel.

Amelia held the bouquet of purple and blue wildflowers as Tabitha gently placed one in her hair in order to complete the look. She had a smaller bouquet of blue flowers and she'd fashioned one of the blooms behind her ear. As Amelia preened herself in the room where they had to wait before the ceremony, Tabitha peeked out of the door at the people congregating in the pews for the ceremony.

"Goodness!" she cried in a whisper, turning to her friend with a grin on her face. "You two brought out practically the entire town. I can't say I'm surprised though."

Amelia felt her heart pounding in her chest. She told herself to remain calm. A lot of people were there, yes, but they were there to share in her joy, not cut her down. "I can do this," she muttered to herself under her breath. "I can do this."

Tabitha gave her a small hug. "Just keep your eyes fixed on Percy and you won't be so nervous anymore."

The music began and that was their cue. There was a sudden "aww" from the crowd gathered there and Amelia and Tabitha looked out of the doorway to see little Ami toddling up the aisle, wearing a bright blue bow. He set the stage for what was sure to be an adorable wedding. Amelia hoped so, anyway.

Tabitha straightened up her posture and slowly marched down the aisle, blue flowers in hand and a wide grin on her face. Next, it was Amelia's turn. She did her best to follow Tabitha's lead. She glanced shyly from side to side as she passed by, looking at the people gathered there but not really lingering on any one face. This way, she couldn't begin overanalyzing anything. She knew that some of the people there knew about her outburst at the store, but she told herself that this was a new day. *They probably don't even think about it anymore. The only one thinking about it is you.*

She looked up at the wedding arch, at the minister, and then her eyes fell upon Percy. He was standing there to the right, looking so dapper and handsome in his Sunday best suit. She smiled and felt her cheeks go hot at just the sight of him there. This man loved her unconditionally. He knew her faults and her past mistakes, and he loved her anyway. Perhaps even all the more for them.

Once she reached the front of the aisle, she turned towards Percy and they took each other's hands.

"Dearly beloved," the minister began. "We are gathered here together on this day to join these two souls in holy matrimony. Mr. Percy Andrews and Mrs. Amelia Hawkins, you have each been wed before and you have now chosen to marry again after suffering such terrible misfortune and loss. It takes a strong and noble heart to continue on in love after facing such tragedies. I ask that you look to one another in your times of grief now. I ask that you see the other as a new dawn, a new chance to create the life that you both truly esteem. As it is written in Peter 4:8 – *Above all, love each other deeply, because love covers over a multitude of sins.*"

Amelia appreciated the Bible quotation he'd chosen, because it somehow masterfully conveyed the way she chose to look at things. *Love and forgiveness for past missteps.* She never thought of Percy's past marriage as anything more than something deserving of sympathy and a part of what made him who he was in the present. Surely he must view her past marriage the same way. What was done was done. She'd focused too long on the wrong things, and he'd been right there for her the whole time in spite of that.

"Amelia Rose Dewitt Hawkins," the minister said, bringing her attention back to the current moment. She gazed lovingly into Percy's loving eyes. "Do you take Percival Nathaniel Andrews as your lawfully wedded husband? To have and to hold, to love and to cherish, to honor and obey, in sickness and in health, in good times and in bad, for richer or poorer, until death do you part?"

Amelia nodded her head quickly, a grin stretching across her lips. "Yes!" she said. "I do!"

The minister turned to Percy, who never once took his eyes off of her. "Percival Nathaniel Andrews, do you take Amelia Rose Dewitt Hawkins as your lawfully wedded wife? To have and to hold, to love and to cherish, to protect and to comfort, in sickness and in health, in good times and in bad, for richer or poorer, until death do you part?"

His smile only grew. "I sure do."

There was a cheer in the pews.

"Then, by the power vested in me by the beloved town on Ogden, I now pronounce you husband and wife. You may kiss the bride."

Amelia and Percy threw their arms around each other at once and kissed. His lips were soft and warm against hers and she felt her heart grow wings and seemingly flutter to and fro about her chest. She was now the new Mrs. Amelia Andrews. A name had never sounded so sweet.

EPILOGUE

THE MONTHS WENT BY FOR AMELIA AND PERCY. THINGS were much more pleasant for them now that she was more self-assured about everything. Her belly grew larger by the day, it seemed, and the symptoms of little Baby Andrews didn't ever entirely go away, but Amelia learned to live with them and take care not to overdo anything. Percy surprised her by taking on the task of cooking, most evenings at least. "I'm no stranger to the kitchen," he pointed out. "I'd been cooking my own meals for years, before we met."

The meals he made were outstanding as well, which made Amelia wonder if she ought to start taking lessons from him. "We should cook together sometime, so you can show me some of your tricks."

"Perhaps," he said, kissing her on the nose as he placed a plate of cheese and bacon grits in front of her. "But only once you are well enough and on your feet again. And only if you're not tired out from taking care of our baby." He winked at her as he sat down beside her.

Our baby. Those were her favorite two words.

When it was time for their baby to be born, Neil Hughes was right there to drive to the doctor and bring him back in order to assist Amelia with the birth. She gave birth on the couch in the living room of their quaint little house.

"It's a girl," the doctor announced. The tiny baby gave a little wail almost as if she approved of the way things had turned out.

She was soon swaddled up in a blanket and nestled into Amelia's arms. She held the baby girl against her chest and cried happily, as Percy petted her hair the way she always loved. "She's so beautiful," he said softly. "Like her mother. What do you want to call her?"

Amelia sniffled a bit. She hadn't given much thought to the name. She'd only thought of what life would be like for her, growing up in this wonderful little town, surrounded by loving friends. "Faith," she said, looking from the baby and into Percy's eyes. "Because she has shown me the importance of never losing faith."

Percy gave her a kiss and then kissed little Faith's forehead as she slept. "Welcome to the world, my darling Faith. You've made me the happiest man in the world. We're so blessed to have you and we'll thank God every day for bringing you into our lives."

THE END

A CHRISTMAS MAIL ORDER BRIDE FOR SAMSON

Montana Valley Brides

A CHRISTMAS MAIL ORDER BRIDE FOR SAMSON

MISSOULA MILLS, MONTANA – 1887

Samson Delaney, a handsome, hard-working lumber mill owner in Missoula Mills, Montana, has grown lonely and longs for a wife to spend his life with. His good friends had been fortunate enough to find their brides through newspaper advertisements, so he decides to ask one of these wives, Mrs. Virginia Monroe, to help him write an advertisement of his own.

Before long, he is receiving letters from women all over the east coast. None impress him as much as the first letter he receives from a young lady by the name of Miss Tabitha McGregor, a lovely former librarian who works at a book shop in New York. The pair exchange letters until, at last, she arrives to be with him.

With Christmas coming soon, Samson decides to mark the occasion by proposing to Tabitha, with the intent to marry her on Christmas morning. Tabitha, on the other hand, begins to start having second thoughts about marrying a man she has only just met.

Will Samson have a bride for the holidays, or will he be left brokenhearted underneath the mistletoe?

CHAPTER 1

SAMSON DELANEY WAS A HARD-WORKING MAN, WITH HIS own rather successful lumber mill. He took great pride in the fact that he belonged to the elite group of millers that had made Missoula Mills, well, *Missoula Mills*. He was thirty-five years old and originally from New York, which was itself a lumber state. There were a lot of trees in Albany, but they were not like the tall cedars, junipers, larches and pines that could be found in the wilds of Montana.

He made his way out west to seek his fortune in 1875 after growing up with his father and older brother serving in the Union army during the war. Luckily, his family survived the war more or less unscathed all things considered, though Samson was a changed man in other ways. He did not have any physical wounds like his brother who lost an arm, nor did he fall ill like so many of his young comrades had in the years that followed. Nevertheless, he emerged a great deal more fearful than he had been previously. Work in his mill did not rattle him, but any sudden noise when he was at leisure could leave him shaken and unable to focus, so scarred by what he had witnessed in the streets and heard about from men who had seen things first hand.

The town of Missoula Mills offered him a much-needed change of pace and respite from city life. As much as he had enjoyed growing up in New York, he was ever so fond of the wilderness and all of its quiet, calm splendor. It did not take him long at all to become a well-known and respected man in town. Everyone trusted that Samson's lumber was sturdy and was the finest that money could buy.

For many years, having a successful business and a good reputation was all that Samson needed. But eventually, loneliness took hold of him. His friends in town were much like him, all of them had come from humble beginnings back in the east, and all of them were managing their own businesses now that they were frontiersmen out west. But there was one thing his friends had that Samson did not; it had not even occurred to him until then. All of his friends had beautiful, new wives.

"Sometimes I really do believe that I would not still have my ranch were it not for my Virginia," Samson's friend Archie told him one night at the saloon. "She brought me peace and hope, and a wonderful son. Until she came along, I thought that owning land and making money was all that mattered."

Samson swallowed back his cup of lemonade, knowing exactly what his friend meant. He could not fully imagine what it would be like to have a wife of his own, of course, but he knew just based on how happy his friend was now that having a woman in one's life tended to change things for the better.

"I was always so shy with women," he confessed to Archie. "My parents would force me to go to parties and meet the eligible ladies, but I never knew what to say beyond the introductions. The war kind of saved me from embarrassment."

Archie threw back his head and laughed loudly, slapping his friend on the back. "That sounds just like you," he said. "Samson, what you need is a wife. And there are ways you can ensure that it goes well for you. Why don't you come over to my house for dinner tomorrow evening? My wife Ginny will be able to help you. She and her friends are mighty helpful when it comes to writing and things of that nature."

Samson blushed a bit. He was not known for being much of a writer. In fact, he could not spell very well, and reading was always a point of frustration for him. Growing up, he had never trained in a profession that would require competent literacy, so he scraped by with the bare minimum. He could keep a ledger of his sales. That was all that he thought he needed. Until now.

"Okay," he said. "Thank you for the invitation. Perhaps

Virginia knows a thing or two about letter-writing. She must, or she would not have met you, right?"

He was no stranger to the mail order bride service. He knew that the majority of his friends had found their wives by taking a chance and mailing off letters to unknown addresses. Samson just did not take too much stock in it working in his favor. He had a hard time connecting with women in person, and an even more difficult time writing, which made him doubt his ability to find a wife as easily as his friends had.

CHAPTER 2

DRESSED IN ONE OF HIS NICER SUITS – A BLUE ONE WITH black trim – Samson arrived at Archie and Virginia Monroe's ranch for their planned dinner. He did not know at all what to expect, though he, of course, had heard nothing but good things about Mrs. Monroe and all of the work she had done to help the community. He felt more than a little ridiculous for needing help from her, but he had a feeling that he would not receive any judgment from someone as notably kind and compassionate as her.

When he knocked on the front door of the manor house, he expected his friend to answer. Instead, he was surprised to be greeted by Virginia. The petite blonde was so beautiful and sweet looking. Samson reached up to remove his hat from his head and then realized that he was not wearing his usual hat because he was wearing his suit. He flushed and then offered his hand in greeting instead.

"It is so nice to see you, Mrs. Monroe," he said politely. "I'm Samson Delaney, your husband's friend from way back when this town was little more than dirt and some rocks."

He was exaggerating of course, but Virginia knew that. She smiled broadly at him and took his hand, giving it a ginger shake. "I have heard much about you, of course. Please come inside and I will pour you some tea. Or would you prefer coffee?"

She led him inside and gestured for him to sit in the living room, upon the couch or perhaps one of the chairs. She was a polite hostess. Samson looked around, recognizing the familiar home of course, and remarking to himself upon how changed for the better it appeared. There were toys in the living room, some blocks and a wooden horse, all belonging to young master Nicky.

"Er, coffee would be wonderful, actually," he said as he sat in one of the chairs near the couch, thinking that couches might be more the lady's preference. "Thank you."

She smiled another beautiful smile at that and then went off to the kitchen to get a kettle going.

So far so good, Samson thought. The woman of the house seemed quite friendly and approachable and he was feeling much more comfortable than he had imagined.

He did not have to wait long before Archie came into the house. The rancher smiled at Samson and removed his dusty leather gloves. "I thought I recognized your carriage outside," he said. "I hope you haven't been waiting long."

Samson rose from his chair in order to politely greet his friend. He shook his head. "No, not long at all. Your wife is fetching some coffee."

"She'll include one for me, I reckon. She knows my schedule well." Archie winked at that, and then he stepped aside and revealed a small boy who was making his way into the house behind his father.

Nicky was an Indian boy of ten years, soon to be eleven. He was adopted by Virginia and Archie from the town's orphanage. When he saw his parents' guest, he smiled. "Hello," he said. "My name is Nicky. You must be Mr. Delaney?"

Samson nodded and offered his hand to the child. They shook and then Nicky took his leave to go and play about with his toys for a bit. He was a hard worker, learning the trade from his father, but he was still very much a child. Samson appreciated that he was able to act his age while still learning how to become a rancher.

Archie sat on the couch and Samson sat back down in his chair. Soon, Virginia returned with a tray of coffee cups, sugar, and some fresh cream. She set it down on the table in front of the couch and sat beside her husband.

"My husband has informed me that you would like to use the mail order bride service to find a wife for yourself," Virginia said.

"Yes, ma'am," Samson said. "The trouble for me is that I

am not so good at correspondence and I reckon I don't rightly know what would suit me."

This seemed to make Virginia feel a new bit of endearment for him. She had been in the same boat herself not that long ago, although from the opposite end. "Would you like me and my friends to help you write an advertisement?" she asked him. "My friend Eliza is a teacher and she could help you write it yourself if you like."

"That would be mighty kind of you," Samson said. "I think that I know what I would like and what I would dislike; I just don't know the right way of putting it. The right words."

After their coffee, they dined together and Archie and Virginia gave Samson some things to think about as he started forming his idea of a perfect bride. He looked at his friend's marriage and the love and respect that they had for each other. When he returned home to his empty house afterwards, he knew right away that he wanted a bride who would give it that womanly touch that turned mere wood and cement into a warm and comforting *home*. He knew all about construction, but he did not know about décor and that feeling of family that exuded from Virginia and Archie's house.

He did not believe that a homemaker would be too much to ask for. Samson just wondered how many homemakers there still were back east. Weren't a lot of the unmarried women working factory jobs now? He feared that no one would want to give up some of their independence in order to marry him and be his. His loneliness was causing him to have low self-esteem. He hoped that some help from Virginia and her friends could change that.

CHAPTER 3

VIRGINIA MET WITH HER FRIENDS AT THE ORPHANAGE THE following day. She told them of Mr. Delaney and his desire for a bride. "He is a very sweet young gentleman. Rather timid, and I think that's a big part of why he is having such trouble on his own. I said that we could look through the papers for him, and possibly help him write an advertisement."

It was a lot to take on, but the four friends were generous and helpful whenever possible. "I think it will be a great deal of fun," Eliza said, "looking at it from the other side."

"Instead of being the one to find the advertisement," Margaret said, "we shall be the ones helping to write it!"

After work, Dorothy picked up a newspaper from her husband's general store. They were always getting the latest newspapers because they were relevant to the interests of the stores' shoppers. She brought it along with her to the sewing circle that the friends had started, at Margaret's home.

Together, they flipped through pages and pages of advertisements, making notes about the sorts of things that Mr. Delaney could try to touch upon when he wrote his own. It was clear to them which of the newspaper ads would have received their attention, and they felt that that information was important to consider as well. Who knew better what women wanted than women themselves?

Once they had a nice, long list of the things Samson should incorporate into his own advertisement, Virginia took up that list as well as the newspaper and brought it all home with her. She wasn't sure when Mr. Delaney would come back to their house, so she placed all of it into an envelope so that it could be delivered to his doorstep. Nicky was glad to help and he brought the envelope over to Mr. Delaney's porch himself.

The miller was in for a surprise. Virginia hoped that it would be considered a help. She was confident that he would be successful if he could only give himself a chance.

When Samson arrived home from his lumber mill, he found a large envelope on his front porch. It didn't have his address written on it, but it bore his name in lovely handwriting that could have only belonged to a woman, for there were no calligraphers that he knew of in town.

He brought the strange envelope inside and carefully

opened it, revealing that it contained a newspaper and a list on parchment that included, in several different hands, some things which he should write in a mail order advertisement. Samson smiled. Virginia and her friends had really come through with some brilliant suggestions. He wished that he had them there with him in this moment so that he would not have to write the ad himself; all the while, second guessing his wording.

The process of advertisement writing, he felt, did not usually take this much time and care, but it was only because he wanted badly to have a wife who fit him as well as those ladies fit their husbands. He was not a perfectionist, but he wanted to find someone who lit a spark within him and made him feel less alone, more whole.

The list for creating a successful advertisement stated that he should try to succinctly describe himself and his position, as well as what he was looking for in his potential bride. He could include a portrait of himself if he so chose, and he should be ready to accurately describe his appearance in the future if he decided not to pay the extra money it took to include a portrait.

Samson's hands shook a bit as he took up a piece of paper and a pen and began to write the advertisement that would change his life and his future forever. He prayed that his bride to be would be looking for a business owner and not Shakespeare.

Successful lumber mill owner in Missoula Mills, Montana Territory, thirty-five years of age, seeks a young lady to be his wife.

Must be interested in household work, friendly and engaging. Must not cling too hard to independence.

He decided to include a portrait of himself, and placed a small photograph into the envelope along with his advertisement draft, so the ladies could offer their critiques of it as well. It was a dapper portrait of himself in a handsome suit, looking like a proper businessman. He hoped that at least one woman out there could find it in her heart to love him even though he thought he was a bit shy.

He sent the envelope off to Archie's house, hoping that it would reach him within a day or two. It was a bit silly to mail it rather than take it over himself, but he wanted the letter to reach Virginia and not be mistaken as something for Archie instead. Although he appreciated his friend's help, he shuddered to think of what his friend truly thought of his awkward attempt to find a bride.

CHAPTER 4

VIRGINIA RECEIVED THE LETTER AND WAS OVERCOME with glee at how sweet Mr. Delaney was. He had followed their instructions very well, though his handwriting left something to be desired. She knew that the newspaper would print it out in its own way, but she feared that some of his handwriting might be unintelligible. She brought his advertisement and portrait along with her to the orphanage so her friends could see.

Eliza tisked a bit. "I can rewrite it for him so it is a bit easier to read," she offered. "And I think we might do away with the independence part. It is a bit much to demand of a young lady."

Dorothy nodded. "I agree," she said. "There is already some measure of a lady giving up her independence simply by responding to such advertisements."

Margaret agreed as well. "It sounds a bit too strict for what he is trying to accomplish," she noted.

Carefully, Eliza rewrote the advertisement, adding her own touch; making it more pleasing to their sensibilities as ladies and former mail order brides.

Successful lumber mill owner in Missoula Mills, Montana. Thirty-five years of age. Seeking a young lady to be his wife. Must be interested in household work as well as assisting in his business as needed. Friendly and engaging.

"What bride does not want to feel as though she is contributing?" Eliza said with a small shrug.

The friends all giggled their agreement and delight at how the advertisement had come out. There was no real need to send it back to Mr. Delaney since they had it crafted in a way that was most suitable, in their experienced minds. Margaret volunteered to take it to the office the next day.

"Oh, how surprised he is going to be," Virginia said. "When he starts receiving letters in response. It makes me so happy to know that we are improving this man's life!"

CHAPTER 5

Samson didn't ask about the advertisement right away. He believed that it had been received by Mrs. Monroe and the lady would let him know if anything was wrong with it. He knew as well that the Monroes were busy with their ranch and their child. However, waiting to hear what had become of it was not easy. The excitement of creating the advertisement had dwindled once he sent it off to be read and edited by his friend's wife. There was nothing for him to do now except wait and hope.

Several weeks went by. Samson let himself become buried in his work, focusing on the lumber business and not giving any further thought to his ad or his desire for a wife. He thought that by working a lot, he would have to spend less time alone. When he was home by himself, that was when his urge to get married was strongest. He started to think, rather defeatedly, that perhaps he did not need to marry after all. Perhaps he just needed to work all the more.

Finally, he couldn't take it anymore. He had to know whether or not Virginia and her friends had approved of his advertisement and where it had gone since then. Was it possible that the ladies had forgotten about it? That did not seem at all like them. He knew that they were busy with their own lives and families, but it was not within their characters to have forgotten about someone whom they had promised to help.

He took his carriage over to Archie's home and nervously knocked on the door. Normally he met his friend at the saloon, but this was a more personal matter and he felt that it should be handled in a more personal and private setting.

"Samson!" Archie exclaimed with a smile upon answering the front door. "Come in, come in."

The two friends went into the living room and sat down in some chairs. "How have you been?" Archie asked. "I have not seen you for some time."

Samson nodded a little. "I have been quite busy of late. I was wondering if your wife might have told you about my newspaper advertisement. She and her friend were assisting me with it, but I have not heard any word about it, nor have I received any reworked version of it."

Archie appeared thoughtful. He was supportive of this endeavor of Samson's, but he did his best to stay out of it because he knew that his wife was enjoying being helpful in the matter. In truth, he was hard at work with his own business and not had really had the proper amount of time to sit down and think of this like Virginia did. Now that he had his own wife and his life was happy and whole, Archie did not like to relive the stress of the mail order bride service, with all of its waiting and nervousness.

"The last I heard of it, Virginia and her friends had changed your advertisement a bit and they were planning to send it off," he told Samson. "She was so excited about it. I assume that the matter has been taken care of."

Virginia came home soon after, surprised to see the guest that was waiting for her in the living room with her husband. "To what do I owe this pleasure?" she asked Samson kindly. "You're here about your advertisement, aren't you?"

Samson was standing and he had removed his hat. He fidgeted a bit with it in his hands. Every time his eyes fell upon Mrs. Monroe, he was reminded exactly how pretty she was. He hoped that someday, not too long in the future, he would have a beautiful and young wife of his own.

"Yes, I am, ma'am," he said to her. "I have been waiting to see if I received a word, and I have not so I thought I might as well come by and check on how things have gone."

Virginia smiled at him. "I am glad that you have come and that you have asked," she said. She sat on the couch and he sat back down in his chair, still fiddling with his hat. She could tell that he was anxious, and she imagined how adorable he would be to some lucky woman back home in the east. "My friend Eliza redrafted it for you and we have sent off the advertisement to be printed in the newspaper. Now we are at perhaps the most difficult part. We must wait. We included your address, so you will receive any responses directly. Oh, and we do hope you will keep us informed and abreast of anything that happens!"

Samson appreciated that the ladies were so caring towards him. They did not get such a glowing reputation for no reason. "Thank you, Mrs. Monroe," he said with a shy smile of his own. "I hope that I shall receive some letters soon, in that case. And of course, I shall let you know what happens. After all, I owe you and it is the least I can do... If you or your friends ever need some lumber, please let me know!"

Virginia laughed gaily at that. "Splendid," she said. "Indeed, we shall. And good luck to you, Mr. Delaney. We are all hoping that you will find a wonderful, perfect bride for yourself."

With that, Samson went back home, feeling much more confident about what would hopefully come next.

CHAPTER 6

About a month later, Samson returned home from his mill to discover a letter on his front porch. This envelope had the pretty handwriting of a lady on it and it smelled faintly of perfume. He was so excited that he almost dropped the envelope into the dust. Hurrying, he brought it inside and sat in the nearest chair so that he could open it and immediately read its contents.

Dear Mr. Delaney,

My name is Tabitha McGregor and I am twenty-four years of age. I live in New York where I am a seller in a small book shop. I found your advertisement very appealing because I have always wanted to explore more of the land in this country and I appreciate a man who owns his own business without being pretentious like businessman one can find aplenty in New York!

In my spare time, I enjoy cooking as well as needlepoint. I am sure that you are receiving so many letters because you seem like such a kind and gentle person. Your photograph was very striking. I have enclosed a portrait of myself so that you may see what I look like. The photograph is a few years old, but I have not changed much, if at all.

I pray that you shall write back to me, even if only to let me know that my letter was well received. Thank you and I wish you well!

Sincerely,

Miss Tabitha McGregor

Samson found himself grinning down at the piece of paper in his hands. She was concerned that he would receive so many letters, but hers was actually the first. He felt that they were well matched and he adored the bit of humor that she had hidden within the lines. This Miss Tabitha McGregor was hoping to find a chance of scenery and a change of pace from New York, and Samson knew more than enough about that.

He went from focusing on the letter to admiring the portrait which she had included. She was a lovely girl with long, light-colored tresses and dark eyes. Samson tried to imagine what she must look like in person, and he liked what he was imagining. She was a real beauty, just like he had been hoping for. He knew that looks were not all that it took to make someone happy, but Miss McGregor seemed to have the kindness and wit to make everything so perfect in his eyes!

Immediately, he took up a pen and wrote back to her. He

knew that she was correct; he would likely receive a lot more letters. However, he wanted to take the time to get to know her better and see if perhaps he had been lucky right from the first.

Dear Miss McGregor,

Thank you kindly for your prompt response to my advertisement. As it turns out, yours was the first that I have received. I do hope that this is cause for celebration and I would very much like to get to know you better. You sound like a wonderful, intelligent young lady. Are you enjoying working in a shop? I am looking for someone who would like to be a homemaker, though of course, I will not disallow some ambition. It is good to have other interests and skills. After all, those are what set people apart as individuals, right? I know some married young ladies here who have a sewing circle and a dress shop, so you would not want for something to do if you came out here.

I do believe that you will find Missoula Mills to your liking. As it just so happens, I originally am from New York myself. I was born in Albany and I spent much of my youth in the city there. At one point, I was an apprentice to one of the businessmen you described. I learned a lot and applied it to my own lumber business out here.

I would like to correspond more with you if you are interested in doing so with me. You are a beautiful and interesting young woman and I would be honored if you allowed me to get to know you more.

Sincerely,
Samson Delaney

He sent his letter off to Miss McGregor in New York the following morning, all the while, wishing that the pony express would be faster.

CHAPTER 7

Life continued as usual for Samson after he sent the letter. He did not know why, but momentarily he had hoped that things might somehow feel different. Before too long, he began receiving letters from other ladies. He responded initially to them as well, but none of them really struck him as much as Miss McGregor's did. He told himself to keep up the enthusiasm just in case things did not work out with his first choice; his first respondent.

After several weeks, he received a new letter from Miss McGregor in New York. Samson smiled at the envelope and imagined that the lady herself was there with him. He took it inside his house along with some other mail. Carefully he opened the envelope so he could read her next letter. He hoped that she had enjoyed his response to her, but he imagined that she would not have written back to him if it was otherwise.

Dear Mr. Delaney,

How relieved and grateful I was to receive your response to my letter! I am truly delighted to know that I was fortunate enough to be the first letter you received. I will not pretend that that makes me the only person that you might wish to correspond with, although it does allow me to hope for the possibility that we shall continue our correspondence and perhaps even meet one day in the not too distant future.

I am very glad to read that there is a dress shop in Missoula Mills, and I appreciate that you have taken the time to tell me about it. If I were to marry, I would love to be a homemaker and help my husband at his business and in his home, but as you said I would like to retain some of my hobbies and interests. I feel that I have been blessed with skills and I want to put them to good use whenever possible. That being said, I think I would be very fulfilled if I was able to work in a dress shop there, or even volunteer my time and service to a sewing circle.

What a small world it is indeed that I should have come upon your advertisement and you are from the same part of America. What are the odds of that? Missoula Mills sounds like a wonderful place full of opportunities and very kind people. I find that I am growing quite restless here. I long to go on an adventure of my own and marry someone who understands and loves me and wants to start a family with me in our new home. I must admit that I did not always feel such a way, but time has made my heart grow fonder towards the ideas of courtship, marriage, and family.

I hope that this letter finds you well. I am so relieved that you found my portrait pleasing. Soon we shall perhaps be able to look upon each other in person. I pray for that day.

Sincerely,

Tabitha McGregor

Samson smiled down at this new letter. He found that he was unable to keep from smiling whenever Miss McGregor was concerned or involved. Life in Missoula Mills was starting to feel very anticipatory for him now that he had these ladies to write letters to and read letters from. However, now that he had received a new letter from Miss McGregor he was starting to believe that his search was at an end and that he had found the right woman to be his wife.

He did not want to jump to that conclusion too quickly and scare her away, of course. He told himself that he should wait at least until the next letter.

Dear Miss McGregor,

You are correct; it must indeed be such a small world, though it often seems so vast. When I first moved out here, I was astounded by all of this unclaimed land and all of this beauteous space. But now that I have been here a while and I have found you, I can see that I am not nearly as desolate as I feel at times. To think that we could have crossed paths before, back when I lived in New York... It boggles the mind a bit, does it not? I could have passed you on the street and I might not have said a thing to you, and now here we are.

Sorry if I am pontificating too much. I agree with you that it would be wonderful if we could meet in the future. It seems as though we have already been writing to each other for so long, though I do think that we owe the pony express for some of that. Months go by between letters, which means that months and months go by in which I can think only of you and how you are doing and what you are thinking about. Can I ever believe that you think of me sometimes? Do you ever find yourself imagining that you are here with me? I imagine such a thing very often if that is not a strange thing to confess.

When I was a boy, my brother went off to war and he used to send letters home to me, to tell me how he was doing and things like that. I remember how much I used to envy him for going off somewhere and writing home. Now it is almost as if I am in that position, with you in New York and me all the way out here. I am grateful that I am not fighting in a war, but that just makes being without you all the more difficult. There is not even a real reason that we should be so far apart, living our different lives. Time and distance are not on my side at present. Dare I dream that you want me to remedy that?

I pray that you are well and happy, even if you are not with me yet.

Sincerely,

Samson

CHAPTER 8

ALTHOUGH THE OTHER WOMEN WHO HAD TAKEN THE TIME to write to Samson were pretty and nice to him, his thoughts were always about Tabitha. After a while, he stopped responding to the other letters, which he felt guilty about but he did not want to lead anyone to the wrong conclusion. He did not want to make them believe that he was going to send along a ticket or a proposal. There was only one young lady who was going to get something like that, and only if she responded to him in a way that made him feel brave enough to do so. He did not want to give his heart to someone if she was not going to give him her heart in return.

At last, he received a letter from Miss McGregor in New York. He was overjoyed to see that her enthusiasm and hopeful optimism about their future together had not dwindled even in the slightest.

Dearest Samson,

I hope it is all right for me to call you by your given name since you so sweetly signed your last letter that way. I am so happy that you are interested in meeting me. I have not been able to stop thinking about you and what life would be like for me on Missoula Mills. I have never lived anywhere other than the city, so it will be quite an experience, but one I very much want to partake in.

You see that? I said will, not would. I am ever so hopeful and excited about the prospect. I hope that you have not changed your mind about me in the interim. I hope that there is not some other eligible would-be bride that might be trying to steal your heart away from me. For my heart is entirely yours, Samson. I want to be with you. Every action that I take now, every bit of money that I earn, I do it all for us now. I do it all so that I may come to you and be with you and help you in your successes and comfort you in your sadness. I want to be with you for everything. I hope that is not too extreme. I simply have never loved someone or felt loved by them. I do believe that I love you, Samson... Even writing your name like that causes me to turn red.

Please write back to me, dearest. I live each day in the hope of meeting you soon.

Sincerest wishes,

Tabitha

Samson was quite taken aback by her passion for him. They had not met properly yet but Tabitha seemed so ready to make the journey and be his wife. He had not proposed to her yet – in truth, he felt that proposing in a letter was not the right way of going about it – but she was already ready to be his. It made him so dizzyingly happy that he almost did not know what to do!

His friends had left his letter correspondence entirely up to him. They did not ask about how it was going or anything like that, thinking that it was his private affair and he would share anything that he wanted them to know. Virginia was very eager to hear how things were going with his prospective bride, but she did not ask about it in case he had received bad news and that bringing it up might hurt his feelings.

Samson knew and appreciated that Archie cared about him and had helped him in this new venture of his, but he did not share the minute details of his correspondence. Archie, for his part, was happy that his friend seemed much happier. He hoped to see him married soon, but he was not going to pry into his life. That simply was not done.

After receiving Tabitha's heartfelt and earnest letter, Samson decided that the time had come. He wanted her to join him out west. He wanted to meet her and show her around the city, and let Virginia and her friends share some of their opportunities with her. He firmly believed that Tabitha's life was going to be made better by moving out to the west and experiencing the beauty of Missoula Mills. Finally, he was never going to have to be alone again! That excited him most of all.

My dearest Tabitha,

You may, of course, call me Samson. I hope that I may call you Tabitha. Since we are friends now and soon to live together, it only seems right that we should speak more familiarly to each other.

Would you do me the honor of joining me out here? I have enclosed a train ticket so that you may more easily travel here. I shall know your answer by whether or not you arrive within the next few weeks. I shall be there at the station to meet you if you come. I look forward to meeting you at long last and I am eternally grateful for how kind and passionate you are in your desire to come here and be with me. I know that soon I shall never be alone again.

Fondest regards and see you soon,

Samson

CHAPTER 9

He sent the letter to Tabitha in early Autumn. By the time that her train was due to arrive, it was nearing Christmastime. Samson worried a bit about the snow, but he knew that everything was going to turn out okay. After all, they had been fortunate to find each other. Clearly, God had a plan for them to be together.

While he waited for his beloved Tabitha to arrive in Missoula Mills, he spent much of the impending holiday time with his friends in town. Decorations were starting to go up everywhere. Virginia had decorated Archie's ranch with a tree and some pine garlands. Their home seemed even more pleasant than usual and his heart swelled a bit when he thought about what his home was going to be like this Christmas, with his new bride.

It was mighty cold during winter. Virginia and her

friends had taken to sewing coats instead of dresses because they were in high demand at the clothing store that Dorothy owned. Samson wondered if he should have mentioned the need for such a thing to his beloved, but he thought that her being from New York would surely mean that she was aware of wintertime being cold. It made him smile just thinking about how she was from the very same place as him.

"I hope that you receive everything your heart has been yearning for this Christmas," Virginia said to him one evening when Samson joined her, Archie and Nicky for dinner. "My friends and I were thinking about having a little Christmas gathering to celebrate. Maybe your Miss McGregor will want to come along and join us in the festivities."

Samson nodded, appreciating the gesture. "I cannot confirm just yet, in case she is too shy or wants to be otherwise occupied, but I thank you for your invitation. I would love to join you if we may."

Virginia smiled and gave a little nod. When next she met with her friends, she was overjoyed to tell them how happy and optimistic Mr. Delaney seemed. "He is almost like a new man. A shinier, happier man. Oh, we have done such good by him. It makes me so proud!"

"Just think," Margaret said in a dreamlike voice. "I bet our husbands were like him, once upon a time. I wonder who they talked to about their excitement at meeting us."

"They probably did not talk to anyone about it," Eliza

said. "I know my poor, sweet Phillip did not say much of anything to anyone until I came along."

"Clint has his sons," Dorothy said. "I am sure that he told them about me, though they disliked the idea for a long time."

Virginia was still smiling delightedly. "Oh, I hope that everything goes well for him," she said. "He is such a nice man. His only fault is that he is shy and lacks confidence in his own personality. But, you know, ever since we helped with his advertisement he has not asked us for help writing. I think he found his voice."

Eliza grinned at that. She was no stranger to that concept. "I pray that he has himself a wonderful new wife soon… Not least of all because it will be nice to have a new friend in town."

Dorothy giggled. "Oh, are we not enough for you anymore?"

"That's why 'Liza spends so much time at the school house," Margaret said as she poked her needle through the fabric she was stitching. "She is trying to replace us." She made a funny face, which made her and the rest of the friends laugh.

CHAPTER 10

On a cold morning in early December, Tabitha was due to arrive. At least, according to Samson's calculations. He had sent her a ticket about a month ago, knowing that she would need a bit of time to pack her things and be on her way. He went to the train station and checked the arrivals, to see if a train was expected to come in from New York. When he was told in the affirmative, he went out to the platform and waited there in his parked carriage. It was far too cold for him to wait whilst standing outside on the platform, as romantic as that image appeared in his mind's eye.

With a loud whistle that caused him to jump in his seat, he saw the big black train as it rolled into the station. He was shaking now with nervous yet giddy excitement. This was the moment that he had been dreaming about for nearly a year. How was it that time had passed so quickly when it felt like it dragged on and on before? Now that they were here in this moment, he felt as though he must have only just woken up from a long and vivid dream.

Samson, however, hoped that it was no dream that Tabitha was on this train. He silently prayed that she had safely arrived in Missoula Mills and she was about to step down onto the very same platform any second now.

When the train stopped, the passengers slowly disembarked.

One of them, a golden-haired beauty, caught his eye and made his heart leap into his throat.

This beauty was his Tabitha.

At once, Samson opened the door to his carriage and stepped out onto the platform. He strode to the lady, careful to keep his gait slow and casual lest he startle her. A conductor was assisting her with a pair of suitcases, laying them at her feet. Samson cleared his throat a little once he was close enough to speak comfortably with her.

That got her attention and she looked up at him with striking, brown eyes. Her skin was like milk and it looked so soft and delicate. She wore a dark blue dress with a brown and black plaid shawl over her head and shoulders. Her long, blonde hair billowed out from the bottom of the shawl and down her back.

To Samson, she was an absolute angel.

"Excuse me, miss," he said gently, smiling in a shy but

friendly way. "Are you by any chance Miss Tabitha McGregor?"

The confused and unreadable look on her face vanished at once, and she smiled. Samson felt a pang just by seeing that smile. Goodness, she was gorgeous. She was light. She was everything.

"Yes," she replied. "You must be Mr. Delaney?"

The way she said his name made it sound altogether new and better than ever before. It sounded like a new word created by a poet. "I am Samson Delaney," he affirmed, knowing that he could never make it sound as magical as she could. "Welcome to Missoula Mills. I am so glad you are finally here." He offered his hand to her and she graciously took it at once. He gave the back of her hand a gentle peck. He no longer felt cold, but he knew that she must so there was no time to delay.

"Please, let me show you to my carriage," he said, giving her his arm so she could walk with him. He took up the suitcases with his other hand, with ease. The large, shiny black carriage was not so far away and soon he was placing the suitcases into the back trunk. Then he gave his hand to her once more and helped her inside. He joined her there, but took up a seat on the opposite bench from her, giving her some space.

Tabitha threw back her shawl and wore it around her neck as a scarf instead, now that she was inside the warm carriage. Samson looked at her lovingly, but did his best not to stare.

"You can stay with Mrs. Monroe's friend Mrs. Wyatt..." He flushed a bit, realizing how confusing all those names must sound to her. "The ladies in town are throwing a Christmas party, to welcome you to town and help you to better situate yourself. Of course, you may have all the time to rest from your journey before that."

Tabitha looked at him with her doe-like eyes. She was very quiet and he believed she was overwhelmed. He hoped some rest would change that.

CHAPTER 11

Margaret had prepared all morning for the arrival of Mr. Delaney and his lovely new presumed-fiancée. She had cleaned her and Stephen's home and decorated it for the upcoming Christmas celebrations. Her tall Christmas tree was in the living room, dressed up nicely with red and gold ribbons. The home's spare bedroom was decorated for their guest, the wardrobe emptied out so that Miss McGregor could place her clothes inside. Margaret was not sure how long the lady would be staying with her, but she was excited at the prospect of a new friend.

Mr. Delaney's carriage arrived outside of the home and he led Miss McGregor up to the front door. He knocked upon it and Margaret happily greeted them. "Hello," she chirped merrily, smiling. "You must be Miss McGregor. It is so wonderful to meet you. Please do come in."

The two ladies sat upon the couch in the living room, meanwhile, Samson handled Tabitha's suitcases, carrying them into the home and placing them in the bedroom for her. "I shall give you ladies some time to get acquainted. I will be back tonight for the party?"

Margaret nodded her approval and he took his leave.

She turned to Tabitha, still smiling. "What do you make of the town so far? My friends and I are quite fond of it and we've only been here for less than a full year."

Tabitha blinked a bit, not quite sure what she should say in answer to that. She had not really had enough time to figure out how she felt about anything yet. The journey to Montana had been long and not very comfortable for her, so it was good to finally be back on solid ground, in a house with a bed. "I am glad to be here at long last," she said. "You are very kind for letting me stay here. After exchanging letters with Mr. Delaney for so long, it is great to finally be here with him."

There was a noticeable hesitancy in what she said. Margaret suspected that Tabitha was feeling shy about things now that everything was really happening. "As he mentioned, my friends and I are hosting a party here this evening. It should be a fun affair, with music and dancing. You are the guest of honor, but of course, you do not have to stay at the party the whole time. I know that you must be exhausted from your travels. I was in your place not so very long ago. I came from Boston to marry my husband, Stephen. He is a doctor."

Tabitha lit up a bit at that information. "And you found it to be a good experience, a worthwhile situation? I must admit that now that I am here, I feel a bit nervous about what happens next."

Margaret laughed lightly. "Oh, yes. I am tremendously happy. All of my friends are. This town has so many wonderful gentlemen in it, and many of them so long for the love of us kindhearted east coast girls."

"And this Mr. Delaney? Is he good? He seemed so kind and thoughtful in his letters, but I must admit that seeing him took my very breath away. I've never met a man like him before. I suppose that is because the only men I've ever known in New York were pompous, stuffy businessmen. He is rather handsome in his own way, is he not?"

Margaret nodded sincerely. "Oh, yes, he is so sweet. He came to my friend Virginia and asked her for help with writing his advertisement. He tries ever so hard. And he does not give up. His lumber mill is a great success in town, but he is not pompous or egotistical at all."

Tabitha smiled. She was glad to know that, though he was handsome and strong, he was not big-headed. He seemed rather dashing to her, which caught her by surprise when he seemed so shy and eager in his letters. She wondered if that man existed within the man who greeted her. That man had seemed so calm and self-assured, which left her feeling a bit out of her station.

She excused herself to go take a nap in her new room. The party sounded like such a splendid opportunity for her to meet some more people in the town – namely Margaret's friends, with whom Tabitha hoped she could ally herself. She looked forward to meeting with Mr. Delaney again at the party as well, and she hoped that he would reveal more of his true nature once things became more relaxed and natural. She supposed that they handled their nervousness in other ways. He, being a man, had to give off a stronger presence. But oh, how she longed to speak with the shy and modest young man who had written to her for those many months...

CHAPTER 12

Samson dressed himself in another of his finest suits, hoping to look dapper and handsome for Tabitha at the party. She had seemed so quiet and demure; not quite what he had been expecting but he found her remarkably charming nonetheless. She was a sweet little thing and he hoped to win her heart. He also hoped that she would be comfortable at Margaret Wyatt's home until she was married to him. He blushed a bit just thinking of it. He knew what he wanted and needed to do; he just hoped that he could find the chance and the bravery to do so.

After Tabitha took a short nap, she found that she was a great deal more enthusiastic about the Christmas party. She came out of her room and downstairs to find Margaret and her husband busily putting out more decorations and snacks for the party-goers who would soon be arriving. "Would you like me to help at all?" Tabitha offered with a smile.

"Oh!" Margaret cried with a laugh. "I did not know you were up so soon. Yes, if you would like to help. The more the merrier."

Tabitha came into the living room and started putting up some bits of pine garland on the mantelpiece as well as the tables. There was more than enough Christmas cheer to go around in the place. After napping, she had worked to tidy herself up a bit from her train ride. Her long, blonde hair was now held up and back in a pretty braid. When she wore her hair this way she looked much more like a woman her age and not some delicate little girl. She hoped that Mr. Delaney had not been taken aback by how innocent she had first appeared. She had not had very many new experiences in her twenty-four years, but she was not as sheltered as she thought she might have looked. Her dark blue dress was velvety with white lace trim, suitable for the holidays for sure. As she cleaned and decorated, she wondered what Margaret's friends were like. She had not had very many friends in New York, especially once they all went off and got married elsewhere so Tabitha was looking forward to forging some new friendships now that she was making Missoula Mills her home.

The guests started coming to the door and Margaret, ever the good hostess, made sure to introduce Miss Tabitha McGregor of New York to everyone.

"So wonderful to finally meet you," Virginia declared,

offering her a full hug instead of the usual polite kisses. "I feel as though we know you already, we've heard so much from Mr. Delaney about you and how much he wanted to have you here with him."

"You are fortunate to have him," Eliza said. "I know he is shy, but he is a good man and he will be very good to you."

"He is very generous," Dorothy conceded. "He helps my husband all the time, and he helped me when I was building my dress shop."

Tabitha smiled at all of the lady friends. "Oh, you're the one with the dress shop," she said excitedly to Dorothy. "I wanted to ask about that. Would you like someone to work there as a shopkeeper sometimes?"

The ladies stood together, thrilled to chat away with Tabitha. Dorothy was more than happy to have someone new to work in her shop. She split her time between there and her husband's shop and, of course, the orphanage so it would be a big help if Tabitha wanted to work with her.

"Of course, the orphanage would always appreciate your help as well," Margaret added. "They can never have enough volunteers."

"How wonderful!" Tabitha said. "Samson – Mr. Delaney – wrote as much to me when we discussed what I may do once I came here. I would very much like to help out in any way I can."

The band arrived and set up in Dr. Wyatt's large ballroom. There were now enough people for music and dancing. But there was no sign yet of Mr. Delaney. Virginia looked pensive. She could tell that Tabitha was eagerly awaiting her beau, buoyed as she was by her conversation with her new friends.

"He will be along soon," she told Tabitha, giving her hand a pat. "He is probably planning to make a grand entrance and sweep you off your feet."

Tabitha's heart quickened at the thought. It seemed everyone at this party was in on this. Everyone was in rapt anticipation about when Mr. Delaney would appear. He really did seem to be quite an important person in this town.

CHAPTER 13

When Samson arrived at the party, he was fashionably late and the dancing was already in full swing. He found the hostess, Margaret, and thanked her for putting it all together. "Everything is just perfect," he told her, admiring all of the decorations.

"Thank you, sir," she said brightly, handing him a cup of hot apple cider. "By the way, your Miss Tabitha is in the library. She was chatting with us before, but then someone went and mentioned that we have quite a lot of books." Margaret giggled a little at that. "I take it she enjoys them. Did you know she used to be a librarian?"

Samson nodded vaguely. "Indeed. She worked in a book shop. Excuse me, please." He went from the living room and found the library. There were not very many people in there. He imagined that had been part of the draw for Tabitha.

The young lady was shy and easily overwhelmed by so many people around her at once. She turned when she heard someone enter the room and her beautiful brown eyes appeared to light up at the sight of Samson.

"Hello there," he said to her in a gentle voice. He had chosen a royal blue suit made of crushed velvet. He appeared quite handsome and dapper again, in Tabitha's eyes, and she appreciated that he was now matching her outfit. She wondered if he had done that on purpose.

"Hello," she said back to him, giving a short curtsy. "I heard that there was a library in the doctor's house so I thought I should explore it a little."

Samson chuckled softly, nodding. "I cannot blame you for that. I hope that these lodgings are to your liking, for the time being."

"Oh yes," Tabitha replied. "Margaret is so kind, and all of her friends are so friendly. I can see that they all wish us well."

She batted her long lashes at him. He gulped a bit, wanting to seize this golden opportunity before it passed him by. Samson went to her and took her hand in his. He knelt before her. "Tabitha – Miss McGregor... I know that I am a timid man. I do not always know the best thing to say and I often rely on the goodness of my friends to help me through. But my letters to you were entirely my own, and that is something I am proud of. I swear to you that I have the best intentions for you and I vow to make you the happiest woman in all of the country."

Tabitha looked down at him, holding her breath. She thought she knew what he was doing, and she found it odd and sort of wonderful that he was doing it so soon!

"Would you please do me the supreme honor...? It would make me so happy if... Aw, heck," Samson gulped again.

"Go on," Tabitha said, giving his hand a gentle squeeze for encouragement. At last, she could see the shyer side of him! And she adored it.

He looked up and into her eyes. She was smiling at him and giving him the sweetest look. He took a deep breath. "Miss McGregor, will you marry me?"

Her little smile turned into a full grin. She nodded at him. "Yes," she said. "Yes, I will."

Samson rose up from the floor and hugged her. She threw her arms around his neck and hugged him back. They were both shaking with excitement and nerves. He had wanted to propose to her right away, and he was proud of himself for not waiting too long.

CHAPTER 14

Tabitha and Samson rejoined the party, walking hand in hand. They both had rosy cheeks after what had occurred. Virginia and her friends could not help but notice; they grinned at each other and at Tabitha. It certainly was going to be a merry Christmas indeed.

Before long, Samson brought Tabitha out onto the dance floor and they danced together, laughing and chatting all the while. She still felt a bit star-struck that this handsome and smooth-talking gentleman wanted to marry her of all people. She was bookish and shy and not used to so much attention. However, she told herself that this was every woman's dream come true, so she should consider herself extremely fortunate.

"Would you like some cider?" he asked her. "I think you must have missed it when they were handing it out." He had left his back in the library, so he thought he would get some for Tabitha whilst he was retrieving his own cup.

"Yes, please," she said with another affectionate smile.

He went off to get the cider and Margaret sidled up to her. "I'd say that you enjoyed my library," she said with a twinkle in her eyes.

Tabitha blushed and nodded a little. "Indeed," she said. She felt that she could trust this kind woman since she had been through the same sort of thing not that long ago. "He asked me to marry him and I have said yes."

Margaret let out a little, "oh!" She clapped her hands together. "There shall be so much to celebrate this Christmas!"

When Samson returned with the ciders, she congratulated him which flustered the shy man a little but he could not keep from grinning.

Suddenly, the music started playing a familiar carol. Everyone joined in singing. *Good King Wenceslas looked out on the Feast of Stephen, When the snow lay round about, deep and crisp and even...*

Tabitha smiled and sang along with all of the others. She did her best to be friendly and spend time with all of these new people. She hoped that she would soon fit in just fine in the town. As she gazed up at Samson, she wondered how long it might take before this all felt real and not like some sort of fairy tale.

CHAPTER 15

BEFORE LEAVING THE PARTY, SAMSON TOOK TABITHA aside once more. "We shall be married on Christmas day," he told her. "And a blessed day it shall be!" He softly pecked a kiss on her cheek, causing her to blush lightly. "I will eagerly await our wedding day." With that, he bid her adieu and she was left with her thoughts once more.

As she helped Margaret clean up from the night's festivities, she bit her lip a little and thought back to the way she had felt when she had been writing to Samson and everything had been such an exciting dream come true. She was beginning to worry that marrying him on Christmas day was going to be a bit too extravagant for her to take. She knew that the mail order business was a rather whirlwind situation as it was, but she was not sure if a big wedding in front of everyone, on one of the holiest of days, was really something that she was comfortable with.

"My friends and I can help you with your dress," Margaret offered to her as they tidied everything back up. "Dorothy owns the shop, as you know. I'm sure we can find a dress there that's to your liking. And if we cannot there's always the option of one of us making it for you ourselves."

Margaret seemed so enthusiastic about the impending wedding. She and her friends were so helpful and eager to please. Their position in the town was obviously prominent to Tabitha, but she hoped that she could take a quieter role in the town. She fancied herself as the unassuming clerk she had always been before.

"I would not want to bring you to any trouble or anything," Tabitha said. "I think a dress that is already made would suit me just fine."

Margaret laughed airily. "I shall talk it over with Dorothy and the other girls. After all, this will be the biggest day of your life."

Tabitha knew that her new friend meant well, but it was a lot of pressure. She was beginning to wonder if this wedding was a good idea. Perhaps Mr. Delaney would have been better off marrying one of the other girls he no doubt had been writing to. She was not really a good wife for someone so well-beloved by everyone in the town. As she had told him, she was uncomfortable being around 'big-wigs' and that sort of thing. Though Samson was a dear heart, he was the closest to a 'big-wig' that this town had.

Fortunately, Tabitha had some time to think about the wedding and try and decide what she wanted. There were a few days before Christmas, and that allowed her to explore the town and experience what working at Dorothy's dress shop was like. She also went and visited the orphanage, realizing that was another great place for her to volunteer her time, as Samson had suggested.

"The children love to be read to," Eliza pointed out. "So, if you feel too shy to play with them, it would be a great help if you could sit beside them and read a story as they try to fall asleep."

Tabitha believed that her new friends really did have her best interests at heart. They paid attention to what she wanted and gave her advice. "It feels so nice to have you all as my friends," she told them one afternoon when they had gathered together in Margaret's house for their sewing circle. "I feel unsure about how I am going to be as a wife to Mr. Delaney, but at least I know that I can depend on you ladies." She started to quietly cry, she was so emotional about finally having a group of supportive lady friends. "I did not come out here thinking that I would find friends, but I am so grateful that I have all of you."

Margaret offered her a smile and a handkerchief for her tears. "There has been so much for you to get used to," she said. "Marriage is an adjustment, and Mr. Delaney is a still a bit of a stranger to you. But in time, you will get to know him and I am certain that you are just going to absolutely love him. Don't get so caught up in how overwhelmed you feel and lose sight of who you came all this way to be with."

It was evident that Tabitha was getting cold feet about her impending nuptials. None of the ladies could really figure out why, but they supposed that she had been a bit overwhelmed with everything. Christmas had likely not helped. It was a beautiful, yet busy, stressful time of year and Tabitha was so very far from home. Marrying a stranger in a strange town surrounded by strangers had to be a rather frightening ordeal. Margaret and her friends had been in similar situations, but they, of course, all had each other to rely on and they did not feel as alone. Through everything, they had always had each other.

"I think we should make a dress for you," Margaret suddenly announced. Dorothy got out her tape measure and the friends proceeded to take Tabitha's measurements.

"I am not sure if I can go through with this," Tabitha said as she stood there being measured. "I am not sure I am ready for marriage. I am not confident that I can stand up there in front of God and everyone on Christmas morning and give myself to this man."

The friends all looked at each other. Margaret decided that the best thing to do was sit down with Tabitha and have a heart-to-heart chat about what exactly the young woman was feeling. She had a sense that it actually had very little to do with Samson Delaney. He was nothing if not gracious towards his new fiancée. He would never do anything to hurt or scare her, and if he knew that she was frightened about their wedding he likely would change the plans. However, what was not certain was if he would gladly do so or if he would be embarrassed and heartbroken.

CHAPTER 16

ONE EVENING, MARGARET DECIDED THAT IT WOULD BE A good idea to pay Mr. Delaney a visit. He greeted her at the door of his home and invited her inside at once. "It smells like snow is in the air," she said, holding her coat tightly around herself.

"To what do I owe this immense pleasure, Mrs. Wyatt?" he asked her, taking her coat and hanging it up as she sat down on his large, deep red sofa. "Is everything all right with my dearest Tabitha?"

He said her name with such reverence, almost as if he was afraid he could break it if he did not say it carefully. Margaret knew that the young gentleman was infatuated with his betrothed, and it made her worry slightly that this was part of the problem. She worried that his feelings were going to be hurt if Tabitha decided that marriage was not actually what she wanted.

"Everything is fine," Margaret said, leaving out some of her doubts and worries so that his feelings would be spared. "Though I do think she is a trifle nervous about the ceremony you have planned. It is quite a lot for a young woman to take in all at once. I know from experience."

Samson suddenly looked worried. He lowered himself into one of the chairs by the sofa. "She has not changed her mind, has she?"

"Oh, no, no," Margaret replied. "She has just expressed that... She wishes that she could get to know you better. She's concerned about marrying a stranger if you can imagine."

He nodded a little. "Oh, I can," he said in a thoughtful voice. "What do you think I should do?" He respected Margaret's views. All of the ladies he had met via his friends were so kind and patient towards him and everyone else he knew; there was no reason not to trust their advice.

Margaret thought about that. Short of rescheduling the wedding, what could he do to help alleviate Tabitha's fears? "Why don't you come meet her after work at the orphanage tomorrow?" she recommended. "A nice gesture like that would go a long way."

Samson smiled. He certainly could do something like that! "That would be nice. I would like to see her more often anyway. Maybe I will bring her a small token of my affection."

"That is a great idea," Margaret said approvingly. "She will really appreciate this surprise, I'm sure." At least Margaret hoped so. Tabitha seemed like the type of person who appreciated kind gestures. It was not that she was an unfeeling person, she was just shy and awkward. Perhaps all she really needed to see was that Samson was more or less the same way.

The following day, Samson went to the mill, as usual, to oversee the workers and make sure that the wood they were producing was up to his strict standards. He left earlier than he normally did so that he could change out of his work suit and into something a bit more presentable for his fiancée. He hoped that she really would appreciate his gesture today. He was starting to feel quite nervous about it. What if she disliked him infringing on her personal workspace? She had once written to him that she did enjoy her ability to work and the independence that it brought her. He had hoped to find a lady who wanted only to be his homemaker, but now he supposed that asking Miss McGregor to stay at home all the time would be so limiting for her. He wanted to make her happy above all. He did not think it was just the Christmas season that made him feel this overwhelming desire to see her smile at him again.

He changed into a fresh, more appropriate suit when he got to his house. The crushed velvet that he had worn for his proposal had been a success, so he decided to wear something similar. He put on a forest green suit this time, with white ruffled trim. He felt a bit like a politician of old.

He hoped that Tabitha would find that appealing and that he didn't look too severe.

CHAPTER 17

When he arrived at the orphanage, bouquet of wild buttercups and bluebells in hand, Samson was amazed by the sheer size of the place. Though he knew of the orphanage and had heard wonderful stories about it – particularly from Nicky, Mrs. Monroe's adopted son – he had not visited it yet himself. Samson liked the idea of children and hoped to have some of his own someday, but he was a bit too shy and uncomfortable around them for him to want to seek them out often.

He took a deep breath and entered the doors of the establishment. Right away, he saw a lady at the front desk and knew that he was likely going to need to place his name there so that Tabitha knew he was there to meet her.

Instead of that even being necessary, Tabitha appeared right away. She looked startled to see him there. Startled but not unhappy. "Mr. Delaney," she said, smiling a bit. "It is so nice to see you here. I did not know that I should expect you."

She felt in such a queer way that being in his presence made everything seem better. She was less apprehensive about their wedding and their coupling when she was actually in the same room as him, breathing the same air. Tabitha looked down and noticed the bouquet of wildflowers in his hand. Her smile brightened. "Are those for me?"

Samson grinned and nodded, handing the bouquet to her. "I was not sure which you would prefer, so I gathered up plenty of both of them."

Tabitha hugged the bouquet to her and sniffed it. She really appreciated this lovely gesture. Samson was trying his best, and it proved to her just how much he cared for her. She still felt shy about marrying him so soon, but she was gradually warming up to the idea.

"I apologize if it seemed as though I was rushing you to the altar," he said. "That was never my intention. If you would like to wait until you feel that you know me better, I will gladly wait for you."

Smiling ever still, she shook her head. "No," she said. "This has been my own issue. It has nothing to do with you, really. I am just not used to any of this, so you must be a bit patient with me. I do want to marry you, and I believe that it will make for a joyous Christmas."

Samson was overjoyed to hear her say that.

Tabitha looked a bit thoughtful then. "...But there is something that you can do that will truly prove your love to me and show how deserving you are of such a wedding."

His eyes widened as he looked at her. "What is it?" he asked. "Please tell me. I shall do anything if it would make you happy."

Tabitha looked back at him and smiled broadly. Her brown eyes had a twinkle to them now, unable to hide her glee at her new idea. "I would like you to meet me here tomorrow morning, dressed up as Saint Nicholas, for the children would be most happy to see him here."

Samson beamed at her, touched that she had thought of such a thing. He laughed and nodded. She was quite a smart one. "I would be happy to," he told her. "I will meet you here, ready to put the children and the staff here into the Christmas spirit."

True to his word, Samson did just that. He went through all of his clothing, finding a red shirt and some red velvet pants amongst some of his old possessions. He put these clothes on, along with a belt, and then made his way to the orphanage. He believed that in this makeshift costume he looked much more like the son of Saint Nicholas because he did not have the white beard that was required.

Still, as soon as he came through the doors and greeted the children at the orphanage, the looks on their faces spelled pure glee. "Santa!" they cried out. All of them wanted a turn sitting on his lap, and he gladly sat there in the main room of the orphanage, allowing them each to take a turn on his leg. Many of the things that the children asked for were toys and treats, but a lot of them asked for new homes as well. That truly tugged at Samson's heartstrings.

"It is a noble thing that you and the other ladies do here," he told Tabitha at the end of the day. "I don't know how you can come here day in and day out and not bring home at least ten of these children."

She chuckled softly. "It is a challenge at times. But they are comfortable and well-fed here. I would love to have a child of my own someday if you are hoping for that." Tabitha looked at him and smiled, blushing a little. She was not sure what kind of mother she would be, but as she was not sure yet what kind of wife she could even be, she would not rule out being a mother someday as well.

"I shall see you in two days," she told him as they walked out of the orphanage, him to return to his carriage and her to meet up with her friends at the dress shop.

"I will try my best not to miss you too much until we meet again, my darling," Samson replied, placing a light kiss on her cheek before they parted.

CHAPTER 18

THE MORNING OF CHRISTMAS, SAMSON ROSE WITH THE sun. He smiled when he realized that today was the day that he was going to make Tabitha his wife. He felt considerably more confident that she was looking forward to this wedding as much as he had been, now that they had spent some more time together. He knew, too, that his work was not going to stop now that they were getting married. He would need to love her and try to make her happy each and every day for the rest of their lives together. Samson was not afraid of this; he was very excited about it.

No longer would he be lonely or unsure of himself. He was going to have a woman in his life who loved him, spent time with him and gave him advice which he felt that he often required. He was overcoming his timidity by marrying this young woman in the town's chapel on Christmas morning. The entire town was going to be there. But that did not matter, as long as Tabitha was by his side he felt confident and sure.

She arose early as well and Margaret, Dorothy, and Eliza helped her with her dress and her bouquet of wildflowers. The ones that Samson had picked for her did not last long, but Dorothy went out and found some fresh ones for Tabitha's wedding day. The hope was that Samson would notice that her wedding bouquet was made up of the very same flowers he had given to Tabitha to help her become more comfortable and relaxed with him. This was Margaret's idea, of course.

The wedding gown that the friends had made for Tabitha was absolutely beautiful. It was long and it shimmered a bit. She wore a long, sheer veil along with it and the image of her in it was so lovely that Dorothy was moved to tears.

"It always me so happy to help create a special day for someone like you," she said.

Margaret, with the help of her husband, hired a carriage to pick Tabitha up and take her to the chapel so that no one else would see her until she was walking down the aisle towards her husband-to-be.

The four friends rode another carriage together, dressed in some of their finest and most colorful gowns. They were serving as Tabitha's bridesmaids, of course. They were always ready to help her if she needed it.

Samson took his shiny, black carriage to the chapel. His

best man was Archie, and little Nicky was there to be the ring bearer. Samson had picked out the prettiest ring he could find for the prettiest wife imaginable. As soon as he arrived at the church, he eagerly met the minister at the altar.

The minister smiled encouragingly at Samson. This day had been a long time coming, and it was one of the most important days for another reason, of course. What better way to celebrate the birth of Jesus Christ than by joining together in holy matrimony?

Once the music began to play from the chapel's small organ, Samson's heart began to race. He could hardly believe that this was all really happening to him. In just a few moments, he was going to have Tabitha as his wife. He was going to be her doting husband.

He watched as, one by one, the ladies marched down the aisle. Eliza in pink followed by Virginia in yellow, Dorothy in green, and Margaret in blue. They were all so lovely and his heart swelled with pride because he could call them all his friends. Then, everyone turned in their seats and he looked up once more at the doorway at the end of the aisle.

Tabitha came into view, a vision in billowing, shimmering white. Samson could hardly contain his joy. She smiled, locking eyes with him there upon the altar, next to the minister. She marched up the aisle, keeping pace with the music and she did not stop smiling the whole time. Only when she was at last by Samson's side did he notice that her face was shiny with tears. He hoped that they were tears of joy, but he had no reason to believe that they were otherwise.

He placed his hand in Tabitha's hand as the minister began the wedding ceremony. "Dearly beloved. We are gathered here on this most glorious of days to celebrate the union of these two souls, Tabitha Eleanor McGregor and Samson Benjamin Delaney. If there is anyone who believes that these two must not be wed, let him speak now or forever hold his silence…"

No one said a word. Samson was so relieved that no one uttered a sound.

"We shall proceed," the minister went on. "As it is said in the book of Ecclesiastes, verse 4:12, *Though one may be overpowered, two can defend themselves. A cord of three strands is not quickly broken.*"

Samson did his best to give all of his attention to the words that the minister said. He had a feeling that all of this, every last word, was important and must be remembered as well as possible for the rest of his life. However, he could not stop looking over at his beautiful Tabitha. He felt so fortunate that God had brought her to him and seen fit that they should be united forevermore.

"Tabitha, do you take this man, Samson Delaney, to be your lawfully wedded husband? To have and to hold, to love and to cherish, to honor and obey, in sickness and in health, for better or worse, until death do you part, for as long as you both shall live?"

Samson swallowed hard. She was the first one to answer

the vow and he really hoped that she would not change her mind. He had done his best to do right by her and let her see the good in him. They would have so much wonderful time together after this day. They would share their first of many Christmases, and for that, he was so grateful. He just had to hear her say those words...

"I do," Tabitha said at last. She bit her lip and looked at him, smiling shyly. "I do."

She had said it twice as if to doubly confirm it, and he loved her even more for it!

The minister focused his attention on Samson now. "Samson, do you take this woman, Tabitha McGregor, to be your lawfully wedded wife? To have and to hold, to love and to cherish, to treasure and protect, in sickness and in health, for better or worse, until death do you part, for as long as you both shall live?"

Samson blushed a little bit. His cheeks hurt so much from smiling, but it did not matter. Nothing else mattered in the world right now. "I do," he said, looking right into Tabitha's eyes so she would truly understand the promise that he was making to her.

Tabitha looked back at him and grinned, tears still slowly careening down her cheeks, unswept away. He could see now, plain as day, that she was just as happy as he was.

"By the power vested in me by our lord and savior Jesus Christ, on this the day of his birth, I now proudly pronounce you husband and wife."

A cheer went up in the chapel.

The minister smiled at Samson. "You may kiss your bride."

Samson moved in closer to Tabitha and carefully removed the veil from the front of her face. He took her small face in his hands and kissed her softly, closing his eyes and just focusing on the feel of her lips on his.

She closed her eyes and kissed him back, love for this man filling her heart.

"I present to you all for the first time, Mr. and Mrs. Delaney!" the minister concluded.

The music began as they marched down the aisle hand in hand during the recessional. Instead of the more traditional music, the organist began playing familiar Christmas songs, and everyone sang along as they left the chapel. There was clearly plenty of joy to go around on that wonderful morning, and for many years to come. Truly, it was a blessed Christmas.

THE END

ABOUT THE AUTHORS

Charity Phillips grew up on a beautiful farm with her three brothers and two sisters in Cherokee County, North Carolina. She fell in love with horses and learned to care for them at an early age. She currently lives just a stone's throw from that gorgeous farm with her loving husband of twelve years and their three beautiful daughters. When Charity isn't dreaming up her next story, she's usually tending to her garden or baking delicious treats for her family.

Faith-Ann Smith has always loved to write. As a child, she enjoyed penning simple tales about prairie life in her home state of Oklahoma. While in college, Faith-Ann became fascinated with American history, particularly of the 19th century, and began to write creative historical fiction in her late twenties. Blessed with a loving husband and two precious children, Faith-Ann enjoys knitting, teaching Sunday School and tending to the flower beds surrounding her home in Nebraska.

To keep up to date with their latest releases, you may visit **www.hopemeadowpublishing.com** and sign up for their newsletter.

FREE STORY!

For a FREE sweet historical romance e-book, please sign up for Hope Meadow Publishing's newsletter at
www.hopemeadowpublishing.com

Made in the USA
Coppell, TX
20 December 2020